QUINN

QUINN

Sometimes, Time Is Not the Great Healer

D R CATHERALL

ISBNs:

978-1-80541-632-6: eBook
978-1-80541-633-3: Paperback
978-1-80541-634-0: Hardcover

TABLE OF CONTENTS

ABOUT THE AUTHOR

David Catherall lives in a small town in the north west of England. He lives with and is controlled by a wife and two large hairy dogs.

CHAPTER 1

Jimmy Quinn, whose youngest son Graham, or to be absolutely accurate, Gunther, (as he was so named by his German mother), once described Jimmy as, "A dirty evil long streak of piss." It was a description which was accurate in many ways, for in fact Jimmy was quite tall for a man of his age, and thin as well, though that had been only in recent years when his addiction to alcohol, heroin and poor meals cooked for himself had lost him the weight he had accumulated during the younger part of his life. Now he lay dead in bed in the top floor single-bedroomed flat on Dumbryden Drive in Wester Hailes and almost within sight of the Edinburgh bypass.

His neighbour, Molly Cullen, had discovered him in bed when she had let herself in his flat after doing his normal 'messages', which she did each morning. Although she was five or six years younger than him she was still fit and active and determined to keep that way, though she had been a widow for over ten years and had no family close by.

Jimmy on the other hand had decided that enough was enough and took to his bed, not through any illness, though he was not the fittest he could have been, simply that he was used to being looked after by a wife or daughter and when his wife had finally had enough and divorced him, he looked on Molly to take care of him. He was a scrounger and an idle sod, who had lived a large part of his life scrounging and thieving as best he could. Finally, he convinced doctors to declare him medically unfit for work and grant him a pension and other social benefits. With what he got from the state he lived a comfortable life, his main expenditure being a daily wrap of heroin and the Racing Post newspaper. Every week he would splash out on a couple of bottles of Buckie and a bottle of cheap whisky. The fortified wine from the good brothers in a Devon monastery was his favourite though.

Molly walked the short distance from her flat across the landing to Jimmy's. Scuff marks from shopping bags she had carried up the stairs had made marks on the walls on the staircase and showed against the dull pastel shades of paintwork the council had last used when decorating. Coming out of her flat onto the landing she went to the window at the end of the wall and looked down on the narrow expanse of lawn below. Kids rusty bikes and lumps of broken wood taken from fences and god knows what littered parts of the lawn. Some of her neighbours cleared away the unsightly items from in front of their own windows, but that's as far as it got for most of them. It wasn't in front of my flat window, so it doesn't matter, was the general feeling. A Cherry Tree, or was it a Hawthorne was blowing white blossom in small clouds onto the roadway outside the block where it gathered in a narrow line of colour in the gutter. The other trees were simply showing green leaves. She glanced at the sky. Clear blue with clumps of clouds scudding across in a biting cold wind. It might be late April, but spring had not yet decided if it was staying or going to make way for a blast of winter. At this time of year, you could never tell. She sniffed and took a key from her coat pocket.

She had lived across the landing from Jimmy for a few years before he had moved in. She knew everyone in the block and everyone knew her. Some of them thought her the salt of the earth, the rest felt she was an interfering old busybody, keen to poke her nose in whether it was wanted or not. A little over five feet tall she was going to be fat. Her brown hair had long given up the ghost and was now predominantly grey, resting in an untidy and unwashed straggle on her head down to the collar of her coat. The years and her life had not been too kind and she took little exercise other than her daily trip to the small supermarket down the road. She walked out onto the landing and pulled her front door closed, shaking the handle to ensure it was locked. Pulling her old brown mid-length woollen coat around her, she stuffed the copy of the Racing Post she had bought earlier into one pocket and checked the other to make sure the small wrap of heroin was safely there.

She took the spare key Jimmy had given her from the pocket with the heroin and inserted it into the front door of Jimmy's flat. She didn't believe Jimmy's excuses about being unable to get out due to his sciatica and COPD and knew it was a lie, but accepted it as she could make a few pounds from the daily errand herself. He would hand over a twenty-pound note and she would return with a wrap of heroin from the kid who hung about outside the bookies and his daily copy of the Racing Post then hand over to him two pounds in change. Jimmy knew he was being fleeced but accepted it as being the cost of his easy life.

But today would be different. Molly opened the front door of his flat and glanced along the corridor to the living room at the end. The door to the living room was open but the door to his bedroom on the left of the corridor was closed.

"Jimmy," she called out. "It's only me. Got your Post." She closed the door behind her with a deft nudge of her foot and flicked on the light switch by the door jamb. The dim lightbulb in the middle of the corridor ceiling illuminated the corridor. There was no noise from the kitchen on the right or the bedroom on the left. "Old buggers still asleep" she muttered to herself.

Her shoes clicked on the sticky ingrained lino floor covering as she walked with her newspaper clutched in her hand and her wrap of drugs in the coat pocket. Halfway down the corridor was a rip in the lino which she was certain he had made himself. The rip was hardly noticeable, but to the unwary, it would trip you and throw you onto your face. She stopped at his bedroom door and cocked her ear to the door to try to make out if he was awake or asleep. There was no noise coming from the room, so she opened the door and pushed it carefully until she could pop her head around to see what he was doing. He was asleep, or appeared to be. Pushing open the door fully she stepped through into the bedroom and stopped, looking down at him lying there in bed.

Jimmy was lying on his back with his eyes and mouth open, yet they appeared to be lifeless. Because they were. Cautiously she took a step forward to see him better. The colour had washed out of his face and what flesh there was had appeared to have sunk down around his scrawny neck.

"Jimmy" she called softly. No reply. "Jimmy" a bit louder. Still no reply. She clutched her worn coat to her, her hand going alternately from her mouth to her pounding heart. Still no reply. She shuffled quietly towards the bed looking down on his still-white bloodless face. The light from the widow by his bed was shaded by the closed thin curtains. She reached an arm across the bed which lay against the wall and beneath the window, and slowly drew the left-hand curtain aside. Two thin blankets and a grubby white sheet were pulled up to his chin. She poked him gently with a finger on the side of his face, but there was no reaction. Placing the Racing Post on the green baize cover of the collapsible card table at the side of his bed she gently placed the back of her hand against the skin of his forehead. It was cold. She pulled back her hand and stood back breathing deeply, looking around the room. Adrenalin pumped through her body and made her eyes shine.

On the table were the remains of his last hit of heroin, a dirty teaspoon, an even dirtier heroin pipe and the silver paper wrap he used to heat up the drug. A disposable lighter was discarded amongst the remains next to a pack of cigarettes and a half-drunk bottle of Buckfast Wine, its sticky top making rings on the green table top.

"Well now Jimmy" she said aloud to herself. "What to do, what to do?" She stood silently for a moment trying to make her heart stop its pounding, not as a sign of respect for her dead neighbour, but to listen for abnormal sounds coming from the rest of the block of flats, to see if anyone else was arriving, or had she been the first to find him? After ten or more seconds of silence, she realised she was alone, she was the first to find the body and it would be up to her to phone the Police and get them involved. It was then she was hit by a strange smell, one she was unable to place. She sniffed the smell and turned to look at him. "Have you shit yourself Jimmy?" she asked the corpse. "Well, I'm not going to find out am I. That's above and beyond."

But first things first. She reached down and scooped up the lighter and cigarettes, thrusting them into her coat pocket, then picked the pipe, the silver wrap and teaspoon and eased them carefully into her other pocket. Apart from today's Racing Post and the half-empty Buckie bottle, the table was clear. As she placed the items in her coat her foot nudged against a tin ashtray on the floor close to the bedhead. Her foot moved it slightly further under the bed. She missed it, partially hidden by the blankets as it was. Looking around the rest of the bedroom she saw what she was looking for hung over the back of the old wooden dining chair at the foot of the bed. Yesterday's shirt and his trousers were slung over the back of the chair. She stepped forward and lifted the trousers. Patting them down she quickly found his wallet stuffed into the back pocket of the garment. Lifting it out a smile creased her face. "Ah Jimmy" she muttered, "What have we here?" Opening the wallet she took all of the thin wad of bank notes from the cheap plastic wallet and stuffed back into it one ten-pound note and a five-pound note.

For a moment she fingered the bank card stuck into one of the pockets of the wallet. Over the past few years, she had been trusted by Jimmy to visit the hole in the wall by the supermarket and withdraw every week or ten days anything between two and three hundred pounds. It was this money he used to give her to buy his drugs and newspaper, as well as the Buckie the whisky and odd bits of groceries. She was tempted to give the hole one extra tug, just for old time's sake, then recalled that Jimmy had told her of a visit during the Sunday afternoon the previous day. A new locum doctor had been to see him to try and wean him off the heroin. She hadn't stayed long.

"Not surprised," Molly thought. "Miserable dirty old bugger would have given her a hard time." But even so. If it came out that the doctor had been to see him in the afternoon then it would be obvious Molly had taken the money if she tried to milk the hole in the wall today.

"Damn you Jimmy. Why couldn't you have waited a day or two? I could have had the lot out of there." An empty wallet would give the Police the thought that he had been robbed, and if he had been robbed then perhaps there was some suspicion about the cause of his death. Putting the wallet back she rehung the trousers on top of the shirt and counted the notes. There was a hundred and forty pounds there in total. She grinned to herself. "Well that will do nicely" she said and placed them into her wallet in her pocket.

Looking carefully around the bedroom for anything else to lift she saw nothing of any value so went through into the living room to cast her eyes around what he had left there. Nothing of any real value met her eye either. A few faded photographs in cheap frames on the fireplace and windowsill, a couple of dirty books, a few pornographic videos, a television and video player were all that Jimmy Quinn had left of any value in this world. Now they would be left for the Police to remove.

The wrap of heroin in her pocket would do well to be re-sold to the dealer, or some other ned on the scheme if the dealer tried to rip her off. Better in her pocket than any other buggers, she thought. She quietly walked back into the bedroom and took one last look at her neighbour. He didn't look normal lying so still on his back with his eyes and mouth open. She gently stepped to the side of the bed and placing two fingers on his eyelids reverently closed them, then placing an index finger under his chin she pushed his mouth closed. Breathing a sigh of relief she took a last look at him. "Bye-bye, Jimmy. Go well you dirty old bugger," she muttered and left.

Walking from his flat and back across the landing she opened the door to her flat and went into the kitchen. Taking the heroin paraphernalia, but not the drug itself, from her pocket she opened the cupboard beneath the sink and stuffed the spoon and paper and pipe into her rubbish bin, then closed the cupboard door. She must remember to take it down to the bins in the bin store by the front door of the flats later. Don't want this to be found in her flat. Returning to her living room she took off her coat, checked that the wrap of heroin she had bought was still in the side pocket, and hung it on a hook behind the door, then sat in her plush armchair by the electric fire. Taking one of Jimmy's cigarettes, she lit it and sat for a few moments blowing smoke to the ceiling where it mingled with the rest of the mottled brown stains. She leaned over and picked up the phone from the side table and phoned the Police, as a good neighbour would, sounding suitably distressed at finding her long-time friend dead in bed. Then she sat back in her easy chair in front of the television, smoked her cigarette and waited. As she blew a plume of smoke out she started to make plans for the hundred-plus pounds she had won. "Life goes on Jimmy" she said, "Life goes on."

CHAPTER 2

Neither Detective Chief Inspector Lewis Maxwell nor Detective Sergeant Joanne Baker could fly an aircraft, so neither a drone nor a pigeon was available to them when they had first received the radio call to go to the address in the three-story block of apartments on the Wester Hailes. So DS Baker drove their unmarked car, unmarked because it belonged to her, and she was only too happy to use it on duty, in view of the welcome and useful mileage allowance for each mile she drove the car whilst on duty. The little over five miles from the centre of the city to the apartment would add up at the end of the month, and contribute significantly to the repayment costs she was paying to the bank for the car purchase. How else would she have been able to afford a three-year-old Volvo S80? When she bought the car she had boasted to her CID colleagues that she had got one over on the car salesman at the Volvo dealership, but the truth was, he had screwed her, in a manner of speaking, but she was more than happy with the car and kept it as spotlessly clean as she could.

As the traffic on the main road out of the city cleared onto Lanark Road she put her foot down and the car accelerated well above the four-lane forty miles an hour speed limit. Maxwell clung onto the grab handle above his head by the front passenger seat, and with one eye on the rapidly changing road scene in front of him and the other on the car speedo, he half turned to Baker in the driving seat.

'Slow down girl' he said. 'The guy's fucking dead, isn't he? He's not going anywhere.' Parked cars and numerous side road junctions made him more than a little nervous. Joanne grinned and turned to flash him a broad white-toothed smile. Maxwell melted a little, she was a good-looking young woman, no matter what else anyone said of her. She was the same height as Maxwell, a little under six feet tall, she had a figure most women would be jealous of, and most men wanted to get their hands on, with short light brown hair and dark brown eyes. Her face was round and her thin lips kept good control of her wide mouth. In the eyes of many, including her boss DCI Maxwell, she was a stunner. Maxwell was happy to be seen in her company, not only for her looks but also for the fact that she was also a very good detective, even though she had only just turned thirty and he was some twenty years older.

'Getting a bit old for this sort of thing are we sir?' she quipped, easing her foot off the pedal and slowing down to something closer to forty. Traffic was light for the time of day, it was late morning, and the five miles from the city took them only a little over fifteen minutes, despite Joanne's itchy heavy right foot. As she pulled the car to a stop in one of the car parking spaces in front of the apartment block, the sun was starting to finally appear from behind the layer of heavy grey cloud which had blown in during the past hour. The sky was clearing and looked like the rest of the day could be good. Though there had been no rain that day, it was coming, they could both feel it. Joanne turned off the engine and unlocked her seat belt to prepare to get out of the car. Maxwell held her back gently with a hand on her arm.

"Just a second Jo," he said, bending to squint up through the windscreen to the upper floors of the dull reddish brown and cream brick block in front of him. The flats were built in a cul de sac with blocks of flats on three sides. In the centre of the close were car parking spaces shaded and beautified by Larch, Beech and a few Cherry trees. Today they were in full bloom and provided shelter over the parked cars, and a nesting place for birds. On two sides of the close of flats were neat piles of scaffolding poles and long lengths of timber. Two of the blocks on the other side of the road had scaffolding built up on the face of the building. Maxwell grunted and nodded to the scaffolding. The structures were devoid of builders or scaffolders. For some reason, they were not working today.

"Looks like you and I are spending more of our hard-earned gelt on doing up these flats." He nodded towards the building work, paused and looked around. "About time." He added.

"These used to be bloody horrible places. When the scheme was first built there was nothing but houses and flats. People had nowhere to go, nothing to do. No wonder they developed into the rat holes they became. Crime was bloody rampant. Different now. Thank god they're pouring money into them. Got schools, community centres, doctors, pubs, play groups, the lot. Becoming a good place to live. Not like it was years ago." He stopped, took a deep breath and continued to look around him.

"Do we know why we are here?" he asked. "I mean, it's just a dead old body, what's there suspicious about it?" She looked back at him and placed her hands on the steering wheel whilst she mentally gathered together the information she had been given on her mobile phone whilst she had sat waiting for him to come from the tobacco shop on the Canongate.

Joanne had sat waiting impatiently in the car parked as it was on double yellow lines. She constantly watched her rearview mirror and looked along the Canongate for the approach of the civilian parking attendants. Nothing would give some of them greater pleasure, she knew than to slap her with a parking fine. It was not as though they were on their doorstep. They were based at the MIT Eastern office at Leith, and yet here they were in the centre of Edinburgh. The excuse for DCI Maxwell to visit the city centre had ostensibly been to deposit a file with the Procurator Fiscal. The truth was he needed to replenish his tobacco, and he could only buy it at the place on Canongate where she had parked outside. As he had leaned back into the passenger seat clutching his package of cut tobacco, she had outlined for him the information which had led them to Wester Hailes.

Now she scratched the side of her nose and glanced across at him. "The community officer felt you wanted to know about this one sir," she said. "He was the first at the scene after a phone call from some biddy who had found him when she went to take his messages. When he radioed it into the control room he specifically asked that you be informed and attend. Control room sent it upstairs to the local CID but they passed it straight on to us as soon as the locals had had a look at the scene. It seems you knew the body from some time back. According to the officer that is." Maxwell glanced across at her, then along the front of the building and back to her before asking, "Who's the beat officer then?" Joanne paused for a moment to check her notebook to bring the information to the fore.

"The Community Officer, sir," she corrected him pointedly, "Is Jack Dwyer,' she said, 'A PC Jack Dwyer. He has stayed on at the flat after the local CID attended and had requested the job be sent upstairs to the MIT.' She paused then added, 'You know him sir?' Maxwell allowed a grim grin to pass over his face and paused for a moment before answering.

'Oh aye, I know Jack. Good bloke. We were on the beat together, in the days before the talking brooches and computers. Thought he'd died off years ago, ought to have done now, the old bugger. He's from the south."

'England?' she asked.

'No. Dumfries" he chuckled. "So who's the stiff then?'
Joanne looked again at her notebook before answering,

"One Jimmy Quinn, sir," Maxwell's face fell and for a
moment he was silent. He turned his face to look at the outside
wall of the flats.

"Fucking old bastard," he murmured. "Beat me to it, did
you?' he said slowly and quietly, his lips scarcely moving. For
a minute neither of them spoke, Joanne knew from the few
years of working with her boss that he would tell her what he
wanted her to know when he was ready, and not before. If she
asked too many questions too early she would be told little or
nothing of any importance, or told to be quiet. Experience is
a grand thing, she thought, waiting for him to speak. Maxwell
reached into the side pocket of his jacket and brought out a
pipe and then a small plastic bag of tobacco which he had
bought from the shop in the city.

'Not going to light it Jo" he said quietly, "So don't get them
in a twist,' Without looking at her he felt a disapproving frown
forming on Joanne's mouth. Looking out again through the
windscreen of the car, he sat still, thinking of what to say to his
detective sergeant. He took a slice of the tobacco and placed
it into the palm of his left hand and started to grind it with the
heel of his right hand until the tobacco lay shredded in his
left palm. Then, taking his pipe in his right hand he carefully
scooped the tobacco into the bowl of the pipe, tamping it
down with the end of his index finger. He placed the pipe
in his mouth and drew on it. There was a good draw. It just
needed lighting now, but that would have to wait until they got

outside the car. Joanne would allow no smoking in her new car. Nor had she allowed it in her old one either. Maxwell was old school, she was new school, but despite that, they worked well together and had a good relationship, provided she did as she was told. The relationship worked though, in spite of his idiosyncrasies, and her excess of keenness and adherence to the rules at times, as he saw it.

Maxwell did not have long to go before drawing his pension after some thirty-two years on the job. Many of those years had been spent in divisional CID, until now, when he had become one of several Chief Inspectors running teams on the Major Investigation Team for the East of Scotland. The new Police Scotland organisation had finally settled down but still had critics, and the whole of the country had been divided into three areas for the investigation of major crimes. Maxwell and Baker worked on the eastern side of the country, which covered Edinburgh down to the Northumberland border of England, whilst the Western area covered Glasgow down to Cumbria on that side of the country. Northern area covered the 'sheep shaggers' of the northern part of the country. Joanne had been working with Maxwell for almost three years now out of her ten years service. She was in her late twenties, almost thirty, and made the hearts of many men race from time to time. Maxwell had paired himself with her on the MIT as a means of keeping the wolves in plain clothing away from her door, and because she came with an excellent service reputation. She was a good copper, and would go a lot further, provided she kept her nose clean, and so far, from his perspective, she had done nothing to blot her copybook.

Joanne looked out of the windscreen at the thin strip of grass struggling to grow between the edge of the building and the parking plot by the pavement and the roadside. She tapped her fingers lightly on the steering wheel whilst she waited patiently for Maxwell to decided what it was she was going to be told. Maxwell lurched sideways and pulled out a stainless steel Zippo lighter from the left-hand pocket of his jacket. He sat idly rubbing his finger over the small black pipe engraved in the bottom corner of the implement and finally drew in a deep breath.

'Well', he finally said. 'Jimmy Quinn.' He paused again and took another breath. 'I didn't know he lived here, used to live in a place off the Canongate. Lived there for years with his wife and kids, then the kids buggered off as soon as they could. It's one of those places that's been done up and gentrified in recent years. Cost you a fortune to live there now. They were slums when Quinn lived there. He just made it worse." He paused again. "Nasty little bastard he was. Wondered where he had got to." He placed a hand on the door handle and started to open the door.

'Wait a minute sir' Joanne exclaimed. 'You need to tell me a bit more than that sir, like what was he good for in his time?' Maxwell sank back in the seat again and turned to look at her. For a few seconds, he said nothing, trying to work out how to tell her why Jimmy Quinn had crossed his path in the past.

'He was good for nothing" he said, "Except fucking his kids," He stared her directly in her eyes. 'And others as well.' Joanne blinked and remained silent for a moment or two before finally letting out her response.

'Oh shit.' She said quietly, then looked away from him back to the grass in front of the apartment block. 'You can light your pipe if you want to sir.' She finally said. Maxwell smiled grimly and nodded his head in thanks as he flicked the Zippo. Holding the flame down across the mouth of his old Peterson pipe, clouds of smoke billowed from it in seconds, and he hastily reached to wind down the window of his door. They were electric and there was no window winder. Joanne turned on the ignition and hit both window buttons on the side of her door. The two front windows slid neatly down and the cloud of smoke blew from the car in seconds in the fresh breeze coursing through the car. Maxwell leaned sideways towards the now open window and puffed on the pipe to get it going properly, blowing the smoke out of the window. For a few seconds, he puffed until it was going properly then held it on the door sill so that the smoke went directly outside.

'He had three kids if I remember correctly,' he continued quietly. 'A boy, then a girl and finally a second boy. As each one of them became four or five he started to abuse them. Carried on until they were ten or eleven by which time the next one was four or five and he started on that one. There were rumours of other kids, relations of some sort who were involved as well, and neighbours and local kids too. Went on for some years. We could never nail the dirty bastard.'

'What about the wife though?' Joanne asked, her eyes wide in a sort of disbelief. 'You said he was married. What did she have to do with anything?' She moved over to the side of the driver's door so that she could more easily sit turned facing her boss. 'Was she involved with it, I mean, she must have been aware of what was going on?' Maxwell grimaced at her.

'Doesn't seem so. She never made any complaints, the kids only told their mates, if they told anybody, and nobody ever came to us. So, what I've just told you was rumour, gossip and neighbourhood tittle-tattle. Nobody said anything. The Police were not the best friends of Quinn and his type, nor any of the neighbours or people he knocked around with. I only picked up on it after it had been going on for some years. A hint here, a story there, nothing definite. Nothing solid. No complaints, No investigations. I just knew he was up to something, but never had anything to go on. I had him in the nick once or twice, gave him a bit of a hard time, but he said nothing, the bastard.' He paused and grinned at her.

'This was in the days before changes in legislation you understand. We had recourse to an ancient act of parliament never taught at the college. It's called the Ways and Means Act. Worked well most of the time, though it got abused a bit.' He paused and looked her directly in the eye. 'I never did anything illegal you understand Jo, never. Maybe smacked him once or twice now and again, frightened the shite out of him a lot, but never planted anything, no rhino whips or waterboarding, never anything too unofficial. Got results at times.' He paused again. "In many ways using the old Ways and Means was due to frustration. We knew someone had committed a crime but though we had a lot of proof could never prove it well enough to get them to court. So we resorted to the Ways and Means Act. Not the best of times. It's better now though in many ways. More resources to help us out, what with forensics and stuff. Much better.' He drew again on his pipe, blowing the smoke out of the open window before continuing.

'Couldn't do anything with him then, ever. It went on for some years. Then the kids left home and the stories stopped. Seems the kids got out as soon as they were able. Abroad, south to England. Anywhere just to get out of his way. Nobody ever nailed him. And now, it seems he's gone and beaten us. Dead.' One of the rumours was he started when he was in his teens. Started hitting on kids where he lived in the Gorbals in Glasgow. Some of the local neds found out and beat the hell out of him. That's how he came to be on our patch. Then suddenly he disappeared for a few years. Turns out he was in the Army, went to Germany, found a woman to marry him and came back to Edinburgh. That's how he started up again." He grinned grimly at her and hit the button on his door, the window rose. 'Come on, let's see how the old shite died shall we?' He opened the passenger door as Joanne hit her window button and got out of the car to join him. He stood in front of the car bonnet waiting for her. She flicked her key fob at the car and the indicators beeped and flashed as the car doors locked. She took the lead into the apartment block striding out to arrive first at the front door. Maxwell gave her blue-jeaned backside an admiring glance, and mentally smacked his wrist for the thought which flashed through his mind. Pack it in you, lecherous old bugger, he said to himself. She's almost old enough to be your daughter and thought of his two daughters. One just finishing university and the other well well-established as a teacher in a high school in the city.

They walked across the narrow rough churned lawn of the doorway to the apartment block. To their right was a wooden door which hid the bin store for the block. They stood for a moment in the doorway knocking dirt from their shoes before Joanne opened the door and entered the block. A concrete staircase ran from the right-hand side of the entry area to the upper floors, whilst on the ground floor itself four different coloured painted doors indicated the presence of four apartments on that floor. Maxwell knew that the second and third floors would be identical to this one. Built in the 60s and 70s to the cheapest budget, all identical. The hallway and staircase walls were covered in plaster, painted cream originally, but now decorated with the graffiti and artwork of the local kids. It was not pleasant to look at, and it was evident from the smell that the entrance hallway had been used as a urinal from time to time. Maxwell's nose curled at the smell as he looked back at the door they had come through. It was made from thick wire mesh-covered glass set in a wooden frame. It did not have a lock on it; where the lock and door handle had been a large rough hole in the wood allowed a draft to blow through from outside. The whole place was open to anyone who wished to come in at any time of day or night. There was no security at all.

'No wonder it's such a bloody tip,' he said to the sergeant. 'Thank god they're paying out to get them spruced up. Let's hope they stay in good nick.' They walked up the stairs, Maxwell showing his seniority of years by the time they had made it to the third floor. He paused on the landing, his breath coming with difficulty. 'Need to say anything about the pipe sir?' Joanne said with a grin.

'Bugger off sergeant,' Maxwell replied with a grin and waved a hand to one of the doors on the landing which was slightly open. 'That's where he'll be.' He said. Joanne stepped a few paces forward to the door and rapped on it with her knuckles. It swung open under the slight pressure and they could hear two voices coming from inside the apartment.

CHAPTER 3

oanne held the door open for her boss and Maxwell eased past her, brushing accidentally against the leather jacket she wore over a white shirt and dark brown V-neck jumper. He ignored her fine figure and murmured an apology as he passed her and walked down the corridor to where the sound of the voices was coming.

'Hello,' he called out. The head and shoulders of an elderly constable came around the doorway at the end of the corridor. Jack Dwyer grinned.

'Bloody hell Lewis. You're not still on the job are you?' He moved into the corridor as the two detectives walked along the short corridor towards him. Dwyer held out his hand. Maxwell reached out and shook it, grinning into the face of his old friend. 'Christ, Jack how many years is it?' he asked.

'Must be about ten now sir,' Dwyer said. Maxwell half turned and held out his arm to Joanne to introduce Joanne.

'This is DS Baker, Jack. She's my Sergeant.' Dwyer nodded a greeting to the attractive young woman and smiled.

'You have my sympathies, Sergeant,' he said smiling. Joanne grinned broadly but did not reply. Maxwell glanced around the entrance to the living room which lay ahead of him but the doorway now was almost blocked by the second voice they had heard, a young uniformed constable who towered over all of them. Maxwell nodded his head in greeting and the young man returned the nod but said nothing.

'So, what have we got Jack?' Maxwell asked. Dwyer turned and walked back into the living cum dining room, the two detectives followed, the young constable hurriedly stepping backwards out of their way. All four stood crowded into the area immediately in front of the open living room door. Before Dwyer could reply Maxwell held up his hand to silence him. 'Just a second Jack' he turned to the young constable.' What's your name son?' he asked. The tall young man replied' Jackson sir, Alan Jackson.'

'Jacko is it?' Maxwell asked grinning.

'Yes sir, amongst other things.' He replied.

'Right Jacko, I want you to go downstairs to DS Bakers car, it's the flash pale blue Volvo without dents right outside the front door. In the boot, you'll find overalls and stuff. Bring three sets up will you?' The young man's head nodded and he looked puzzled. 'You'll be on guard outside the door of the flat to stop anyone coming in. OK?'

'Right sir,' he replied with a disappointed look on his face. Maxwell grinned at him,

'Don't worry Jacko, you'll get your chance in time. There's enough stiffs to go around this city for everybody to have one eventually.' Jackson eased his large bulk between the others and took the car keys from Joanne's outstretched hand. He walked off down the corridor. Maxwell turned to PC Dwyer. 'So, where is the bastard then Jack?' Maxwell asked.

'Bedroom sir' replied Dwyer, pointing to the room back along the corridor they had just walked past.

'OK. Let's hang on until young master Jacko gets back shall we?' He looked around the living room and took in the rather sparse furniture. A two-seater sofa in a tweed mixture fabric covering and a single matching chair were arranged in front of a wall-mounted electric fire, the chair was to the right as they had come in through the door. The settee was placed facing the fire. Under a large picture window on the left wall was an old-fashioned Formica-topped drop leaf table with three similarly old-fashioned white painted wooden chairs placed neatly under the three free sides. Behind one of the chairs was a metal walking frame pushed against the wall, and behind that against the wall, an aluminium adjustable walking stick. A newspaper lay on the table with a pen from a local William Hills bookmakers open at the inside back pages on the racing pages.

In front of the fire was a very old worn rug made from pieces of cast-off rags and clothing. Nothing like that was sold in shops, it was homemade. In former times Maxwell recalled, everyone had a rug like that. The wife of the family would make them with a rugging hook from cast-off and old clothing. It was the only form of carpet available to the working people who lived in the city, and then Wester Hailes, in times gone by. Now there weren't many of them around. Maxwell nudged it thoughtfully with his foot.

In the right-hand corner of the room was a small low table with a modern flat-screen television on it, beneath it an old video player, and by its side a small radio, and CD player. The remotes for both television and video lay on the table in front of the television, gathering dust. The fireplace had a mock oak wood surround fitted to the wall with a shelf, some four inches wide, running along the top. In the centre was a small gold-coloured carriage clock and to either side of the clock were standing several cheaply framed photographs. Larger photographs were affixed to the wall above the fireplace, and as Maxwell and Baker turned around to examine the rest of the room they saw other photos on the other walls. All were framed in a mixture of cheap plastic, wood or plastic designed to look like metal. Joanne's lips moved silently as she looked at each wall and counted the images on the three walls.

'Twenty-four, sir.' She said quietly,' Including the ones on the fireplace.' Maxwell nodded his head silently and looked around the collection of photos on the three walls, turning to take them all in, wall by wall.

'Quite a collection isn't it?' he said quietly. 'Looks like they go back probably fifty years or so judging by the things some of them are wearing.' He paused to look again at the ones on the fireplace wall and then those behind him on the opposite wall. 'And kids,' he said, 'Lots of them have got kids in them with him and other people.' He drew in a deep breath and looked across at Dwyer. 'The bastard never stopped did he Jack?'

The older constable followed his glance around the room and shook his head slowly as he moved from wall to wall.

'Looks like it, sir. Some of them look like his own kids but most of them don't seem to be connected.' The three of them stood turning around in a group each one taking in some differing aspect of the images they saw before them on the walls, trying to understand what lay behind it. Each of them thinking the same thing, that Jimmy Quinn had not stopped abusing children even when he had left the centre of the city and moved out onto the 'scheme.' Even when he had divorced his wife. Perhaps it had been easier for him then, living alone in the flat, with no one to put a brake on his activities.

'Sergeant Baker' The voice of the young police officer standing in the front doorway echoed down the corridor. Joanne turned and walked to the door, returning a minute later with three sets of white forensic overalls in her hands. Handing one each to the other two men the three of them struggled into the flimsy white one-piece coveralls, and pulled on blue plastic over shoes and thin blue rubber gloves. Maxwell walked to the corridor and called to the constable. 'Don't let anybody in Jacko unless you tell me first. Got it?' he said.

'Yes sir.' Jackson replied and pulled the front door of the flat closed.

'Right,' said Maxwell. 'Let's see what we've got shall we?' He led the other two from the living room to the corridor and with one blue gloved finger pushed open the door to the bedroom which was slightly ajar. A faint metallic smell wafted out of the room into the corridor and caught in the nostrils of all three of them. Maxwell took a deep breath and exhaled, then stepped through into the room followed by DS Baker. Constable Dwyer stayed out in the corridor watching the two detectives through the open doorway as they stood taking in what lay in the room. He had already been into the room and knew how small it was, not big enough for three people and the furniture which was in there.

The two detectives looked around the room but were immediately drawn to the dead body lying in the single bed under the window. At the side of the bed was a collapsible wooden card table with a green baize top. A half-empty bottle of Buckfast Wine stood on the table along with a half-empty bottle of whisky. The screw top of the Buckfast lay by its side. At the head of the bed was a small cream-painted wooden bedside cabinet on which stood an illuminated bedside lamp and a pair of half-moon reading glasses. The small drawer at the top of the cabinet was partially opened. Maxwell looked into the drawer without touching it. Inside was a pad of betting slips from William Hill in Wester Hailes and three small blue pens with the bookmaker's name on them.

Maxwell turned his head towards Jack Dwyer in the doorway. 'How far to the bookies Jack?' he asked pointing to the pad of betting slips. Dwyer pondered the question for a moment or so before answering,

'Under a mile, I would think. Take him some time to walk there with his walking stick or frame, if he ever used them. Maybe the frame and stick were just for show and to persuade the DHSS' he replied. Maxwell nodded in agreement.

'Aye. Could be right there. Still about a mile though.' he replied.

Most of the space in the drawer was taken up with several strips of prescription tablets of differing types of pills and the boxes they came from. Maxwell took a silver Cross ballpoint pen from his inside pocket and gently poked one of the boxes of pills, it bulged open, revealing that inside were two identical strips of pills, still in their foil wrapping. A front door key with a plastic tag on it marked, 'Front Door spare' was jammed at the front of the drawer.

Against the right-hand wall at the foot of the bed as the two detectives came into the room was a flat-pack single wardrobe in a Birch-coloured wood. Opposite the window wall was a cream hand-painted three-drawer chest of drawers. On top were four photographs standing in frames, a black plastic comb with grey hair clinging to it, and a dark blue Salbutamol inhaler. On the floor standing by the side of the bed and in easy reach of the bed's occupant lay an opened can of Irn Bru, Scotland's second most popular drink after whisky, according to A G Barr, the drinks manufacturer. Two more unopened cans of the drink were close to it on the floor but to one side of the opened one. A fourth can, apparently empty, lay on its side just under the bed. Also on its side was a second half bottle of Famous Grouse whisky, its screw top firmly in position, the bottle was half empty. On the floor by the side of the bed was a rug similar to the one in the living room, it lay flat and unruffled on the floor. Lying half on the rug and half under the bed was a copy of the Daily Record newspaper, its pages skewed across the rug, and a cheap metal ashtray full of cigarette ends.

Lying under a grubby white sheet, two worn brown woollen blankets and a pink candlewick bedspread lay the body of Jimmy Quinn. Maxwell needed only one look to confirm that it was indeed he. 'Jack. A minute please.' he called to the officer standing outside. The door pushed open and PC Dwyer stepped over the threshold of the room and stopped. Maxwell half-turned. 'It's him alright isn't it?' he said.

'Aye sir, you're right. No mistaking that evil little sod is there?' replied Dwyer. Maxwell turned back to look at the body, nodding his head in agreement. The first part of the identification was complete.

'So then Jack, what makes you think the death of this bastard warrants the time and effort of two of the country's best-loved and most hard-working detectives? Seems like he just went to bed, had a good drink of Grouse and Irn Bru and died. No hatchet sticking out of his head as far as I can see, no immediate signs of gunshot wounds, his neck doesn't look like someone has taken a chiv to it. So what makes you suspicious Jack? Or did you just want me to see him for Auld Lang Syne?' He turned and smiled grimly at Dwyer. Dwyer pointed to the point where the covers came up to the neck of the body in the bed.

'Just pull the cover back sir, but gently now.' He said. Maxwell looked at his old friend quizzically and then at Baker.

'What do you reckon we should do Jo?' he asked lightly.

'I think you should perhaps do as the constable says, and stop pissing about sir.' She said lightly. Maxwell grinned at her and turned back to Dwyer.

'You see what I'm up against these days Jack. No respect. No bloody respect at all. What's the world coming to? Wasn't like that in our day was it Jack?'

"You're right there sir," Jack replied. 'Aye, different days sir. When men were men, and sheep were scared.' Maxwell bent over the body and gently took hold of the sheet, blankets and counterpane in both his hands and slowly peeled them back until they lay on Quinn's chest, slowly revealing the pyjama-clad body underneath. Jimmy Quinn was dead, of that there was no doubt. The colour had gone from his face completely and his closed eyes had sunk into their sockets. The skin on his face was stretched taught across the underlying bone structure and a rim of deep purple blood had already started to form at the back of his neck where it touched the pillow. The thin strands of white hair which remained on his head were lying swept neatly across the bald majority of his head and the top of his forehead. In addition, Jimmy Quinn's hands were crossed over his chest in a formal funereal position of repose, all ready for an undertaker. Joanne pointed to his hands.

'Not normal that, is it sir?' she asked.

'No. Looks like he had bad rheumatoid arthritis, doesn't it? Can't see him having been able to drag the blankets and sheet up to his chin like that.' Quinn's fingers were twisted and swollen at the knuckles, the veins standing out on the back of the hands like blue railway lines. Jimmy Quinn was dead alright.

The three officers looked down on the corpse, each with differing thoughts. Maxwell was the first to break the silence.

'Well now. Was he killed and placed like this, or did someone find him dead and put him into this position? What do we think?' He said glancing sideways at his detective sergeant. Joanne stood upright from the bent-over position she had been standing in to observe the body.

'Hard to say without seeing everything sir.' She replied quietly. 'Could be either. But I do think his hands have been placed in this position since death.' Dwyer coughed gently. Joanne glanced at the officer and saw he was suppressing a grin. She looked back at the body.

'Maybe you should look at the rest of him sir,' Dwyer said. Maxwell turned to look at him and saw the thin smile on his face. He frowned and turned back to look at the body. Taking the bedclothes again he continued to pull them back off the body until they lay in a heap at the foot of the bed. The metallic smell they had first noticed on entering the flat now wafted strongly into their faces. It was the smell of blood. Joanne gasped. Maxwell grunted. Dwyer gave a subdued laugh.

'Puts a bit of a different light on the subject now doesn't it sir?' he said. Maxwell nodded his head silently, looking carefully at the fully exposed body lying on the bed. Exposed was the appropriate word to use. Jimmy Quinn's pyjama pants had been pulled down and were lying in a rumpled heap around his ankles, still with the feet in the legs, but to all intents almost removed. His bare legs, his penis and his hips were fully exposed to the light, only his pyjama coat covered his body down to below his waist, and this had been fastened from the neck to the bottom, and lay on his body in a neat array. Blood covered all the exposed parts of his body from the inside of his thighs down to his knees and had soaked into the bottom sheet and mattress and had also stained into the sheet and blankets which had lain on top of him. Maxwell gently lifted the counterpane from the other bedclothes and saw the blood had only just soaked through the sheet and two blankets which lay immediately on top of the body. They had not soaked through to the counterpane. Quinn lay with his legs slightly apart at the feet and it appeared that the blood had come from a small cut on the inside of his left thigh. The cut was clear to see, as was the implement which had probably caused it, a wooden handled thin-bladed knife with a hollow ground edge. The blade was six and a half inches long and tapered to a fine point from the handle. Three stainless steel rivets punctured the four-inch long black wooden handle which held the two halves together. There was no blood visible on the top surface of the knife which they could see. It appeared that the knife had been placed close to the cut on the thigh and on top of the pool of blood lying between his legs after it had been used to create the small cut on the inner left thigh. The knife was lying directly in line with the shrivelled limp form of the old man's penis. The tip of the blade was facing his scrotum and the handle his feet. Along the underside of the legs and buttocks lay a thin layer of the same deep red discolouration they had seen on the neck.

Maxwell pointed to the surface of the knife, Joanne bent forward to see more closely what he was pointing to.

'See that? Looks like the knife was placed there after the blood had stopped flowing. It's settled into the blood a little, but not completely fallen into the blood flow whilst it was still very liquid. Could have been placed there sometime after the body had stopped bleeding out.' Joanne nodded her head silently. The blood had indeed settled around the knife, forming a slight meniscus effect around the edge of the blade and handle. Gently she touched the pool of blood with her index finger, there was a very slight tension against the digit, which sprung back into a flat surface when she released it. Similar to the skin on cold custard, she thought.

'Rule out suicide sir?' Joanne asked quietly. A stifled snort came from PC Dwyer behind her, followed by a cover-up cough.

'Smart arse,' said Maxwell. 'But yes, at this stage I think we can rule out suicide.' He stood up straight again and called through to the corridor behind them. 'PC Jackson' he shouted. The sound of the front door opening came down the corridor to them. 'Sir?' Jackson called back.

'Get the doctor here, and scenes of crime will you please Jacko? Give them my name. Tell them I want four if possible, including photographers and video.'

'Roger that sir.' Jackson replied and started to close door as he reached for his personal radio. He paused for a moment before speaking into his radio. 'Excuse me sir' he said. Maxwell looked round at the young officer and lifted his head in a questioning gesture. 'Sorry sir, but I don't know your name.' The young man flushed red from the shirt collar to his ears. Maxwell glanced at Dwyer who was turning away with a broad grin on his face.

'Yes. You're right officer. My fault. I should have introduced myself when I asked your name. I am Detective Chief Inspector Maxwell, Major Investigation Team at Leith. And this is Detective Sergeant Barker of the MIT as well,' said Maxwell, and smiled warmly at the officer, who nodded his head and made away along the corridor, feeling not quite as stupid as he had a moment before. Maxwell turned to PC Dwyer.

'What you smirking at? At least he had the nouse to ask. Won't die wondering that lad.' PC Dwyer wiped the grin from his face and nodded in agreement. Maxwell turned to his Detective Sergeant. 'Right Jo, I want the circus out for this one. I want you to call the Procurator for me, tell him what we've got and get the go-ahead from him. Find out if he's coming to see this or not. Don't suppose he will. Young Jackson is dealing with the doctor and SOCO, I want you to get a team out to cordon this place off and start house to house, just in case anybody saw anything. Get hold of the press office. See if they can be of some help on this one.' Turning to Dwyer he said, 'I want you involved Jack. You know this old bugger from way back same as I do. Not only that, the folk on the estate will know you. Possible that some of them even trust you.

Get onto the intelligence office and records, see if they have anything at all. Questioning, thieving, indecent assault, drunk and refusing to fight, pulled in for flashing, anything at all.' He paused for a moment thinking and then said, 'Take yourself off to the closes off Canongate. That's where he started out. Maybe someone there still remembers something from when he lived there. Perhaps now the bastard is dead they will feel happier about shopping him. Always providing there is anyone left from his time there. Dig around Jack. There will be something somewhere.' PC Dwyer nodded his head in agreement.

Just at that moment, a clod of wet mud thudded against the window of the living room, causing all three of them to duck down involuntarily and look towards the window. Grinning sheepishly Joanne went over to the window to see a youth of mid-teens legging it away down the close. 'Locals' she said. 'Just the one.'

'Wonder if that was for us or Quinn' said Maxwell glancing at the other two officers. 'Either way it means somebody knows something about him, and might be prepared to talk to us.'

CHAPTER 4

The following morning DS Baker was seated in her boss's chair at his large wooden desk sifting through the photographs which had been removed the previous day from the walls and furniture in Quinn's flat. She was trying to categorise them into some sort of order and entering the details on a spreadsheet which she had started on Maxwell's computer. Behind her, the sun shone through the large window of the room making it easy to view the images in her hand, but difficult at times, because of the sun, to see the screen in front of her. She moved her head from side to side as she typed one entry into the list after another. There was a double tap on the partially open office door. Joanne looked up from her desk. It was one of her junior colleagues, Detective Constable David Jones. He stood in the doorway with his hand on the door handle.

'Boss not in Sarg?' he asked. Joanne made as though to carry out a thorough search of the office, including under the desk, before grinning at him.

'Appears not Davie. Appears not. Anything I can do for you?' The young detective constable smiled broadly at his good-looking boss.

'Respecting your senior position within the hierarchy of this force boss, and not wishing to get myself into any more trouble than I can easily do, I will refrain from stating the obvious.' He said. 'However, I have this for the DCI.' He was brandishing a plain unsealed white foolscap envelope in his free hand. Joanne rested her chin on her knuckles and her elbows on the desk.

'Care to enlighten me, oh thou great and spotty unwashed one?' she said. He grinned and stepped forward, handing her the envelope.

'It's the post mortem report on Quinn. Just come in.' He said. 'Leave it with you, ok?' Joanne's eyes lit up as she reached for the envelope.

'Aye, no problem. Thanks, Davie.' She took the envelope from him and removed several sheets of paper from inside and started to read them. David hung about to see what she would tell him. 'On your way young man, on your way.' She said in his direction without looking up from the forms. 'Close the door as you go now.' The DC snorted and walked out of the office, closing the door behind him as he did so. Joanne smiled to herself and started to read the report.

She read the whole of the report twice and then started to read a third time, this time making notes on a pad of A4 paper on the desk in front of her. She stopped her writing and carefully moved the stacks of photos she was working on to one side, taking care to ensure they kept in the same piles as she was creating. After working for some minutes on the pad she saved her work on the computer and started a new form for the contents of the post-mortem, copying down her notes from the A4 pad, noting further items of interest and significance. As she started to read again the report from Dr Macpherson the pathologist, she heard familiar footsteps coming along the corridor towards the office. She knew the footsteps belonged to DCI Maxwell and looked up as the door swung open. She started to rise to her feet to vacate his seat. Maxwell waved her down as he unfastened the grey mackintosh he was wearing. Though bright and blue sky outside, it was still only late spring and chilly. Maxwell hung up the coat on a wooden coat hanger in the corner of the room behind the door.

'Sir ye down Jo, sit ye down,' he said as he drew up a hard-backed chair from the far wall and placed it in front of his desk. As he swung his legs around to move closer to the desk he banged his knees heavily against the solid wooden vanity board and yelped in pain. 'Shit' he said. 'Sorry Jo. Forgot that this board thing is there.' He bent to rub at his painful knees. 'So, what do we have then?' nodding at the photos and the post-mortem report he could see on his desk in front of her. Joanne turned the report around and slid it across the desk to him.

'See for yourself sir' she said. 'Interesting and a bit weird if you ask me.' Maxwell bent down to read the report in silence. 'Fancy a coffee, sir?' Joanne asked.

'Mm. Aye, ok.' The DCI answered absently as he started to try and digest what he was reading. Joanne rose from the desk and went to a light brown wooden desk set against the side of the office wall. It was cluttered with files, a coffee-making machine, a kettle and a clutch of mugs bearing the logos of various Scottish football teams. Having mugs from all the major teams meant never causing offence to visitors by giving them the wrong one. She grinned and half turned to face her boss,

'Ah the old perky copulator' she said. Maxwell just grunted, unaware of the old joke she was attempting to resurrect. She turned back to the machine and turned it on, then put sugars in two of the mugs and returned to her side of the desk. Maxwell looked up.

'Do you make any sense of this Jo?' he asked. He placed the report on the desk in front of him and leaned back in the chair, brushing back the greying hair from his forehead. Joanne took the report from in front of him and glanced once again at the contents.

'It's a strange one isn't it?' she said and started to read aloud bits from it. 'Thin, undernourished but not excessively so, clean and well looked after. Clean pyjamas, unstained.' She looked up at Maxwell, 'Could mean he took care of himself or someone else was coming in to see he washed and such.' She carried on. 'Clean hands and fingernails, hair washed and combed, what there was of it, some trace of lividity, but not as much as would have been expected.' She paused again and looked up grinning. 'Oh excuse me, my dear Doctor Finlay, did you not see the rather large pool of blood he was lying in?' Maxwell grinned at the attempt of mimicking the television series receptionist of the same name. He stood up from the desk and walked over to the coffee machine which had started to make loud glouping noises. The noise threatened to block out their conversation. He stood by the desk and poured out the two mugs of coffee and stirred them with a rather stained teaspoon lying on the side of the desk. Lifting the two mugs he took one and placed it alongside Joanne's side of the desk and walked back to his seat. Joanne continued to read extracts from the report.

'Spondylolysis of the spine. Rheumatoid arthritis in his hands and knees, osteoarthritis in other bits as well and COPD.' She looked across the desk. 'Good' she said quietly, 'That means the evil sod was in pain. Old fracture of the orbital maxilla. That's his cheekbone yes?' she asked. Maxwell nodded his head and considered this for a moment.

'As I recall, obtained when he lived in Glasgow in his younger years before he wished himself on us. Believed to have been tampering with kids in his neighbourhood and the locals gave him some Glasgow justice.' He sat back and drank from the mug in his hand and sat for a moment trying to recall exactly what he had heard at the time, all those years ago. The memory suddenly came back to him.

'Aye, that's right.' he said as the memory returned. 'I remember now. He got himself roughed over by a group of neds from the area he lived in, not far from the docks in the Gorbals. Glasgow Police reckoned they caught him touching up one of their kids and gave him the gypsies warning. Ended up in hospital for a few days, but sadly was released and pretty soon afterwards turned up on our patch.' He drank from his mug again then placed it on the desk in front of him. Joanne was silent for a moment then asked,

'So when did you first run into him sir?' she said. Maxwell frowned as he tried to recall exactly when it had been when he first came across Quinn.

'It must have been in the early eighties I think. Yes, must have been. I hadn't been long on the job, along with Jack Dwyer, and we were sent to some sort of disturbance in one of the closes off the Canongate, not far from where you live now. Course, that was before the whole area was gentrified. 'Fore the likes of you took up residence.' Joanne grinned and ignored the comment, simply waving a hand gently for him to continue. He paused to recall more of the incident and carried on.

'It was a domestic. His wife had given him a good hiding one night and he was bleeding a fair bit from his nose, as I remember. She was a vicious little sort. A skinny little German lass. He met her there when he was in the forces. Anyway, she had laid into him and he came off worst.' He sipped again from his mug before continuing. 'Nothing came of it. She refused to make any sort of statement saying it was just a Friday night sort out, and he wouldn't say a thing, so we left it at that. Sounded like she gave him a good hiding for all the right reasons at the time. But he kept coming up over the years.'

'In what way sir?' Joanne asked drinking from the black coffee. Maxwell considered the question for a minute before carrying on.

'You've got to realise, things were different then, Policing that is. Jack and I worked together in uniform in that area of the city for some time before they split us up. Then we were on different shifts, but we occasionally pooled whatever information came to light, and kept our eyes open for him. From time to time we would get a snippet of information here and there from people who lived in the area and we'd share it. Nobody liked the Police then, especially from that area, not even the law-abiding ones, but the one thing they had in common was that they would not abide anybody who was a kiddy fiddler, as they called them then, Paedophiles nowadays. So from time to time Jack or I would get a sniff of something about him, and keep an eye out for him.' He drank again from the mug.

'Not a bad brew Detective Sergeant,' he said nodding appreciatively at the coffee, 'If you ever need a proper job I could find you one.'

'Get on with it sir.' Joanne said lightly, grinning at her boss.

'So. then I was promoted to CID in the city, and Jack stayed on the beat before sometime later getting sent out to the Wild West. Not sure how long that's been, must be ten years or more.' Joanne interrupted him.

'Just a minute sir, did you say his wife was German?'

'I think so, why?'

'One of the photos from the flat is of a bloke in army uniform and what is obviously a bride. A wedding photograph, but I am sure there was some German writing in the background, maybe a signpost or a sign on the side of a building. I just remember it was out of place a bit in his sort of flat. So that might well have been him on his wedding day in Germany.' She started to rummage through the closest of the piles of photos on the desk at her side and pulled out one of them which was in a frame. 'There' she said, handing over the photo. Maxwell stared at it for a minute before looking up at her.

'You are a right little sharp-eyed detective aren't you?' he said. 'That's Jimmy Quinn alright, and that does look like a German sign in the background.' He put the photo down on the desk. 'So that, presumably, is Mrs Jimmy then. So, what else does the good doctor tell us from his butchery of Quinn?' Joanne continued to read bits from the report.

'Well, in addition to the broken cheekbone he also had old fractures of his arms, both of them, ribs, several of them, and a depressed skull fracture. Sounds like his mates from Glasgow did a real job on him. I mean, that could have almost been attempted murder couldn't it?' Maxwell nodded his head.

'Could have been, if he had opened his mouth, which he didn't, and wouldn't have if he really had given them cause to kick him around a bit. Sounds like our Jimmy started his abusing quite early.' He paused as something crossed his mind. 'Before he went to Germany in fact, before he joined the army.' Joanne considered this for a moment then asked,

'If he was doing it before he joined the army and went to Germany, you would have thought that he would have packed it in when he came home with a wife, wouldn't you?' she asked.

'Maybe, maybe not. You can never tell. It gets set into their minds as being alright, as being normal, from an early age. Maybe he was abused as a child and it was part of life for him. Maybe his dad started on him and he saw nothing wrong with doing it to other kids. Easier in some ways than trying to find himself an adult to make love to.' He stopped and took up his mug again peering into it. 'Would you believe it' he said, 'This mug's empty Joanne.' Joanne sighed and got up from her chair, picking up his mug and taking it with her own to the side table. She refilled both of them and set them down once more and sat for a moment in silent contemplation. Maxwell did not disturb her, aware that she was turning something over in her mind, and willing to give her the opportunity to voice her own thoughts.

'I don't buy that sir.' She said. 'If he was abused as a child and started to abuse other children when he grew to, say puberty or early teens, then that in itself was his normal way of life. You are right about it not being the normal taboo in which the rest of us regard child molestation, but it wouldn't necessarily mean that when he found a wife he would stop it. I think he would have carried on with or without a wife. He would just have become a bit more cunning to make sure she never found out, and perhaps the hiding she had given him when you first met him proves that she had found out and had given him a beating herself.'

'Is this you and your studying for the psychology degree then Sergeant?' he asked with a grin. Joanne blushed and took a long sip from her mug. She had come into the Police with a

47

degree in Criminal Law and was now studying part-time with the Open University for a degree in Criminology and Psychology. Juggling the job and the study was not easy, but Joanne was determined to see it through. Whilst it was something of a joke in the department, nobody thought it was funny, and many admired her dedication to running a six-year course alongside the normal day-to-day work of being a detective.

Maxwell considered what she had said and turned it over in his mind. Would Jimmy Quinn have carried on molesting children after he was married? Would he have molested his own children as they grew older? That certainly doesn't conflict with rumours he had heard during his time as a young copper in the city centre.

'OK.' He said, 'Carry on with reading the post-mortem report. Let's get as much of the overall picture first before we start digging.' Joanne found the part of the page she had previously reached and was about to continue when there was a double knock on the door.

'Come in' Maxwell called out. The door opened partially and the young detective who had delivered the post-mortem report appeared around the doors edge. He found who he was looking for and said to Maxwell,

'Sorry to interrupt sir, but we've turned up some more photos from the flat. Do you want them here?' Maxwell stood up and went to the door, his hand extended for whatever the detective had concealed behind the door. Two heavy white supermarket carrier bags appeared round the door clasped in the young DCs hand. Maxwell took them.

'Jesus, what's in here?' he asked.

'Just albums sir, photos, not records.'

'Right, thanks, Davie.' Maxwell strained to lift the two bags onto his desk with one hand and Joanne rose to take them from him.

'Bloody hell' she said, 'How many are there?' They emptied the bags onto the desk, there were four large cheap fabric-covered brown albums, stuffed with photographs, both loose and stuck on pages in the books.

'This is going to keep you busy Jo' said Maxwell, as they turned pages in the books, and flicked over odd photos one after the other. For a few moments, they both looked casually at their individual books and finally put them to one side with the remainder of the images taken from the flat.

'Right, on with the report Jo. One thing at a time eh?' Joanne cleared her throat and resumed her selective reading of the post-mortem report.

'Now we come to the good bits. Stomach contents.' She paused and laughed, a dry humourless laugh, then looked up at her boss.

'Irn Bru. Irn bloody Bru.' She said. Traces of whisky, no food at all, just Irn Bru. Oh, and Buckie as well.' Maxwell sat forward in his chair.

'He never said it was Irn Bru, not in his report, did he?' he asked incredulously.

'No sir, that was in a note to his report sir. Said that the stomach was empty apart from what appeared to be Irn Bru, Buckfast Wine and whisky, and a few small grains of what appears to be a white medication. No food. Nothing else.' She replaced the report down on the desk. 'That appears to be it, sir. Says he has sent the blood and the nasty bits away for toxicology and that the results should be through later today, with luck, or tomorrow at the latest.'

'Right. Not a lot more we can do until we get the bloods and bits back is there? So, I want you to keep on sorting and classifying the photos. Let's see what comes up from them.' He stopped as Joanne looked at him aghast at the task she had been given. 'Alright then, I'll get someone in to give you a hand then. Happy now?'

'Thank you, sir. Should only take about two weeks.' She dropped her hand to the right pocket of her jacket and fumbled around for a sweet.

'Alright then, if it makes you feel less hard done by I'll put young Davie on to give you a hand then. Midget Gems sergeant?' Maxwell enquired looking at the sweet packet in her hand.

'Yes sir. They are available, and can be purchased, in most high street shops these days, sir.' She replied as she handed three sweets over to him into his hand outstretched over the desk.

'Well, if you won't let me smoke, this is what you need to be supplying me with then.' He said. She grinned and popped two of the sweets into her own mouth. Maxwell pushed his chair back from the desk.

'One final thing Jo.' She looked at him quizzically.

'Sir?' she said.

'Any cause of death mentioned, you know, just as an afterthought?'

'Well, yes sir, there is sir, but I thought you weren't that interested.' She fumbled through the pages until she found the appropriate paragraph and made a great play of running a finger down the pages until finally stopping close to the bottom on the final page.

'Heart failure. Stab in the leg a contributory factor, along with possible heroin misuse.' Maxwell grinned at her and got up out of his chair straightening his jacket.

'Right then. You and me. Lunch. And I'm buying.' Joanne slumped back in her chair as though in a feint. He pointed a finger at her across the desk. 'And any more of that and you can forget it.' Joanne rose from her chair and fastened her jacket as they left the office.

'What's it to be sir, Compass or Credo?' she asked, naming two restaurants across the road from the station. Maxwell turned and locked the door behind them as they started walking along the corridor to the lift.

CHAPTER 5

The Leith Police canteen was similar in many ways to many of the remaining Police canteens across the breadth of the country. So many had been closed down, along with the police stations. Bad lighting, a limited menu and in need of decorating. Permeated by the smell of chips and washing up. Not a happy place.

'Should have known better,' Joanne mumbled through the Tuna and cress sandwich she was chewing on. Maxwell looked up from the white plate in front of him containing two unhealthy-looking meat pies.

'It's rude to talk with your mouth full. Didn't your mother never teach you that?' Joanne swallowed the mouthful and took a drink from a bottle of water at the side of the sandwich.

'Take you out for lunch, you said, I'm paying, you said. I don't know how your Anne copes with you at times. You are the sort who gives the Scots a bad name you know.' She put the plastic bottle down on the table heavily. Maxwell shook his head sadly.

'I never said we were going out, just that lunch was on me.' He pointed to his plate and then to her sandwich. 'See? Lunch.' They ate on in silence for a few minutes until they were joined by Jack Dwyer striding over to their table.

'They said I could find you here.' He looked from the plate to the sandwich and grinned. 'My how well you eat here in Leith' he said.

Maxwell looked up from his plate. 'What is it you want Jack? We were just enjoying a nice quiet break from all the backbreaking work we have been doing here whilst you have been out in the fresh air of Wester Hailes.' PC Dwyer leaned against the back of one of the spare chairs at the table and moved his head closer to the two officers.

'I think I might have turned something up this morning on the house-to-house.' He said quietly, then paused waiting for a reaction. When none was apparently forthcoming he continued.

'A day or so before yesterday one of the biddies in the block across from Quinn's saw a woman going into the block. Never seen her before she says. And that means she has never been seen in the city before if this old dear is anything to go by.' He paused and indicated the mug of black coffee by Maxwell's plate. 'That fresh coffee sir?' he asked. Maxwell waved towards it and Dwyer picked it up before carrying on. 'So. This visitor arrived about late morning the day before Quinn was found. Middle-aged, well dressed, five foot six or so, a bit chunky, so the lady says. Arrived on foot, no car, and a female.' Maxwell listened for more but that was it.

'That makes it Saturday or maybe Sunday morning when she arrived? Nothing else Jack? No idea how long she stayed for?' he asked. Dwyer put on a thinking face and suddenly lifted his index finger.

'Oh yes. The only other thing was sir, she was wearing black calf-length boots and a full-length red duffle coat.' He stood back from the chair and waited for a response.

'That's brilliant Jack. Well done. Thanks.' said Maxwell his face clouding over. He looked across at Joanne. 'You do realise what this means don't you?' he said. He glanced from one to the other, they both shook their heads. 'This ever gets out it's going to be the bloody Red Riding Hood Murder.' They both grinned. Dwyer continued.

'Nothing much else I'm afraid. She was carrying a black shoulder bag, but she said that the woman's face was hidden by the hood on the duffle coat, only saw her from the back, and the hood was pulled up. But she said it looked expensive, woollen, not a cheap one, and it was a proper duffle coat, the ones with the wooden buttons, not an anorak sort of thing. It was down almost to her knees. Says she didn't see the woman coming out of the block, and that's unusual. She's one of these women with bugger all else to do. In fairness, she is getting on a bit and a little infirm, so it's not too surprising she spends most of her day peering out the window. But she is sure she didn't see the woman coming out the block. Which is not to say she didn't come out at some time later in the day, is it?'

'You're right Jack. She could have been there all night for all the old woman saw. I suppose.'

"I think you could do with having another word with this old dear sir," Dwyer said.

"Any particular reason?" Maxwell asked.

"Seems that she went in to see Quinn later in the evening as she normally does, just to check he was alright. He was fine. Gave him a glass of Buckie and then left." That would be about ten o'clock. Said there was nothing wrong with him."

Maxwell glanced across at his DS. "What do you reckon Jo?" he asked. "Could she have done him in and left for the night?"

Joanne shook her head. "The blood was not sufficiently coagulated by the time Jack here found him, there was quite a skin on it but it wasn't solid. If she did him in then it should have been solid by the time Jack arrived. Whoever did for Quinn must have done it in the early part of the Monday morning or late Sunday evening." Maxwell reached into his jacket pocket to bring out his pipe, then remembering where he was, folded his hands together across his slightly expanding waistline and sat back in the chair, thinking. After a few moments, he looked up at the two others watching him and indicated Joanne's empty sandwich pack. 'You finished then?' he asked.

'Couldn't eat another thing sir, completely stuffed.' She said cynically, pushing back her chair from the table. Maxwell stood up and patted Dwyer on the shoulder.

'That's good Jack. Thanks for coming up to find me. Sounds like you've been up to your old tricks of being a proper copper again. Get you in trouble one of these days. We'll get something moving to try and find this lady. There must be a car somewhere. If she is a stranger to Wester Hailes then she must have come in a car, the bus service is too bloody complicated for a stranger to use.' He and Joanne left Jack at the table as they walked out of the canteen. PC Dwyer picked up the second untouched meat pie on Maxwell's plate and started to eat.

CHAPTER 6

When they arrived back at his office Maxwell indicated for Joanne to resume her position in his chair, to carry on sorting the photographs they had taken from Quinn's flat.

She seated herself back in the chair and started anew on the task. A few of the photographs had a date written in pen on the reverse of them, some of them included a place where the image was taken. She had just started her task when the door opened and young Davie Carswell, the young detective who had been to the office earlier, came in and pulled up a chair alongside her to help in her task. Joanne explained to him her system of sorting the images and together they worked on arranging the images into some sort form of recognisable groups.

Maxwell settled down in his chair on the far side of the desk, pulled the telephone towards him and spoke at length to the supervisor of the city ANPR operations room. When he finally finished his conversation and replaced the receiver Joanne was looking pointedly across the desk at him.

'Why only cameras from the M8 and city centre sir?' she asked. Maxwell stared at her and thought for a moment before speaking,

'If the Lady in Red was a stranger, the chances are that she would be coming from the north, the west or the east, and M8 and the city centre cover the main roads in doesn't it? Can't see her having come from the south, just the Pentland hills there isn't there?' He paused for a moment as she continued to look fixedly at him. Maxwell finally nodded his head. 'You're right Jo. Pentland hills as well then.' He picked up the phone and added the roads from the south of the city to the list of cameras to be checked. Joanne sniffed and grinned at her colleague working with the photos.

'They don't call me Chris de Burgh for nothing you know.' she quipped. Davie looked at her quizzically. 'I don't get it.' it said.

'Too young ' she replied and bent on with her work.

'Don't go getting big-headed now,' he whispered chuckling.

'Lady in Red,' she chortled quietly to her colleague. 'He gets worse you know. Never going to live that down.'

Maxwell finished his call, replaced the receiver on its cradle, and sat back watching the two younger detectives working away in front of him sorting the photographs. Eventually, he pushed back his chair and stretched his back.

'Just off to the incident room. Back in a minute,' he said and walked from the room.

In the small incident room which had been set up along the corridor, two uniform constables, a detective and a civilian were bent over computers and telephones. The room was cramped, only just big enough for the four of them. They looked up from their work and nodded an acknowledgement at their boss, then turned back quietly to the work they were collating; entering details from statements taken by the house-to-house team onto the HOLMES 2 software. Maxwell walked over to a large-scale map of The Lothian and Borders area pinned on the wall and looked at the location of Wester Hailes in relation to the rest of the city and the major roads in and out of the whole area. It could have been the M8, he thought to himself, or maybe somewhere else.

He spent an hour talking with the officers in the incident room bringing himself up to date on the various witness statements already gathered by the small team on the ground. The team was not a big one, the murder of an old man did not warrant a massive allocation of officers and resources, so said the brass, and on this occasion, he was inclined to agree with them. If there were too many bodies they would only start to trip up over each other. Anyway, who would miss this nasty little old pervert? He thought to himself and immediately answered the question. Well, his kids for starters, and his ex-wife might be interested. Maxwell took a pad from one of the desks and made a few notes on it as he walked around the room, glancing down now and again at entries being made into the software program. He perched his behind on the corner of a desk at the front of the room and looked at the scribbled notes he had made. The eldest boy lived in the Caribbean somewhere, so he was probably out of the question unless he had come back in the past few days.

Check eldest boy home, he wrote. The girl was next. *Daughter, where does she live? Married, single, kids?* Youngest boy. *How old, where does he live?* It suddenly came home to him how complicated this was becoming, yet again. But there again, he thought, murders were never really straightforward, simple and uncomplicated unless it was a family affair, which was often the case. He carried on making notes.

Rheumatoid arthritis, osteoarthritis, spondylolysis, - medication, doctor, social worker?

Betting office, William Hill office? Nearest one?

He looked up as he wrote the last note to himself. 'You got a telephone directory here?' he asked of the uniform officer nearest to him.

'No sir, I can Google it if you want sir.' He replied. Maxwell sighed and gave him the name of William Hill the bookmaker and asked him for the nearest one to Dumbryden Drive in Wester Hailes. The officer bent over his keyboard and within a few seconds called out, 'Want to have a look, sir? There's three or four in easy driving distance.' Maxwell looked up from his notepad, a surprised look on his face.

'Bloody hell,' he said, 'That was sharp.' The officer nodded, grinning.

'Aye, it is that sir. The power of the wonderful Interweb,' he added. Maxwell looked at him quizzically and then said,

'I want the nearest bookies for a decrepit old man with arthritis to walk to,' he said and walked over to look at the flat screen monitor the young officer was trying to turn towards him. On the screen was a Google Map of the area showing quite clearly that the bookmakers closest to where Quinn had lived was almost a mile from his home, on Westside Plaza. Maxwell stared at the map for a moment then stood upright.

'He's never going to manage that, not seven-tenths of a mile, not with a walking frame. Might do it if he was desperate enough though. But why would you be that desperate to struggle down three flights of concrete stairs then walk almost a mile just to put a bet on?' he said almost to himself. He rested his hand for a moment on the officer's shoulder and thanked him, then walked out of the office taking the notepad with him.

As he entered his own office he glanced down at his wristwatch.

'Shit,' he said. Joanne looked up. 'Got the end of play briefing in half an hour. Anything on the photos yet?' Joanne indicated one of the piles by her side.

'I started out trying to sort them by date, but pretty soon something struck me, sir. Come and have a look for yourself.' Maxwell walked around to her side of the desk and looked over her shoulder at the piles of images she now laid out one by one on the desk in front of her.

'See anything special about these sir?' she asked. Maxwell studied them for a moment then pointed to one of two men in army uniform, one of them was Quinn. Then he pointed to another one of Quinn and his wife taken at their wedding, presumably in Germany, and finally one of Quinn with his wife and a child outside the castle in Edinburgh.

'Well,' he said,' About the only thing that hits me is the quality of the photos. This one of him in the army, and the one of him and his wife are not the same quality as the other one the pair. Bit blurred, discoloured a little, and whoever took it nearly chopped their feet off. The one at the castle is clear and crisp. Different people taking the photos, yes?' Joanne shook her head.

'Might be two different people, but I think they were also taken using different cameras. Here, take a look at these others.' She pulled two or three more towards the front of the desk and laid them side by side, pulling one or others to the fore to demonstrate the differences she had mentioned. The quality of the images differed completely. Some of them were crisp and well focussed and equally well posed whilst others were blurred and off-centre. There was also a great difference in size. The blurred ones appeared to be of a uniform size. Maxwell took one off the desk and turned it over. It had the paper maker's name on the reverse side, Kodak. The photos of a better quality were also of uneven size. He took one and turned that over. There was nothing on the back to indicate the maker of the paper. Maxwell replaced the images on the desk, touching them gently with his finger, pushing them from side to side. 'What do you think Jo?' he asked. She sat back in her chair before answering.

'I think they were taken by two people with two different cameras, over a period of years. One of them was a good amateur photographer, probably did his own developing and printing,' she indicated one of the larger clearer images with her forefinger.' The other smaller ones were taken by somebody with a bog standard camera who took his films to Boots to get them printed. Overall I think that they span about forty-odd years from the ones in the army to this one of him and his wife in their middle age.' Maxwell studied the two photos she had indicated in front of her which she had brought from the piles at her side. His eyes moved from one to the other comparing the paper, the quality and the composition. He let out a long sigh and patted Jo on the shoulder.

'Well done Jo. I think you are right there. So what does this mean then if you are right?' She sat back in her chair again and for a moment gathered her thoughts.

'If we assume that the whole of this lot,' she waved her hand over the mess of photos on the desk. 'If this lot is taken by the same two people, these two people,' she pointed to Quinn and the other man in army uniform. 'Then their relationship went on for a long time, maybe forty years, maybe starting when they were both in the army.' She paused to think again. 'And if Quinn was a paedophile all that time it could well be that this other guy was doing it too, or at least knew about it. See how a lot of the photos have Quinn and a child in it, sometimes it looks like his own children, others with a different child. The second guy is here with his wife in Germany, look.' She pulled a second wedding photo from the pile and pointed to the two figures in it. One a man in British army uniform, who was not Quinn, at his side was a young attractive woman dressed in a similar wedding dress to that in Quinn's wedding photo. 'Perhaps they both met girls in Germany whilst on service there, married them and brought them back to the UK at the end of their term of service.' She paused to let her boss think about it for a moment, then slid a photo from the pile and placed it to sit at the foot of the others on the table. It was an image of a child. A very pretty girl with soft curly hair and dressed in a frilly white dress. She appeared to be about eighteen months old and was seated on a rug in front of a fireplace and looking up at the camera. Something was disturbing about the child's gaze. She was looking over the shoulder of whoever was taking the photo and looked either puzzled or frightened. Not overly frightened, but it was an unsettling look for the two detectives to view. Joanne tapped the image in front of them.

'This was taken by the same person who took the good ones, sir. Size, quality, all the same. Maybe this was the daughter of Quinn's army friend, in which case this could have been taken in his home at that time.' Maxwell moved his gaze from the image to others in the two piles of photographs, gently moving one and then another before finally saying,

'I think you could be right there Jo. It adds up doesn't it? They meet in the army, go to Germany, meet two girls there, get married, bring them back home, start families and Quinn starts on with his paedophilia again.' He drew a deep breath. 'Was the second guy involved with him though or did he just take photos, and if so what sort of photos did he take? We can't simply assume he was a paedophile like Quinn, though it is possible of course. Those bastards tend to be attracted to each other don't they?' He glanced again at his watch. 'Look, Jo, come through to the briefing, both you and Davie. This is something I need to bring up there and I'll need you in case there are any questions to be fielded.' Both officers nodded their heads and started to gather together the piles of photographs off the desk to take through to the incident room. Jo turned to her colleague.

'That sounds promising, doesn't it? Fancy a brew?' she asked. He shook his head as he rose from his chair.

'No thanks Sarg, I think I'll nip downstairs for a quick smoke before the fun starts.' He patted his jacket pocket and eased round the desk to the office door. Joanne smiled at him and as he was leaving the office said,

'Davie, keep this under your hat for the time being. If this gets out and the boss finds out, there will be blood on the walls before he's finished.' Carswell nodded and grinned.

'Don't worry. I can keep it shut.' He said.

CHAPTER 7

Maxwell walked into the major briefing room on the top floor of the station and strode to the front of the room. Behind him were floor-to-ceiling windows overlooking Queen Charlotte Street which at that time of day let in little light, the sun was shining in the opposite direction and cast few shadows into the room. Three rows of chairs were arranged facing the window wall where a large white video screen had been lowered from the ceiling. DS Baker and DC Carswell followed him into the room and seated themselves on the end of the front row, clasping some of the photographs they had been examining. The rest of the rows were filling up with officers from the murder squad and they were buzzing with comments amongst themselves about what they had been doing that day. Behind the chairs was space. This was, so far, a small incident group. Maxwell placed the A4 pad he was carrying on the table at the front of the room and perched himself on the edge of the table.

'Right. Let's have your attention then ladies, gentlemen, and others.' Silence fell over the room. Maxwell cast his eyes over the group of people, many of whom he had known for many years, and one or two others who were new to him.

'First thing. The murder, and that's official, it is a murder, is not going to be cleared up in two days. I think we are here for a bit of a long haul.' He paused to let it sink in. Better to give them the bad news straight off, he thought.

'Second thing. There are rumours, and I've heard them, that the murder victim was a paedophile. I want to hear nothing more about this subject unless you as individuals are tasked with investigating any possible connection the victim had to any paedophiles in the city. If this sort of thing leaks out to the press then I will find whoever is responsible and they will be moved off the enquiry immediately.' He paused to let this sink in.

'Am I making myself clear here?' He paused again and a murmur of comment came from one or two in the seats.

'When I discover who that person is they will not only be moved off the squad, they will be moved from CID, and if I can manage it, they will be moved off the job.' The murmur rose again, a little louder this time. Maxwell looked again at each person in front of him before continuing.

'I cannot emphasise to you how important this is. If we allow the public, and the press in particular, to start to think that Jimmy Quinn was a paedophile then we can expect at least one more, maybe more, murders. You know the local neds here in the city as well as I do. Many of us were born here, or at least live here now. You know what they are like. They will think they have carte blanche to declare open season on anybody they feel is a paedophile, whether they are or not. It will become open warfare on settling old scores, whether they are paedophiles or not. I want this buttoned up under wraps.' He paused again then carried on.

'Am I making myself crystal on this? You all know from previous experience that as soon as something like this leaks out the world and his mate starts to flood us with useless information, trying to spike their palls, and working off old grudges. I don't want this investigation mired over with hundreds of useless phone calls which have then to be followed up. There are enough so-called paedophile hunter groups out there without adding more rumours to their little brains.' There were one or two murmured comments and a nodding of heads generally amongst the group.

'Right, onwards and upwards. So far we have a body with a stab wound in the leg as a possible cause of death. Lived alone, as far as we can tell. Bad physical health and used a walking frame or walking stick to get around. PC Dwyer, the Community Beat Officer,' Maxwell's eyes searched the room until he found Jack Dwyer seated in the back row. Maxwell nodded in his direction, PC Dwyer raised his hand.

'Jack Dwyer has already come up with a stranger entering the apartment block a day or so before the body was found. How significant this is we need to establish.' Maxwell reached around and picked the pad off the table and read from it. He looked up from the pad and nodded at Jack Dwyer.

'Jack, I want you and young Davie Jackson to go back and see the neighbour. Get a statement from her. OK?' Dwyer nodded his head.

'DS Milton'. Maxwell looked around, a hand was raised silently on the back row. 'Go and see his GP at the Wester Hailes Medical Practice. DS Baker can give you the address and hopefully the name of his doctor. From the post-mortem, it seems he suffered from quite a lot of complaints. Check with his doctor on the last time he went in there and what the doctor last prescribed him with. I want a full list of his current prescribed medicines.' Milton nodded his head silently, noting down in his notebook details of the task.

'Next. It could be that Quinn was visited by social care people. I want someone to tackle Social Services about this. Find out if he was on their books and if so, did he have any care people going in to see him on a daily basis. I don't see how he could have had them on a daily basis as it was a neighbour who reported he hadn't been seen, but we need to check.' A hand raised at the end of the middle row. Maxwell nodded at the detective with the raised hand.

'DC Molyneux, you can do that for me if you will.' The young blonde woman detective nodded her head.

'That's almost it for this evening. I hope tomorrow we will have more as and when the full forensic and PM reports come in. Just to keep you right up to date though, we have a preliminary PM report, should have the full one in the morning sometime. Also, I hope we will have the forensic report then as well. So far there is precious little come down from the heights, other than they can't find any fingerprints. I am sure they will though.' He glanced down at his list and then at Joanne and Carswell on the front row.

'Finally, DS Baker and DC Carswell have been sifting through a lot of photos which were found in the flat. Some of them on the walls and furniture, but also a lot were found in three old photo albums. They are categorising them to find out who and what is involved in them.' He grinned at Joanne before saying, 'Bit of a ball-breaking task, but DS Baker is just the person for that.' A ring of ribald laughter rang across the small group. Maxwell smiled apologetically at his aide before carrying on. She sniffed and gave him a dirty look. He placed the pad back on the table behind him and waited for the comments to die down.

'Right. Before we pack in for this evening, let me fill you in on Quinn a little bit, and his activities in the past. Very briefly, he appears to have had a history of abusing children. Jack Dwyer and I first came across him when we were new to the job. So that's probably twenty-odd years ago. It could be that he has carried on with these activities over the years, even though he has no convictions. It could also be that he started long before he came here. Perhaps in Glasgow. I know he was suspected of one job once upon a time. Don't forget, he was an old man when he died, but so far nothing has come to light. It might be that these photos can point us one way or another in the direction of what he was doing during the time he lived at Wester Hailes, and maybe before that. We have no idea, but it is something I feel we should be pursuing at this stage, and that is what DS Baker and DC Jackson are going to be carrying one with today. The body was staged in a peculiar way with the knife used in the killing placed on top of his blood after death, and the rest of his body neatly arranged for us to find. It's fairly clear this is not a random break-in and killing. The flat was clean and tidy, as was the body. This has been a very deliberate murder and arrangement of the body after death. Somebody hated Quinn, perhaps we will soon have a list of people who hated him enough to kill him, perhaps it is connected with his former activities as a paedophile. These people do not calm down and go away. He has lived on our patch for over ten years." He paused and allowed a rueful grin to crease his face.

"He lived, incidentally, not all that far from the Wester Hailes Police Station. Cheeky bugger. For those of you continuing on house to house today I want you to bear these facts in mind. He came from the city centre a little over ten years ago, we will find out exactly when that was later. He did get around before he became invalid. Let's see if anything comes to light about his activities before he slowed down.'

Maxwell stopped and consulted his pad once more before looking across the centre row of chairs.

'DS McMillan, get yourself along to the William Hills bookies on the Plaza on Wester Hailes. There was a pad of betting slips from the firm found in his flat. Find out how often he went in there, how much he tended to spend. Did he go alone or was there a carer with him?' McMillan nodded his head and scribbled the detail into his notebook.

'Next. DCs Broughton and Jones.' Two heads next to each other lifted. 'I want you to go through local records and SCRO files to compile a list of known Edinburgh paedophiles. See if any of them are linked to Quinn at any time. Finally. There is a suggestion from the photos in his flat that Quinn had a long-term relationship with a man he met in the army, probably doing National Service judging from the style of uniform and their ages. I want someone to chase down the Army records and see what they can come up with. Volunteers?' He lifted his hand and pointed at the raised hand of a middle-aged DC in the middle row. 'Fine. Thanks, Alex.' He said.

Maxwell glanced from Jack Dwyer to Baker and finally Carswell before asking the rest of the room,

'Anybody got anything to ask or tell us before we wrap up for the night?' There was a general shaking of heads and feet started to move in their seats.

'Right ladies and gentlemen, until tomorrow morning I wish you goodnight. Apart from those on the night shift.' He grinned and two of the officers in the room groaned. They were it, the night shift.

Back in his office, he turned to Jo as she entered behind him.

'Covered everything do you think?' he asked. She nodded her head, placing the photos down on the desk in front of him.

'I think so sir, nothing else concrete to say at this stage is there? she said. Maxwell shook his head before answering.

'Right. I'm off home. Early start in the morning. I want the forensic, SOCO and PM reports here first thing if at all possible Jo. Got that?' Joanne nodded her head. Maxwell took his coat from the rack behind the door, pushed his arms into the sleeves and left the office.

'Got it, sir. See you in the morning.' She said to his disappearing back. She slid the loose photographs into three large brown envelopes and placed them in the open safe in the corner of the room, then slammed the door shut and locked it with a large key from her key ring. DC Carswell, who fancied his chances with Joanne helped her on with her coat.

'Thank you, kind sir,' she said beaming a smile at him.

'Fancy a drink on the way home Sarg? He asked quietly. Joanne smiled at his young face. Too young for me, she thought.

'Thanks, David, not tonight. I fancy a nice quiet drive home, get myself a takeaway and settle down with a bottle of red.' She smiled again at the disappointment on his face. He shrugged on his coat and walked from the office, turning to wait as she locked the door.

At the front door of the station, their ways parted as he went for his car, and Joanne walked off towards her car parked near the end of the street, enjoying the abnormally fine early spring sunshine.

CHAPTER 8

Jo's drive to her home was pleasant and not very long. Traffic for once was light and her new car was becoming more of a joy to drive each day. She resisted the temptation to put her foot down and instead used the drive home as a time to unwind a bit. The spring evening was beautiful and the weather fine. The sky was blue and clear. Not a cloud to be seen. So unlike the normal grisly Edinburgh weather, she thought. Arriving at the apartment block she locked the car and entered the building. She climbed the three flights of steps from the street level to her front door and pushed her key into the lock. Stepping through into the short hallway she took off her coat and hung it by a hook close to the door and went through into the small kitchen, kicking off her shoes as she did. She found a clean glass on the draining board by the sink and poured into it a good two inches of Highland Park, and regarded it with a smile before adding a dash of cold water and sipping from it. 'All the way from Orkney to my wee home in Edinburgh,' she said to herself and went through into the living room where her laptop lay on the floor by the side of a large three-seater fabric cushioned sofa. She sank into the sofa swinging her legs up until she was almost lying full length on it. She sipped again from the glass of life then hauled the computer to her knees and flipped open the lid.

Booting up the machine she went to her e-mails first and deleted all the crap she had delivered during the day, leaving only one from her father who lived in Inverness to be dealt with later, and one from her bank telling her that her monthly statement was ready for her to view online. She clicked on Google Chrome and typed in COPD into the search engine area, and whilst that was finding seventeen and a half million entries in less than 0.4 seconds, she selected some music on her Windows Media player. She browsed through the list of CDs she had downloaded onto the machine and eventually selected Karl Jenkins, Adiemus, Dances of Time, and clicked on the first piece in the list. As she sat back and listened to the music playing from the two miniature blue tooth speakers on the fireplace, she spent the next thirty minutes alternately sipping from the heavenly brew from Orkney and learning all about the COPD complaint and how it would have affected the breathing of Jimmy Quinn, until someone had removed that physical necessity from him just a couple of days before.

The glass was over half empty when her head started to nod down to her chest, but she caught it in time and saved the whisky from spilling onto her jeans. She closed the laptop, mentally promising her father she would reply to his e-mail later, and replaced it on its normal shelf, on the floor. Several times during the evening she caught herself almost falling asleep so eventually decided to make an early night of it and was soon snuggled into her duvet not long after the decision was made.

Her radio alarm woke her at 6.30 the following morning. Eyes closed she reached on autopilot for the off button, but hit the snooze button instead, and fell back to sleep. When it went off a second time it was to hear a DJ on Radio Two being unbearably happy and cheerful. 'Bastard,' she muttered to herself and reluctantly pushed the duvet aside. A minute later she was sitting on the toilet in the bathroom along from her bedroom. The full-length mirror she had installed on the back side of the door showed her what she feared most. It was going to take some effort to make all that better, she thought. Her hair was sticking from her head a bit like a rough Albert Einstein on speed, and the thought went through her mind that if every world leader saw themselves like this each morning, then there would be second thoughts on making war or pissing off the neighbours. Her pyjama trousers were rumpled around her ankles, and her white legs and thighs glistened in the morning light from the bathroom window. Her eyes were still partially glued together and she knew that she had spent most of the sleeping hours on her back with her mouth open. The inside of her mouth and most of her throat felt as dry and rough as the bottom of the hamster cage she had had as a child. She yawned and made her way to the shower in an effort to become alive once more.

Twenty minutes later she stood before the sink in the kitchen waiting for the kettle to boil, she realised that a steady pouring of rain was falling on the kitchen window. Not a real downpour, just a steady heavy drizzle. Experience had told her it would probably last until lunchtime at least and would be just as capable of ruining her hairstyle as any heavy torrent. She flicked off the kettle and made a brew of instant coffee. With mug in hand, she scuttled through to the wardrobe in the bedroom and found suitable clothes.

Shortly before eight o'clock she had managed to bag a parking spot just off the back of Constitution Street, and hurried into Maxwell's office, hot, out of breath and soaking wet. Her hair resembled a cross between a Deer Hound, a scarecrow and a hedgehog. Her boss sat at his desk and glanced up as she walked in, then did a double take at the hairstyle. He burst out laughing for a moment then was silenced by the look of murder on Joanne's face. She ruffled her hand through the mop of hair which was still appearing to have a life of its own.

'Morning sir.' she said. Maxwell simply nodded his head and concentrated on the papers in front of him on the desk. 'Coffee sir?' Joanne asked. Maxwell nodded his head again and held out the empty mug from the desk in front of him, concentrating on the reports. She took off the wet coat, hung it on the hanger behind the door, turned on the space machine on the desk against the wall and spooned sugar into her mug and into the one her boss had handed her. She stood quietly for a moment thinking and waiting for the machine to do its work and provide life-giving liquid. Maxwell looked up from his desk, his laughter now under control, barely.

'The first forensic report is in Jo. Some interesting reading in it.' Jo turned and placed one of the mugs of coffee on his desk and stood for a moment sipping from hers, waiting for him to continue.

'Did you see any Quinine in the drugs on Quinn's bedside table the other day?' Jo shook her head.

'No sir. Not that I can remember, but I didn't make a note of everything.'

'There was a strip of twelve tabs in the drawer with a couple missing. How did he get malaria in Scotland I wonder? The tablets do tie in with something else.' He picked up another report from his desk and waved it at Joanne.' Blood tests show he had a low level of Quinine sulphate in his blood, and traces of Sildenafil, whatever that is, along with the Irn Bru, the Buckie and the whisky.' He raised his hand to forestall any comment from her and picking up the SOCO report carried on.

'SOCO also found an empty envelope under the rug by the side of his bed and three more photographs.' Joanne's head lifted. Maxwell continued.

'Three photos, coloured ones, look like Polaroid, taken some time ago. All of the small girls in a state of undress.' Joanne put down the mug of coffee and held out her hand for the images Maxwell was holding out for her. They were just as he described them to her. They appeared to be children about five or six years of age, all without any clothing from the waist upwards. She turned them over one at a time to find anything to identify them, but the backs were clear.

'Going off what bits of clothing they still were wearing I would bet they were taken sometime in the eighties,' she said. "Did we come across a Polaroid camera in the flat sir? She asked.

'No. No trace of any cameras at all.' he said. 'The inside of the envelope showed no signs of paper, ink or DNA. The only sign of life were two hairs which they say came from a cat.' Joanne stared at him.

'A cat? You have to be kidding me, sir.' She said, almost choking on the hot coffee.

'Wish I was' he muttered. 'This is getting bloody farcical. Little Red Riding Hood, now cat hairs. Somebody has written this as a script for a second-rate TV series and somehow it's got out of hand.' He grimaced as he placed his mug on the desk.

'Anyway, there's more. The envelope had most of the stamp torn off, but there is a bit of the postmark still visible. It reads LAN. Any thoughts?' He looked up at her expectantly. Joanne considered his question for a moment before answering.

'Only thing coming to mind immediately is Lanark or Lanarkshire.' Jo replied. Maxwell nodded and glanced at his wristwatch before pushing back from his desk.

'Right. Let's get onto the morning brief, shall we? There's other stuff in this report I need to spell out as well.' He walked from the room carrying the report in his hand. Joanne followed him clutching a notepad in her hand.

In the briefing room, the group of detectives on duty were wandering in, some with mugs in their hands.

'Right, come on, settle down ladies and gents.' Maxwell said, positioning himself at the front of the room. The bodies settled into silence, Maxwell looked around to see if everyone was present. It appeared so.

'OK. First of all, anything from the night shift last night?' No one said anything. 'Right. I've had part of the forensic and SOCO reports and the final post-mortem report from the pathologist. There are some interesting pieces for us there.' He turned to Jo and motioned for her to pin up the three images of the girls on the whiteboard at the side of the room where he was standing.

'These are three little girls, don't know who they are, where or when they were taken. I want someone to chase them down. Seems pretty obvious that Quinn was involved with them in some way or other some years ago. If he was, then whoever killed him might also be connected with them. Judging from the few clothes the girls are wearing DS Barker feels they might have been taken in the 1980s. So bear that in mind.' He paused for a moment to let the information sink in, then continued.

'So far, we have pretty much nothing more to indicate who the killer might have been, so it's worth looking at. Any volunteers?' A hand went up in the middle of the room the room. Maxwell nodded at a young woman detective. 'Thank you, Jenny. You and Andy give it a go will you?' The detective nodded. "Will do sir," she said. Maxwell continued.

'Next, an envelope was found in the same location as these photographs.' He held up the white foolscap envelope for the room to see.

'Typewritten address, postmark and stamp ripped off, no return address, and the envelope was empty, except for a couple of hairs from a cat.' He paused to allow a ripple of sniggers to run through the room. When it had died a natural death he carried on.

'The envelope might have been used in delivering the three photos. Has a partial postmark of L. A. N. on it which is still visible. Possibly Lanark or Lanarkshire. When you are looking for the three girls Jenny, please bear this envelope in mind.'

The noise in the room rose a little as the officers discussed what had been said.

'Right, last thing. Quinn was not killed by the knife found on his body.'

'Not the avenging angel was it sir?' quipped a voice from the back. Maxwell smiled.

'Might have been, but what I am telling you must not go any further than this room. The knife found in the blood between his legs was not responsible for making the cut in his thigh. It was done by either a surgical blade, like a scalpel or maybe an old-fashioned cutthroat razor. The blood was let out by a definite cut, not a stab.' The noise level rose again.

'Sir. What does this tell us, are we looking for an associate of his who was a surgeon, or barber, or what?' came a voice from the back. Maxwell grinned ruefully.

'What it means is we have bugger all to go on so far, and it's not getting much clearer.' He stood up from the edge of the table he had been perched on and gathered his files together.

'One final thing this morning.' The noise died off. 'There are no traces of any fingerprints at the scene apart from those belonging to Jimmy Quinn, and an odd one which probably comes from the neighbour who found him, Molly Cullen, nothing else. Which means we are dealing with a very methodical person who has gone to some trouble to ensure he left nothing behind. No fingerprints, no DNA, so far.' He paused for a moment then said,

'Right. Those of you seeing the doctor, the betting shop, and Alex doing the army records, get yourselves off there now. Jenny and Andy, you get off to check on the photos. Those of you on house to house, I want you to concentrate on any of the local yobs seen in the vicinity.' He pointed to one of the detectives in the second row.

'Andy. A minute with you after please.' The room broke up and the detectives dispersed. Maxwell and Joanne together with the detective he had spoken to went back into his office. Maxwell perched on the edge of his desk.

'Andy. I want you to do some background into Quinn's finances. I don't think for one minute he was flush with money, but I want to find out what his income was like, did he have any unusual sources of cash, how he paid for things etc. Somewhere amongst the contents of his flat are bank statements, see what turns up there and maybe get onto his bank. Use your charm if need be.' He grinned at the young man.

'Shouldn't be a problem, sir. Bags of charm.' The young man replied.

'Aye, I know. Oozing with it. Get on with you.' Andy grinned and nodding, left the room.

Maxwell and Joanne sipped on yet another coffee in silence, each engrossed in their aspect of the investigation when there was a knock on the office door and a man walked in. Maxwell rose from his desk, his hand extended across the desk.

'Alan, good to see you, man. Sit yourself down.' He pointed to the chair in front of his desk and the civilian, Alan Macready, sat himself down in the seat, panting a little.

'See you haven't given up the weed then Alan?' The tall overweight man grinned at Maxwell.

'You neither by the sound of it.' Macready was a former detective who had worked in the scenes of crimes department prior to retirement and had immediately re-joined in a civilian capacity as a senior technician. His experience could not be bought for a ransom.

'Thought you might like a bit more information on the photos sir,' he said. Joanne, seated behind him at the table filled with photos turned around.

'More the merrier sir,' she said politely to Macready, indicating the piles of photos on her desk. Though he was a civilian Jo was keen to observe his previous rank in the force, out of deference and not a little bit of charm. Macready smiled back at her,

'Not a 'sir' any longer thanks Joanne, just plain old mister. Are you dealing with the photos from the flat?' he asked her. Joanne nodded her head and indicated the piles behind her.

Macready glanced at the various photos and stood to examine them more closely. He picked up one of them and held it for them both to see.

'This was taken on a bog standard Brownie type of camera. Nothing special about it at all.' He replaced it on the pile and took up another one, holding it close to his eyes.

'This one is like the other landscape and industrial scenes. It was taken with a 35mm film camera.' He pointed to the bottom left edge of the photo where there was a small white mark protruding into the image.

'See that?' he said. 'Means that there was some sort of fault with the winding mechanism which caused a small scratch on all of the images taken with this camera. Each time the film was wound on the winding mechanism sprocket caught on the edge of the film and made this mark.' He put the image back and took one of the portraits from the table.

'This one, this was taken with something like a Hasselblad or Mamiya. Used a tripod and lighting as well.'

'Bloody hell Mac, can you tell all that from just looking at them?' Maxwell blurted out.

'Well, it does help if you've got years of experience in photography.' He grinned and took up one of the landscapes to hold it alongside one of the portraits.

'See the portrait? Right. See how the left part of the face is quite clear and in bright sunshine whilst the right-hand side is in darkness?' He looked from one to the other until they nodded their heads.

'This is artificial lighting. You rarely get photos taken indoors with that sort of clear definition of light. Had to be staged indoors, with additional lights. Which means he was a keen amateur or a professional. These cameras are not cheap even today when they have been superseded by digital cameras. There are a lot of amateurs who prefer to still use film and process them themselves. Part of the hobby aspect of the thing really.' Macready looked again from one to the other and then carried on.

'Take a look at the quality of the ordinary ones, the Brownie ones. Same format and the same developer and printer, probably Boots or more recently Max Speilmann. Not the same as the others. Which means to me that there were two people involved, not just two cameras. You wouldn't normally use a bog standard camera if you had access to a high-quality Hasselblad, Mamiya or Nikon or something like that. Maxwell sat looking blankly across the desk at Macready until eventually, Macready waved a hand across his face.

'Hello. Anyone home?' he said. Maxwell blinked and looked at Macready and then Joanne.

'I'm just wondering where this gets us, if anywhere,' he said. 'Tell me what you think of these Mac.' Macready rose from his seat and went to bend over the piles of images in front of Joanne, he starred from one pile to the next for a moment or two, then indicating one of them he said,

'Right. This one, the portraits and pictures of groups of people. In the main, taken by the person with the Hasselblad or Mamiya. The buildings and scenery I would say are taken by, let's say a Canon or Nikon 35 mm. A lot of the portraits show artificial lighting, especially the ones taken indoors, but even some of the ones taken outside show fill-in flash at times. He hasn't relied entirely on natural light. The size of them indicates that they were developed and printed by either a professional photographer or someone with a very good amateur setup to do the work. The rest are chemists stuff.' He sat back down in his seat.

'So, I'll say it again. In my opinion, there are two photographers here. One using the Kodak style of camera, the other using one of two professional quality cameras, and he knew how to use them.' Macready sat back in his chair for Maxwell or Joanne to comment. Eventually, Maxwell spoke.

'So where the hell does this leave us then? I still don't see we are any closer to finding whoever killed Quinn, or whoever took the photos.'

'Sir. We might be able to get a bit closer if we can identify any of the buildings or the landscapes involved. It could be worth asking one of the crew to look at them to see if the places or buildings ring a bell with anyone, particularly anybody from the Lanarkshire area.' Maxwell sat forward and moved some of the papers on his desk before finally nodding in agreement.

'OK. We'll put it to them, he said, see if anyone recognises anything. Let's wait until the briefing tonight and see if anything turns up from the stuff they've been looking at.' He turned to Macready.

'You've been a big help, Mac, thanks a lot.' Macready rose from his seat, 'Anytime sir, anytime.' He turned to smile at Joanne then walked out of the room, closing the door behind him.

When he had left the room Joanne turned to Maxwell. 'I think I've got a timeline and possible scenario for this lot sir,' she said, indicating the piles of photos. Maxwell looked up from his desk and walked around to hers, and stood looking at the piles Joanne had made of some of the images. 'Go on then. I'm all ears.'

She pointed to the two men in uniform. 'This is where the two men start. Back in the late 50's or early 60's. Had to be 'cos National Service ended in 1963. They meet up and go to Germany in the army.' She pointed to one of the big images of a gothic-looking church. 'I think this is Germany, looks nothing really like an English or Scottish church. Too much ornate stuff on the outside, and if you look carefully in the background there appears to be a few piles of rubble. Perhaps war damage." Maxwell examined the buildings in the photos, his eyes moving from one to the other and back again. 'OK.' he said, 'Carry on.'

'They meet up with two local girls and end up getting married to them in Germany.' She pointed to the two men in uniform looking very starched alongside two young brides. 'When they come out of the army they split up, perhaps. Certainly, Quinn comes back to Scotland.' she points to two images of Quinn and his wife outside the main entrance to Edinburgh Castle.

'Good quality photo of the happy couple, taken by his mate. Maybe showing him around the city as a sort of touristy guide. Maybe on a holiday visit here.' Maxwell nodded his head in agreement. Next, she pointed to a series of small 'Boots' photos of Quinn's wife with first one then two and finally three children.

'See these, taken at different times, different dress or coat she is wearing, but the places in the background are still in Edinburgh, or I think one of them might be in the Pentland Hills or somewhere near.' Joanne selected another photo of two women, one was Quinn's wife, the other a stranger. She pointed to another one of the 'mate' together with the stranger.

'This I think is Quinn's mate with his wife, after they come back to Scotland. Better class of suit the bloke is wearing, she is wearing a nice hat, quite fashionable. Maybe on holiday with Quinn and missus Q.' Joanne sifted through one of the other piles.

'This is the mate with a girl, then a young boy and finally a baby. The woman is nowhere to be seen.' Joanne sat down on her chair and cast her hands over the whole series of images on the table.

'The whole lot are taken over about forty years, judging from the clothes, the cars in the background of one or two of them, and the state of some of the buildings. If you look at the landscapes and building scapes, some of the buildings are being demolished. Could be in the 80s when coal and steel were dying in the Lanarkshire area.'

Maxwell stared silently at the photos for a while, grunting as he touched first one then another.

'This is good Jo. Very good. I think we need to be talking to the kids, and see where they were living around this time. They might just be able to throw some light on who the mystery friend was.' He paused for a moment then added,

'The other thing is, that the other photos of the three small girls, could be a relation of one of them if the girls were assaulted by Quinn at some time. Perhaps his mate was involved with it.'

CHAPTER 9

Later that afternoon the briefing room was buzzing as once more the detectives returned from their enquiries that day. Maxwell took up his position at the front of the group, Joanne sat in the front row. Davie Carswell had taken himself off to the back row, the memory of his embarrassment of asking Joanne for a date still a bit too raw in his mind.

'Right. What pearls have you got for me, ladies and gents?' Maxwell began perched in his usual spot on the corner of the table at the front of the room. A hand went up. It was Jack Dwyer.

'Sir. We went to revisit the neighbour who saw the woman going to Quinn's flat. Turns out it wasn't the Sunday morning but the previous Friday morning. Same time though, 10.30.'

'How does that change things then?' asked Maxwell more to himself. Before he could go on he was interrupted by the detective who had visited Quinn's doctor.

'Might be able to help out sir. We went to see the doctor. Got a full list of the medicines he was being prescribed.' The officer paused and looked down at his notes.

'The doctor paid a visit to Quinn on Friday morning, about 10.30.'

Maxwell interrupted. 'Well, that's good. Maybe our good doctor saw someone else near the flat.'

'Doubt it, sir, although might be a possibility. The doctor's name is Mansoor, Dr Shenaz Mansoor. A very attractive Pakistani lady. About five foot eight inches tall, and on Friday she was wearing a red duffle coat, and carrying a black shoulder bag. She had it in the surgery when we called. Seems like Jack Dwyer's neighbour witness saw the doctor going in there.' A groan went up from the room.

'Are you saying that the doctor is the person who killed Quinn?'

'No sir. Not saying anything like that. Just that if she is ruled out then at least we know who Jack's witness saw.' Maxwell looked down at his notes for a minute.

'What does she have to say about prescribing Quinine for him?' The detective studied his notes and had a whispered conversation with his colleague.

'Nothing sir. She never mentioned Quinine. It isn't on the prescription list she gave us.' He held up a handwritten list of drugs. Maxwell stared for a moment then said,

'Well our friend Quinn had small traces of some Quinine in his stomach, and the blood showed some of the drug. The pathologist estimates about one or two grams, which could be three or four of the tablets we found in the drawer by his bedside. But those weren't Quinine. Whatever it was might have been enough to kill him, certainly enough to give him a bad night's sleep.' Maxwell stood up from his perching position slapped the file he was carrying down on the table and looked at Joanne.

'I want you to get onto the pathologist in the morning and find out if this amount of Quinine would kill him. I've never heard of it being used to kill someone, but I suppose an overdose of any drug will kill you. Find out what the fatal dose would be.' He glanced around the room before carrying on.

'Right. This is a bit more like it. Tomorrow I want you to go and see his kids. One of them, a woman, lives out at Queensferry and the youngest son somewhere near Wester Hailes, not sure where. Jo will have the address. Next, I want you all at some point during the day to look at some of the photos taken from his flat. They are a mixture of countryside and towns, they might be one or other of the towns in the Lanarkshire region. Derelict buildings, hills, that sort of thing. Let's try and pinpoint where they are. That might give us an idea of where Quinn and his mate got to. At this stage, we could be thinking that his mate lived somewhere not too far away from Quinn and his wife. Take a look too at the three photos of young girls on the whiteboard. They were found along with an envelope in Quinn's flat. It seems like he was abusing kids somewhere in this area, or Glasgow. The only thing to go off on the envelope is a partial postmark of LAN, which we are thinking could be Lanark or Lanarkshire. Could be New Lanark. Take a look, see what you think. Any ideas, then you come and hot foot to me straight away. Now, any questions?' He paused for a moment, but his instructions were clear.

'Right, off you go, and remember to put everything in for the people on Holmes. No point in you getting some pearl and not sharing it.'

The group filtered out of the room one by one, stopping by the whiteboard to view the images and envelope pinned up there. One of the officers, a stranger to Maxwell, came up to him.

'Excuse me, sir.' Maxwell looked at him quizzically.

'Sorry, but I don't think I know you officer.' Maxwell said.

'DC Jones sir, Brian Jones. I've recently transferred in from Greater Manchester force in England sir.'

'Ah. Saw the light did you Jones?' Maxwell said jovially.

'Indeed sir. And a beautiful light it is sir. Especially when seen through a glass of malt.' Maxwell laughed at the younger officer's impudence.

'Go on with you man. What's on your mind?'

'I just took a glance at some of the landscapes, sir. I'm not a hundred per cent sure, but I think that some of them are of Lancashire. Not Lanarkshire. One of them looks like a few of the hills I used to walk around before I came up to Edinburgh. I lived not far from hills like those. They look very familiar sir. I'd like to have a closer look at them if I could.'

'Bloody right you can Brian. First thing tomorrow you have a look at the rest of the photos we've got and let's see what there is to it. Even if it's not where you think, at least we will have ruled it out.' The young man left Maxwell at the front of the room. Both were bearing wide grins of satisfaction.

Back in Maxwell's office, Joanne was putting what she hoped were the finishing touches to the piles of photos seized from Quinn's flat. Something was troubling her and she didn't know what. Something in what had been said did not ring true, and it bothered her. She sat looking out of the window trying to remember what had been said at the briefing and why she should be troubled. Maxwell opened the door and walked straight to the coffee machine on the side desk. He glanced round at Joanne.

'Problem Jo?' he asked. 'Something on your mind?'

'Yes,' she said, 'And no.' She looked up at him from her seat. 'There is something from the briefing which bugged me and I can't think what it was. Bloody annoying. Maxwell poured two mugs of coffee and placed one in front of Joanne. 'Any idea what it was?' he asked.

'Not yet, but I think it will come.' She glanced down at the coffee. 'How many sugars did you put in this?' she asked nodding towards the mug in her hand.

'Sorry. Forgot. None.' he grinned. Joanne rose from her seat and stepped to the coffee machine. As she was scooping the second teaspoon into her mug she stopped and turned round.

'Got it, sir.' Maxwell looked up from his desk and smiled.

'Indeed you do Joanne, but what about the case?' he grinned mischievously. She shook her head ruefully. 'Men!' she muttered playfully.

'Sorry Jo.' her boss said. 'Carry on. What is it that suddenly hit you?'

'Quinn was found Monday morning by his neighbour.' She ticked the item off on the fingers of her left hand. She raised a second finger. 'Doctor Mansoor visited Quinn on Friday morning. Seen by Molly Cullen the nosey neighbour.' A third finger was raised.

'When we went to see him late Monday morning the blood was still semi-liquid and the knife was still lying on top of the blood.' She paused and for a moment allowed a broad smile to light up her face. A fourth finger was raised.

'So. He had to have been killed sometime late on Sunday night or during the early hours of Monday morning. It could not have been Doctor Mansoor, she was last there on Friday. Unless she came back to see him on Sunday evening or early Monday morning.' She paused again.

'If she was the one who killed him.'

Maxwell stared at the four upright fingers on her left hand and mentally ticked them off one at a time.

'You're right Jo. You are right. She could not have killed him unless she went back to the flat again after the Friday visit.' He put the mug of coffee down on the desk.

'Let's see if Jack Dwyer has anything more today.' He reached for the telephone on the desk and quickly replaced it.

'Shit. I only have his mobile number.' He reached into the inside pocket of his jacket and pulled out a mobile. After clicking a few buttons Jack answered the phone.

'Jack, Lewis Maxwell here. Listen. Your old neighbour Molly, can you arrange for me and DS Barker to come and see her this afternoon.' He listened to the PC for a few seconds.

'It's important Jack, but I don't want you spilling anything to her. Just tell her we are following up to confirm some of the information she gave us. This afternoon if you can make it.' He listened to the reply and clicked off the call.

'Sorted. Jack's going to fix it for this afternoon.' He smiled broadly at Joanne. 'Well done you. More coffee?'

'No thanks, sir. Not finished this one yet.' She turned back to the photos in front of her on the desk and what the English DC had said. Now, she thought they made some sort of sense. Let's hope the Englishman can either make some identification or rule them out. She turned to try and make some order from them. As she worked on the files the office door was pushed open and Danny Riccardo walked in and smiled broadly at her.

'Hi Sarg' he said and walked over to Maxwell's desk where he too was working on one of the files. Riccardo was six feet tall and slim with short-cut black hair and clean shaven. Dressed, as usual, in a dark blue three-piece suit with a blue shirt and pink tie, he made Joanne's blood pressure rise each time she saw him. As he stood bending over the boss's desk pointing to one of the files Joanne quietly swung her chair round and leched for a moment at his tight firm backside. She felt her pulse rate increase and her face started to flush. Quickly she turned back. Oh if only, she thought. If only he wasn't married. Now there's a man for her. To prevent herself embarrassing herself further she folded her files and picked up her bag from the floor by her side.

'I'll get off now boss,' she said. Maxwell nodded in her direction and grunted his farewell. Joanne walked down the corridor, glad to have escaped.

CHAPTER 10

Margaretha Bowen, who was born Quinn, the daughter of Jimmy and Renate, lived in a house which had been built on the sloping side of a hill some miles to the southeast of Edinburgh, in golf club country. All around the house were open stretches of green golf clubs, rich, gently rising and falling farmland, and the largest high-security mental hospital in Scotland. The front door of her house was painted a deep green and matched the frames of the windows all around the house. A job lot of paint some time ago. A small garden at the front of the house was bisected by a steep concrete laid path to the front door, whilst around the back of the house was a slightly larger garden, at the bottom of which was a slender tree which fought every year for survival against the winds and rain which blew relentlessly across the open countryside. The garden was bordered by wooden fences and looked out over the farms which surrounded the place. Margaretha stood in the living room of the house looking out over the garden to the houses on the opposite side of the quiet road and watched as an unmarked police car pulled to a halt outside her home. She was drinking some red wine from a bottle which had been left over from the previous night, even though it was only late morning. Since the arrival two days before of the marked police car with the two women occupants who had told her of the death of her father, she had been expecting such a visit. The front door of the house opposite slowly opened and half a face eyed the two plainclothes officers who now approached her path.

With some difficulty the man first, then the woman, negotiated the child's broken pram straddling the path and gently eased aside a rusty wheel from a bicycle which lay in the muddy patch which once had been a lawn. Margaretha lifted the bottle from her lips and wiped a dribble of red wine clear from her chin with the arm of her cardigan pulled down over her hand. She was expecting them, either CID or Child Protection, she thought. The drinking was nothing unusual, merely that today she had started earlier, and was one of the reasons her husband of eight years had finally had enough of the fighting and arguments which normally accompanied it. He had left two years ago, and now she was alone. There were no children from the marriage, her second, something she had insisted on from both husbands before either of her two marriages had ever taken place. No children.

Maxwell and Joanne both pulled their coats around themselves as they waited for the front door to be answered. Having first asked the team to interview the kids of Jimmy Quinn, Maxwell had decided this morning it should be he and Joanne who made the first approach to them. The wind was biting and a thin persistent rain had started to fall. It was waiting for nobody, and soon, despite only being there a minute or so, they were both wet.

Margaretha opened the door and gestured for them both to enter.

'It's a bit damp out there' Maxwell said with a wan smile.

'Go through into the lounge' Margaretha replied, indicating a door to the left of the short corridor. They both walked through, unfastening their coats as they did so. The lounge was quite large and well furnished, though both detectives noticed the almost empty bottle of red wine standing on a small table to the side of one of the two armchairs straddling the fireplace. Introductions were made, but tea, coffee and wine declined before they settled down to talk to her about her life with her parents, in particular her father Jimmy Quinn.

Margaretha sat on one of the armchairs whilst Maxwell and his DS sat on the three-seater sofa facing the fire. Margaretha was dressed in grubby tracksuit bottoms and a thin obligatory black tee shirt with the logo of an obscure pop group on the front. She was in her mid-fifties but looked considerably older. Her hair was mousey-coloured, uncombed and unwashed. She leaned back in the chair nursing a mug of tea, which on seeing the condition of it, Joanne was glad she had refused the offer. Joanne was in the corner of the sofa furthest from the woman, able to see the bomb site of the back garden through the dining room window, whilst Maxwell sat in the other corner facing Margaretha. Joanne slid a photo from the brown file she had taken from her briefcase and placed it on a coffee table in front of her and pushed it across to Margaretha. It was one of the photos of the two men in army uniform.

'Do you know who the man with your father is Margaretha?' she asked kindly. The woman bent down to closely examine the photo, and after only a couple of seconds shook her head. 'No idea. Doesn't look like my dad either. Never seen that before.' Joanne took back the photo and replaced it with one of the Quinn family, all five of them.

'How about this one, does this ring any bells with you, like who took it?' For a moment Margaretha fought the effects of the wine last night and this morning suppressed a sudden barbed wire belch of acid and tried to clear her head. She again examined the image and slowly shook her head.

'I think that must have been taken when we were on holiday somewhere.' She said. Joanne repeated the performance with seven or eight of the photos. The only thing Margaretha could remember was possibly the place where the photos were taken, never who the strangers in the images were, nor exactly where they had been taken. Maxwell sensed they were going to draw a blank with her and decided to call it a day.

'Look, Mrs Bowen,' he said finally, 'We are trying to find the person who killed your father. You are one of the few people who might be able to tell us more about him, his life and who he knocked around with.' She stared him blankly in the face and said nothing.

'Well, if you can think of anything will you get in touch with us then?' he said in desperation.

'We're off to see your young brother next in Oxgangs, see if he can help us at all.' She sat back in her chair and replaced the mug on the table, crossing her arms before spitting out.

'You'll get nothing off that mad bastard,' she snapped. 'He's off his fucking head most the time on weed or smack or white lightening or bucky. He's as mad as a fucking hatter that one.' It was the only time during their interview that the two detectives sensed any life or truth in what the sad, prematurely old, drunken woman had said.

Maxwell and Joanne rose from their chairs and, gathering their files to them, took their leave of Margaretha. As they thankfully sat down in the car looking back up at the front door and the figure standing back in the window with a new bottle of red wine to her lips, Joanne commented quietly,

'Wonder why her husbands got a divorce? No staying power do you think?' Maxwell chuckled as she started the engine and drove off.

'Let's hope the young brother is a bit better than her,' he said as she made her way off the small estate and onto the main road leading back towards the city.

'Wonder what made her like she is now,' commented Joanne after a few minute's drive. Maxwell sat silently in the passenger seat then pulled out his pipe from his jacket pocket. Seeing her reproving sideways glance, he replaced it.

'It's hard to know really. Nobody starts out life like that do they? Nobody starts life thinking that this is the sort of life I am going to end up with, and makes plans to settle down for a life of difficulty and hardship. Are you sort of suggesting that her parents had a lot to do with it and that maybe she is the result?' he asked.

'Well, it makes more sense than just believing that she was made that way. Lack of upbringing, parental control and guidance would go a long way to understanding how she became like that in her teenage years, but then something stops her breaking out and reforming herself into a normal human being later on in life, didn't it? A lack of guidance or model to form yourself on.' She paused and then carried on. 'From a psychological angle,' she began before Maxwell interrupted her.

'Aye aye, here's the degree course coming out again is it?' Maxwell quipped lightly.

'It's a thought though sir. She denies even knowing her parents in the photos. Her brothers and her parents were friends as well, and yet she was there. Not once did she even acknowledge that they were part of her family or that she even knew them. Now that's strange. Very strange. That takes something pretty drastic to happen in her life for her to deny any knowledge of them like that.' She paused for a moment before continuing.

'She was part of whatever happened during the times when those photos were taken. It was her life, as well as those of her parents and brothers. If what happened to her was bad, then it could account for her complete refusal to accept that she was there in the photos, that she was even there, that she was part of the family.' Joanne pulled the car to the side of the road on the outskirts of the city and they sat with the engine ticking over thinking.

'So, are you saying that she might have been abused as a child by Quinn, along with her brothers as well?' Maxwell asked.

'It's a likelihood isn't it sir? Or at least a possibility. You came across him sometime after he moved to the city after his army service. If it was believed before then for him to be abusing children, but you were unable to crack him. That would be in the 1970s, yes?' Maxwell nodded his head and interrupted her flow.

'More to it than that Jo.' He said and opened the passenger door of the car and got out.

'Yes. Unfortunately, there's more to it than that.' The fine misty rain was falling again. He took his pipe from his coat pocket and pulled his mackintosh around him and lit the pipe, stretching his back and legs to ease their aching. Joanne had joined him by the side of the car.

'What do you mean sir, there was more to it?' she asked gently. Maxwell looked sideways at her and took the pipe from his mouth.

'The powers that be wouldn't let us charge him. The thought was that there wasn't enough evidence and that by the time we got him to court the kid would be too scared to testify, and anyway, it was only a kid off the schemes.' He said it quietly and looked down silently at the ground, unaware that the rain was starting to come down heavier now and was falling directly down the neck of his jacket. Joanne was silent too for a moment, trying to find the right thing to say. Everyone knew of the years of neglect and cover-up which had gone on with various public figures and people in power and their abuse of children, but for her, here was an incidence of an ordinary person, a bus driver, who was afforded the same benefit of avoiding prosecution. Just because it was easier to do nothing. It was shocking, but she wasn't shocked by it. No longer. Knowing the sort of mentality which had been common in the police and society at that time, she believed and accepted what her boss had said. But now, there was nothing to be gained by her also castigating Maxwell. He was paying the price, she thought, and probably had done for many years. Joanne stepped close to her boss and touched him gently on the arm.

'That's over sir. Society has changed. We're going for them now. Now we've got a chance to nail him firmly in his coffin for what he did, whether it was to her, her brothers, other kids or whoever, and with whoever else.' She drew a deep breath and looked around at the countryside disappearing into the outskirts of the city.

'The daughter shows many of the signs of an abused child growing up into an adult, who lacks any sort of signs of empathy, concern or even acceptance of what has happened to her. I don't think we are ever going to get her to admit what he did to her, ever. Maybe in time other members of her family might drag it out of her, but she only has one brother left alive close to her, the other brother has taken himself off to Bermuda, hasn't he? That in itself could suggest he too wanted to get away from the home environment, why? The other brother, from what the uniforms who went to notify him about

Quinn's death told me, he seems even worse than Margaretha. One of them commented that he would be better off in the State Hospital out near where we've just been.' She smiled at him and started to move back to the car.

'Going to stand there puffing that nasty evil little thing all day sir?'

Maxwell grinned at her. 'Beats chocolate any day though.'

The trip across country to the Oxgangs estate, similar in many ways to Wester Hailes, with the aid of the car's sat-nav, was made to Gunther Quinn's address in a little over forty-five minutes. It was a building almost identical to the one Jimmy Quinn had lived and died in, five floors of flats instead of four, with car parking areas in front of the main front door. As they drew up in the parking spot Joanne turned to Maxwell.

'Déjà vu or what?' she said. Maxwell just nodded his head and made to get out of the car, noting the twitching curtains on two of the ground-floor flats.

'Make sure you lock the car doors, Joanne. I think the natives have spotted us.'

CHAPTER 11

Gunther's flat on the Oxgangs estate was similar to Jimmy Quinn's flat in some ways, but different in many others. To start with the block of flats had a lift, which failed to work no matter how hard or often they hit the call button, so they had to take the stairs again. The stairs smelled just like the ones in Quinn's block, but Gunther's flat was on the third floor of the building. They were both out of breath by the time they reached the landing with its four front doors. They stood there for a moment regaining their breath and looking around themselves at the four identical doors before Joanne finally pushed the bell on the one belonging to Gunther Quinn.

It took a minute before they heard unsteady footsteps coming along the corridor and before a disfigured eye peered at them through the spy hole fitted in the door. After a few seconds scrutiny the door opened, secured on a chain to the door jamb. Half a face peered into the crack between the jamb and door.

'Police' said Maxwell. 'We've come about your father's death Mr Quinn.' He and Joanne held out their warrant cards for Gunther to examine, which he did slowly and closely before finally releasing the chain and opening the door.

'Can't be too careful, could be anybody.' he said, glancing behind the two officers as they walked past him into the flat. He walked off along the corridor pushing past them both, leaving the two detectives to follow on behind. Joanne closed the front door behind them. Gunther Quinn led them into the living room. The flat was identical in layout to that of Quinn Senior, though that appeared to be the only similarity. The living room overlooked wide expanses of greenery with tall deciduous and conifer trees planted close up to the buildings. Although it was possible to see the neighbouring blocks of flats and other houses on the estate, it was also possible to imagine you were in a green and pleasant land. If it had not been for the reputation which the estate had acquired for drugs and violence.

The room was dominated by a large hi-fi and television system taking up one wall at right angles to the window wall. Speakers half as tall as themselves bookended the system and made it hard to open the door from the corridor, whilst a small sofa and two easy chairs together with a dining table and two wooden upright chairs almost filled the room, so there was no easy way to negotiate a way around to sit themselves down when Gunther told them to. The floor was littered with old magazines and a few books, whilst the walls were adorned with garish prints from concerts held during the

Edinburgh festival from many years before. As the two police officers took their seats on the sofa both looked sideways at each other, recognising the pungent and lingering smell of marijuana, but said nothing.

Gunther Quinn appeared to be in his late forties or early fifties, though it was difficult to be precise. He was over six feet tall and undernourished to be almost anorexic. His thin grey hair was curled untidily over his ears. At some time or other in his youth, it was obvious someone had taken a dislike to his nose. It was still crookedly bent where it had been broken, possibly twice judging from the bends in it. He had watery blue eyes which darted from one of them to the other all the time when it wasn't looking out of the window or darting around the room. He tried hard to keep his hands under control, but most of the time they exercised a life of their own, twitching and flailing around as he spoke. He wore old and worn blue jeans with rips in the knees and below a side pocket. He sported a long-sleeved jumper which sagged over his wrists and had constantly to be pushed back away from his hands. No socks or shoes. His feet were clean, as was his other visible skin. Neither of them felt it necessary to delve any closer to see what the rest of him was like. As Maxwell started to talk Gunther suddenly held up his hand for silence and rose quickly from the seat he had occupied by the side of a wall-mounted three-bar electric fire which should have been condemned many years ago as a health risk. Maxwell fell silent as instructed and they both watched curiously as Gunther went to the hi-fi system and chose a CD from one of several piles lying by the CD player. He placed the CD into the mouth of the machine and heavy metal music filled the flat. Gunther turned up the volume and retook his seat by the fire.

'Bugs, you know. The bastard downstairs has me bugged you see,' he said, his eyes flitting down to the flat below. It was impossible to think, never mind talk with the volume so high. Joanne stood and reached for the volume knob and turned it down.

'You daft so and so,' she said smiling at him.

'Do you not think we came prepared?' Gunther looked at her questioningly. Joanne reached into the inside pocket of her jacket and pulled from it her smartphone. She held it up for him to see, but not so close as he could easily make out the icons on the screen.

'We have come prepared Gunther. All our phones are equipped with a jamming device app. Only for the police, but it works well.' For a moment Gunther was silent then the look on his face turned first to amazement then burst into a broad grin.

'Man that's bloody marvellous. Where can I get hold of one?' He reached out for her to hand the phone to him. She put the phone back in her pocket and resumed her seat.

'Sorry Gunther. It's for police and security forces only. But believe me, it works. Nobody can eavesdrop on us whilst I have that switched on. It constantly emits a frequently changing variable high and low-frequency sonic wavelength which interrupts any sort of device used to listen to others.' She settled back in her chair and nodded towards the hi-fi system. Gunther stood and turned off the machine. Their ears returned to normal. His look changed from delight to belief then consternation.

'My name's not Gunther. I changed it some time ago. I like to be known as Graham now.' Maxwell sat forward.

'Graham?' he asked, 'Why Graham?'

'I never liked Gunther. Too German. To warlike.' His eyes flickered from one to the other whilst his hands flittered and fluttered on his knees.

'Started when I was painting. Used to do miniatures on seashells and stuff and sell them down by Spring Gardens. Made a lot from it, well enough to keep the world from the door. Don't do it now.' He indicated his shaking hands.

'Too much blaw over the years. Not that I do much now. Too expensive you know.' He laughed nervously, and stood from his seat by the window, nervously casting a glance down to the street as he walked over to the far side of the room.

'So, it's not me you need to speak to then, is it?' he said, nervously licking his lips and lifting from one foot to the other.

'Graham, your father was James Quinn wasn't he?' Joanne asked. He nodded his head nervously.

'Aye. He was my father. But I never done him though. Wasn't me.' His face was starting to sweat due to the temperature in the room but more because of the brief questioning. Joanne wafted her hand at him to sit himself down.

'Graham. Sit yourself down now. We haven't come to accuse you of your father's death. We just want to get some background information about your father which might help us find his killer,' Joanne said. Gunther sat down, holding his hands tightly under control between his knees. She brought out the army photo of Quinn with the other man.

'Who is the other man along with your father, Graham?' He glanced at the image quickly then looked away.

'Don't know. Never seen him.' He replied sharply. She put that one away and took out a family photo of the Quinns.

'And where was this taken Graham?' she asked. Quinn studied it for a few seconds then said,

'I can't remember. Looks familiar obviously, but I'm not sure.' She tried him with the photo of the young girl with the other army man.

'How about this group then? Do you know who she is?' He shook his head vigorously.

'Never seen her. Don't know who she is.' He stuttered. Joanne showed him several more of the images, none of which he admitted to knowing or recognising.

'Why are you lying to us Gunther?' asked Maxwell, his voice somewhat louder than Joanne had used.

'I'm not lying man. I don't know them. No idea who they are or where they were taken. Sure they were my family, but I've had so much blow over the years a lot of it up here has gone now.' He tapped the side of his head with his fingers. 'My memory ain't what it was.'

Joanne looked at her boss who turned back to Quinn. Maxwell tapped the photo of the stranger with the young girl.

'This man might have killed your father Graham. Don't you want to help us get him?'

'Couldn't be him, he's dead.' He blurted out and flicked his eyes from one to the other when he realised what he had said.

'And how do you know he's dead Graham?' Maxwell asked quietly. Quinn stood again and then sat down immediately when he quickly realised that he was not capable of holding himself steady.

'Got a letter' he stuttered, from a mate in the south. Told me he'd heard a friend of my dad's was dead, and asked if this was him. Sent a photo. Didn't recognise it at the time, but later when I'd sobered up a bit I realised it was a friend of my dad. Don't know who he is though.' He paused. 'Or where he lives, lived.' He fumbled around in his pockets and brought forth a small polythene bag of roll-up tobacco and some papers and tried to start to roll himself a cigarette. A large portion of the tobacco spluttered onto the miserable warn carpet on the floor as he made several attempts to roll himself a cigarette. In the end, he had himself a cigarette. Snatching a lighter off the table he lit the cigarette and blew a cloud of smoke over their heads. Maxwell rose to his feet looking towards Joanne as he did so. He nodded briefly at her towards the door, she shook her head and winked at him. Maxwell resumed his seat, not knowing what his junior officer had in mind, but sufficiently trusting in her judgement to know it was worthwhile following her instinct, wherever it might lead.

'Graham,' she said in a friendly fashion, opening her notebook as if preparing to take down whatever he said.

'Tell me, how long have you lived in Edinburgh?' Quinn looked suspiciously at her for a moment then answered the question cautiously. He continued to answer the few questions Joanne asked for the next half hour, but in the main Jo simply allowed the conversation to go wherever he wished it to go. He told them of his drug addiction, his friend and supplier Jimmy who occasionally ran 'messages' for him, the neighbour in the flat below who once installed a video and listening device in his bathroom so he could watch him using the shower and toilet. He broke into his story once to go through into the kitchen where he secretly, he thought, took a long drink from a litre bottle of White Lightening cider before resuming his position in the living room.

For over an hour, they allowed him almost uninterrupted free rein of his verbal wanderings, telling them all about his life, where he had lived, the people who had upset him during his life, how he had got his own back on them and generally how wonderful he was, and how, with his superior intellect he had baffled them in their efforts to bring him down. He lied and moaned about life and people, groaned about his health and the way the social services and health professionals had let him down, about the way his friends had attempted to control him and made his life hell, whereas his enemies had been masterfully outwitted and fooled by his superior brain. He told them of the times he had been 'Sectioned' under the Mental Health Act, but had successfully talked his way around the psychiatrists and psychologists to get out of the wards he had been on. For over an hour, he poured out all that had happened to him in his life, how life and the government had conspired to outwit him yet he still survived and would continue to do so.

At the end of the time, both Joanne and Maxwell were feeling brain-dead and physically drained. They could stand his meanderings no longer. Joanne glanced sideways at her boss and nodded slightly at him. He took the hint and stood up from his seat looking at his watch as he did so.

'Well, Graham. As enjoyable as it has been talking to you today I am afraid that DS Baker and myself do have to be going now.' Joanne got to her feet and the two of them stepped into the corridor, Joanne in the lead with Maxwell behind. Gunther's voice carried on talking behind them as they attempted to leave the flat. Once started his 'off' switch was hard to find. Halfway down the corridor Maxwell suddenly stopped, causing Quinn to bump into him. He turned so that the two men stood almost nose to nose.

'One last thing Graham. Did your father ever sexually assault you or your sister and brother? Quinn blanched and screeched in pain, and stepped hurriedly back from the tall detective, banging into the corridor wall.

'He never. No! Never! He never touched me! Not me! Never touched me. Not me. Now fuck off. Fuck off. You've got to go now. Fuck off!' He danced on one foot then the other in terror waving his hands at Maxwell until they finally left the flat, closing the door behind them. Downstairs the two detectives sat in the car in silence before Joanne started up the engine.

Maxwell sucked on his dead pipe for a moment then turned with a grin to Joanne. 'A constantly changing variable high and low-frequency sonic wavelength,' he said. 'That was something else, Jo. Ten out of ten for bullshit. It was a bit of a reaction though wasn't it?'

'A cracker.' She said.

'So tell me Detective Sergeant Baker, why did we sit through over an hour of unmitigated shite from that mad bastard back there? Do you have a death wish or something?' Joanne sat looking through the windscreen for a moment, gently tapping the steering wheel before finally flicking the windscreen wipers on and off to remove the layer of think drizzle which had started to fall before replying.

'Mad bastard is a bit politically incorrect don't you think sir?' she said.

'I would prefer to describe him as suffering from severe and enduring mental health problems, specifically, I think he might have already been diagnosed with, and at some time in the near past, treated for, paranoid schizophrenia, narcissistic delusions and drug-induced psychosis.' She turned and grinned at Maxwell.

'Apart from that, just your average mad bastard druggie sir.'

'Dangerous?'

'More than likely. He didn't get that broken nose and the scars on his knuckles from opening a tin of peas, sir. My feeling is that he should probably be more at home and better treated if he lived closer to his dear sister.' Maxwell stared at her in silence, his jaw dropping slightly open. Joanne grinned and gently pushed a finger against his lower jaw closing it. Maxwell pulled his head away.

'You cannot be serious? They'd kill each other.' He saw the grin on her face.

'You have a weird sense of humour at times don't you Jo?' he said taking a bag of midget gems from the left-hand pocket of his jacket and holding it out to Joanne for her to take one.

'I'm serious sir. Closer to his sister, but not with his sister. The State Hospital is not all that far from where she lives. I'll bet a lot of the houses on that estate were originally built for officers who work at the hospital.' She peeped into the bag and routed around to take three black ones.

'Oi! Pack it in. You get what's on the top, don't go fishing for the black ones. You saying the hospital is for the likes of him? I thought it was just a straightforward mental hospital.'

'Forensic cases, as they are termed sir. Seriously mentally ill and violent, whether convicted of a crime or not. I think it would fit Gunther Quinn to a tee.' Joanne smiled a grim smile and popped all three into her mouth before driving off back to the station on Queen Charlotte Street.

CHAPTER 12

The two of them sat in Maxwell's office later after lunch reading through once again the various reports submitted by SOCO, forensics and the pathologist.

'Jo. Do a search on Sildenafil will you?' Maxwell said. 'Let me know all about it. It was found in his blood, but our dear doctor has neglected to tell us mere mortals what the hell it is.' Maxwell continued to read through the final report sent to him that morning by the pathologist. He suddenly let out a low moan.

'Oh, Jesus Christ.' He said and slumped back in his chair, a look of disbelief on his face. Joanne looked up from her computer screen and turned around to face him. He glanced down again at the report.

'I have all day sir, but would prefer not to wait that long.' Jo said sardonically. Maxwell snorted and looked at her again.

'The pathologist found two unusual things in his blood. The first was heroin, the second was traces of semen on Quinn's upper thigh, the left inner thigh to be precise.'

'Semen?'

'Seems so.' He said grinning.

'You are serious?'

'Seems so.'

'Sir. Pack it in. Does he say who it belonged to?'

'There wasn't a lot of it, but it appears from the DNA that the stain was from one James Quinn. Matches the blood on the body and other DNA traces from him found in the flat. The strange thing is though that they are the only DNA traces found in the entire flat. No other DNA traces, no fingerprints. Nothing.' He read on further in the report ignoring the periodic questions from Joanne. At last, he reached the part of the report he was seeking. He held up his hand for her to be quiet and read on from the report.

'There are extensive traces of acetic acid on his thighs, cans of Irn Bru, bottle of Buckfast wine.' He breathed in deeply and continued, 'The knife, his legs, door handles, kettle, wood surfaces in the kitchen and living room, in fact, almost every bloody where someone would leave a fingerprint or DNA trace. Shit!' He slammed down the report on the desk and stood up, going over to the coffee machine and angrily flicking the on-off switch.

'So, whoever has done it knows all about how to remove traces of their presence at the scene.' He paused then turning to Joanne questioned, 'Acetic acid? Where the hell would he get that?' Joanne turned back to the computer and Googled acetic acid. In seconds she had a suggestion.

'Vinegar sir?' she suggested. Maxwell chewed on a midge gem for a minute then asked,

'You think a doctor would know all that sort of stuff, but plain old simple vinegar to get rid of the DNA? Can't see it. And where does he get the heroin from? Who was getting it for him, and how much was in his blood?"

'Last question first Jo' he replied.

'Could have got the heroin anywhere on the Wester Hailes estate. How does he get it? Could be Molly Cullen. She regularly ran his messages for him, could have picked it up on the way. How much was there? Well, the pathologist suggests there was not enough to kill him and yet enough to suggest he was a regular user. So he's been using it for some time."

'You think his GP has done him in sir? She could have done it if she was used to visiting him. Comes into the flat in broad daylight wearing a bright red duffle coat and carrying a black shoulder bag. Gives him a quick J Arthur as a thank you for being a child molester and general pain in the backside all these years, then wipes everything in the flat down apart from him, and buggers off into the night. Well, yes, I see how you might think that sir.' She stopped and looked at him in silence, grinning.

'Alright smart arse. Just a thought.' He said and turned to pour sugar into mugs and added coffee. Joanne looked back to her computer where her search results for Sildenafil were displayed. She clicked on the first link and read the page for a minute or so.

'This is good,' she said.

'What've you found now Jo?'

'Sildenafil. Main constituent of, guess what?'

'No idea. Viagra?' he grinned. She turned to stare at him in disbelief.

'You deliberately winding me up sir?'

'What do you mean?'

'It's exactly that.' She read from the web page.

'Sildenafil is also known as Viagra and is used to treat erectile dysfunction.' Maxwell walked to her desk and looked at the web page she was reading, and read it over her shoulder.

'There's more to me than just a pretty face you know, Detective Sergeant Baker,' Maxwell said, and moved back to his desk. Placing his coffee on the desk he sat down in his chair and regarded her over the desk.

'What the hell does this mean then Jo? We have someone coming into his flat, makes himself at home, gives Quinn a whisky and Buckie, feeds him with Viagra, gives him a quick hand shank, sticks a blade of some sort in him then covers him over so the blood doesn't spurt out everywhere, then calmly wipes the place down with vinegar and buggers off. All without anyone seeing hide nor hair of him. You couldn't make it up could you?' He shook his head in disbelief.

'I am not looking forward to telling the troops this little bit of a gem tonight, what?'

Joanne smiled broadly at his potential discomfort. 'Could be interesting sir.' She said eventually.

'Bugger off Jo, this isn't funny. I just hope they get over the funny side of it and get onto the real work quickly. We're getting nowhere fast with this one.' He glanced at his watch.

'Come on. Time we were off to see the lovely Molly Cullen. Nearly that time of day again Josephine.' She grimaced at him and his incorrect use of her name then rose from her seat, collecting her files together for the evening briefing on their return from Wester Hailes.

*   *   *

Molly Cullen waved them into her flat after carefully looking through the spy hole in the front door of her flat.

'Come in now. Go through to the living room, sit yourself down' she said, almost entirely in one breath. Maxwell led the way through and perched on the edge of the sofa, leaving Jo to occupy the other corner. Maxwell beamed at her and asked how she was after finding her neighbour dead the other day.

'Oh it was a shock to be sure,' she said,

'But I can't say it surprised me. He was not a well man you know Inspector. Hadn't been for some years. It's why I did the messages for him.' she carried on. Once into her stride, it was hard to stop her. Eventually, Joanne pointedly looked at the wristwatch on her arm and glanced over to her boss.

'Sir,' she said quietly. Maxwell glanced back.

'Yes, you're right. We must press on.' He turned back to Molly and said,

'I'm sorry to rush you Mrs Cullen, but you mentioned the doctor visiting the other day before you found Jimmy dead.'

Molly reached to the side table by her chair and took a cigarette from one of two packs lying there. Lighting it with a small disposable light she pulled a cloud out to the fireplace.

Jo made a mental note of the two brands on the table but said nothing. She sat forward in her chair.

'Aye, that's right. Sunday afternoon, like I told the uniform the other day. She was a nice-looking young woman. Though at my age, everybody looks young.' She grinned and paused to take a breath.

'She was Asian you know.' No sense of disapproval or censure in her voice. She had overcome her years of normal upbringing in the city and regarded an Asian doctor as normal nowadays.

Maxwell looked sideways at Joanne and took a deep breath before carrying on.

'Tell me again Mrs Cullen. The doctor came on Sunday morning. I thought you told the constable it was Friday morning.' She looked at him quizzically for a second or two then said.

'Aye. The Asian doctor came on Friday morning. Bonny lass she was. But when I went in to see Jimmy on Sunday night before he went to bed he told me a new doctor had been to see him. A locum he said, from the surgery, he said. Some sort of drug rehabilitation scheme she was attached to. Well, that's what he told me.' There was a moment's silence as she looked from one to the other and then said,

'Is there something wrong detective?'

'No, Molly, nothing wrong. Just trying to get something sorted in my head.' he said smiling at her.

'So this second doctor. Did Jimmy tell you what she looked like, what she was wearing?' Molly thought for a moment, taking the odd drag from the cigarette.

'No. Nothing really. Just that she was a bit older than the Asian lass and English. That was about it. Said she'd be back to see him again in a week or so about the drugs.'

The two detectives looked from one to the other. Maxwell raised an eyebrow. Jo shook her head from side to side slowly.

'Right then Molly. You've been a great help and we've taken up a lot of your time. Thanks very much for your time and the information. I'm sure it will be very helpful. We'll be off now.' He rose from the sofa as did Joanne. They made their way to the front door down the corridor and let themselves out onto the landing, casting a cursory glance to the locked door of Jimmy Quinn's flat.

Joanne drove back to the MIT office in almost silence.

'So. Jimmy's a heroin user. Has a visitor from England who gives him a quick one and then sticks a knife in his femoral artery and wishes him a good night. Is that about the strength of it Joanne, do you think?' Maxwell said as Joanne negotiated the building traffic along the roads back into the city and nodded her head.

'Sounds like a good story sir' she commented. They lapsed into silent thought for the remainder of the journey.

CHAPTER 13

The briefing room once more was half full, as Maxwell and Joanne took their places at the front of the audience.

'Right ladies and gents, let's get on with it. The pubs are still open for a bit longer yet. So, what have we got today?' Maxwell began.

A young DC named Jack Douglas raised his hand.

'Sir. I'm struggling with the army. I went over to Glasgow this morning to the army records office there. A bit unhelpful. Said their other office was at Lytham St Anne's near Blackpool in Lancashire, and they might be able to help more. So, can I be off there in the morning? Shouldn't take me more than a couple of days.' A loud laugh rose from the men and women in the room. Maxwell smiled broadly.

'Aye of course lad, take a week if you want. Now just you tell us what the hell Glasgow had to say.'

'Well. I eventually got some sense out of them. Turns out that only some of their records are online right now, but they were able to help me out.' The officer looked down at his notes before continuing.

'Seems that at the time Jimmy Quinn was called up there were 19 others in the same intake, they were all posted to Oswestry in Shropshire, in England.'

'Aye, we know where Shropshire is. Get on with it.'

'Of the twenty, twelve are dead. Four are disabled getting an army pension and living in Scotland. Four others are alive and living in Scotland, they are not getting a pension. The ones on pension stayed on for twenty-two years of service after the national service had ended. Seems that of the original twenty-seven were from England or Wales, the other thirteen from Scotland.'

'Hang on. Let's get this straight. There were twenty to start with, four disabled living in Scotland, four not disabled living in Scotland after twenty-two years of service, and twelve dead. Have I got that right?' He paused for a moment doing some mental arithmetic.

'How many were from England?' The detective read his notes once more.

'Three from London, two from Lancashire and two from Manchester.'

'So, what do we know about them?'

'All dead sir.'

'Shit. All of them? Never mind, of course they are. They'd be old buggers by now anyway, same as Quinn if they were still alive. So were you able to find out anything about them, particularly the ones from Lancashire?'

'The two from Lancashire sir, well one was from a place just outside of Blackpool, and the other from a place called Accrington.' A voice broke from the group, it was Brian Jones, the officer who had moved to Police Scotland from Greater Manchester Police.

'Sir. Accrington is in the same neck of the woods as what I thought the landscape photos were from.' Maxwell broke into a broad smile.

'Right. Now that's more positive. Sounds like a better day than DS Baker and I have had.' He perched himself back on the desk and glanced at Joanne sitting in the front row.

'Right. Brian I'd like you to have a closer look at the images Jo has got of the landscapes and see if anything more comes to mind. If it does then you have my permission to shoot off there and try and place whatever you can. Let's see if we can place the man in the place shall we?' He rose from the edge of the desk, a satisfied look on his face.

'OK. Ladies and gentlemen. Some more information has come to light from the pathologist. Sit back and listen, you'll like this, not a lot, but you'll like it.' A few snorts of laughter came from his attempt at humour.

'Jimmy Quinn died of loss of blood caused by a deliberate cut, not a stab, but a deliberate cut to the femoral artery in his left leg. He bled out under cover of the blankets which apparently were pulled over him whilst he bled out.' He paused to allow this to sink in before continuing.

'This is strange though. There are no signs of a struggle on the bed. He was lying there very peacefully. So, was he unconscious? He had large amounts of Irn Bru, Buckfast wine and whisky in his stomach, so he probably was well-oiled when he went. His blood also contained quite a small amount of Quinine, which you will probably associate with mosquitoes and malaria. Why he had been administered Quinine in such amounts is not clear at the moment, if he was in fact administered it, rather than taking it himself. That is something Joanne will chase tomorrow. In addition, he had traces of Viagra in his blood and semen on his inner right thigh.' The room erupted in sarcastic laughter which Maxwell calmed down after a few seconds.

'And' he paused to ensure they were listening.

'An amount of heroin.' Murmurs came from the assembled ranks.

'So now we have to find out who was supplying him. The amount was not enough to kill him but enough to suggest he was a regular user. It paints a very strange picture of how and why he died. We might have something in here about the motive for his death, or not. We might also have some pointers towards who killed him, or not. The red duffle-coated doctor seen going into his flat on the Friday morning before he was found on Monday, might well have been responsible for giving him the drugs, but would she have given him any sexual relief as well, or did he do it himself? I have my doubts about that, especially in view of the severe rheumatoid arthritis in his hands, but let's not rule it out completely. If he was capable of using his walking stick and Zimmer frame then he might well have been capable of giving himself a quick.... well, you get the picture. If the doctor was aware of his previous sexual abuse of children then she might have taken it upon herself to rid the world of the nasty little bastard as a public service, but why masturbate him?' The room buzzed again with muted conversations until Maxwell quietened them all again.

'OK. One further spanner to throw in the works. DS Barker and I have just come back from seeing the neighbour who found him. She tells of having visited Quinn the night before he apparently died. He told her that he had been visited on the Sunday afternoon by a locum doctor who had something to do with drug rehab.' Again a murmur rose from the gathered detectives.

'So, we need to be looking at who he was getting the drugs from, who the new visitor was and where is the evidence in his flat of any heroin. My feelings are that PC Dwyer's friendly neighbour Molly Cullen could have a lot to do with the supply.' He turned to Jack Dwyer.

'Jack. I want you to follow up on this if you would. You're local in that area, so it makes more sense with your local knowledge to dig in there rather than tying up my highly experienced and very expensive detectives. Christ he could have walked past your nick any time.'

'I'll get onto it in the morning sir,' Dwyer replied. Maxwell nodded at him and carried on with his briefing.

'The flat was clean. I mean, cleaned out of DNA and fingerprints. Nothing at all other than those of Quinn. Whoever did it knew what we would be looking for, and went to some lengths to clean up after themselves. So we probably aren't dealing with one of the local neds or druggies, though God knows that place is a breeding ground for druggies, and neds as well".

He turned to the officer who had searched the army records.

'Jack. I want you to keep pushing the Lancashire records office, see if you can get an address for him when he was in the army, any addresses since then, any family, work etc.' He turned to the rest of the room.

'Right. Anything else from anyone else then? No? One last thing. Brian, can you pop into my office on your way out please?' He pointed to DC Jones, the officer formerly from Greater Manchester Police.

Back in his office with Joanne, Brian Jones stood before Maxwell's desk. He nodded at the young officer,

'Sit yourself down Brian, you're not in any bother.' Jones sat down on the straight back chair in front of the desk and relaxed.

'You're off to Lancashire tomorrow. I want you to have a look at the last address we have for the army bloke who joined up with Quinn. Make sure you have it from the DC doing the army check, will you? If what we know is right, then he might still have family there, someone who might know more about Quinn or any other associates he or Quinn had after coming out of the army. But. I don't want you making any real enquiries, just see what there is around if anything. If he was associated with Quinn then we don't want the relatives getting wound up. They might have been the subject of Quinn's attention if the two families were close together. Is that understood?'

'Yes sir, quite clear.' He shifted in his seat a little.

'Look, sir, I've got a few mates in the area in the job. How would it be if I asked around, see if anyone remembers anything or if anything is going on which is still current?'

Maxwell thought for a moment then said,

'I appreciate your thinking Brian, but no. Not for the time being. Just keep it low-key. If anything does turn up then we have to do this investigation through the right channels, and at the moment I'm not too clear on what those channels are. So, hang fire for the time being. One last thing, are you alright going in your car? You can take a personal radio with you, but not a force radio.' Jones nodded his head,

'That's fine sir. Not a problem. Be interesting to see what the range of these personal radios is,' Alan said, and left the office, smiling warmly at Joanne seated near to the door.

CHAPTER 14

Brian Jones left home early the following morning, having risen at 6.00 am. He had looked closely the previous night at the photos in the incident room and picked two or three to take with him. His home was on the outskirts of the city not far from the city ring road, so by 7.00 am he was showered, dressed, filled with caffeine and driving along the A720 dual carriageway and heading for the junction with the A702, south towards England. The early morning sun was shining brightly into the left of his car over his shoulder as he picked up the fast, very quiet road to the south, a beautiful day for a good 400-mile round trip to Lancashire.

Along the A702 he put his foot down in the four-year-old Vauxhall Insignia he was still buying on a finance deal. He booted the car to well over 85 mph along the wide and dipping road and sped through the gentle hills south of the city. Constantly watching his mirrors for his 'brothers-in-law', the ones with the high-powered, high-vis cars and motorcycles. He worked the blast out of his system after half an hour and settled down to a steady 65 mph through the small towns and villages along his route, enjoying the sights, the weather and the fact that he had a day out of the office and the city he had come to love. He slid one CD after another into the car's player and tapped along to Queen and Queen Anthems. By 8.15 am he had almost reached the A74 M close to the small village of Abingdon. He looked around him as he drove through the quiet village for a cafe to pull into for a coffee and breakfast. Failing to find one he was disappointed and drove on, picking up the motorway shortly afterwards and carrying on down to Gretna where he pulled off for a short break at a service area, and enjoyed the best bacon butty in Scotland, in his opinion.

He flew on south through the Lake District, enjoying the luxury of an abnormally quiet run down through the mountains, with glimpses of lakes and then the sea close to the motorway. Sunshine glinted off hints of water in the far distance as the Irish Sea at Morecambe Bay flitted in and out of his view between the hills. It was a beautiful day. Southbound traffic picked up as he came close to Preston and he metaphorically switched his mind back into gear, taking the off slip on the A59 near Blackburn. Still avoiding the major conurbations, he swept out along the Ribble Valley, bypassing Whalley, and heading on out towards Clitheroe. As he checked out junction after junction and familiar roundabouts, he looked out for the side road he knew would take him over the Nick O' Pendle and the south side of Pendle Hill.

He turned right off the main A59 onto the narrow tree-decked country lane to the Nick, and carefully watched sheep by the side of the road as he wound his way up through the moorland fields. The sheep were notorious suicides, well known for running from the poor grassland at the roadside into the path of oncoming cars. Being so far off his patch now, he did not want to damage his car. At the top of the steep winding road at the summit of the Nick, he pulled over into a disused quarry which had become a car park in recent years, and switched off the car engine. He got out of the car and stood listening to the car engine ticking as it started to cool, pulling his coat around him. Despite the fine weather and sunshine, it was still cool on the summit of Pendle, though wonderfully peaceful and quiet. He listened for a minute to the Curlews and Grouse flying high off the heather and the sound of sheep and cattle somewhere close by. He grinned at the memories of witches' parties and the like which he had been to in years past in Newchurch and Sabden. Memories of drunken sessions in country pubs, where he and his mates had ended up sleeping over, rather than risk death by car crash while driving home.

For almost twenty minutes he stood close to the side of his car looking first one way then another trying to place once again in his mind's eye the hills and townships he could see around him. The weather was good and the sky was clear blue. A few high clouds hurried along in a high-level wind. The far towns in the West Riding of Yorkshire he could see were visible, though only through a feint haze, the closer ones in Lancashire were viewable; the smog and fog of industrial Lancashire had disappeared many years ago, along with the industry. A blast of wind coming from along the length of Pendle made him suddenly shiver and he felt the need for a pee. Looking down the road in the direction of Sabden he saw no trace of vehicles approaching. He cocked his head in the direction of the top of the Nick not far away and listened as best he could above the slight breeze and odd sheep, for the sound of traffic approaching. He could hear nothing from the Clitheroe side of the hill. So confident was he in his solitude that he turned his back to the wind blowing off Pendle, unzipped his flies and started to relieve himself close to the rear wheel of the car. He was just getting into the stride of things when the sound of a high-powered motorcycle sounded from the Clitheroe direction. He whipped around to look in the direction the noise was fast approaching and sprayed warm pee over his hand, thus reminding him of one of his father's sayings,

'Never pee into the wind, you'll only get your own back.' He pushed hard to finish and made himself decent again before the bike arrived in view. As he zipped his trousers two big green Kawasaki bikes came flying over the summit of the hill, the front wheel of the first off the ground. It banged down hard onto the road surface and the rider glanced sideways at Alan as he flashed by. Alan watched from behind the back of the car as the second bike went by, and silently cursed both riders as he shook traces of urine from his hand. He took out his handkerchief and wiped his hands before giving himself a mental reminder to wash them at the first toilets he came to.

Starting up the car's engine, he turned the heater to full and directed the air ducts as best he could to the moist patches between his thighs. He drove on down the fast steep road on the far side of Pendle Hill into the village of Sabden, then followed the twisty gully-like narrow road out and up the hill on the far side. The road ran low between fields and stepped high on either side of the road, with bushes and small trees overhanging dry stone walls on the edges of the fields into the roadway, making it difficult to drive at any real speed. He wound his way slowly up the far side of the hill from the valley bottom, hastily pulling into the left to stop for an oncoming car, almost bending the bodywork of the car on the walls which acted as boundary for some of the way. Almost at the summit of the next hill on the far side of Sabden was a council car park set back from the road, with a red and white painted barrier two metres high set across the entrance to the rough, unmade parking area. He stopped on the edge of the parking area after he had circled around it. For a moment he sat looking back at the Nick from where he had come. The wind had grown since he had left his spot on the summit, and now a bank of high clouds was drifting south across the summit line of Pendle Hill. The whole of the hill was spread out in front of him in, its familiar whale-like skyline silhouette visible. From the left, where he had driven over, to the right and the distinctive edge of Pendle, the ground rose gradually, and from this distance, it appeared to rise smoothly. He knew from past knowledge of walking it that the surface was anything but smooth, and the gradient was shallow only from that direction. Starting from Newchurch or one of the other villages, the walk up Pendle Hill was hard and steep. The ground from the Nick was rough and peaty in places, rough and tufted in others. The pathway from the Nick to the summit was good but rutted with the tracks of sheep which grazed there during the warmer months and in more recent years the deep tracks of 'pleasure' dirt bikes. From where he sat, the right-hand end of the hill ended in a sudden steep hill down into the valley floor near the villages of Barley and Newchurch. Witch country, he reminded himself.

Alan reached into the brown folder which lay on the back seat of the car and pulled from it several of the landscape photos Joanne had shown him and allowed to bring with him. He held them up in front of the windscreen, comparing what was in the photo with what he saw appearing before him in the landscape. He finally stopped with one which matched almost exactly what he was seeing in front of him. In the image was the edge of a hill, which was unmistakeably Pendle, and spread out to the right of the photo was what he saw in front of him. Smaller, lower hills and valleys stretched away to the east, and a ridgeway on the far horizon. This was where the photographer had taken the photo, which confirmed what Alan had first felt when he had seen the images in Maxwell's office. The photographer came from this part of Lancashire, or certainly, was familiar with it on an intimate basis. A knowledge which would only come from regular walking in the hills, which meant he lived somewhere nearby, or certainly within easy driving distance.

Alan glanced at his watch, it was a little past noon. If he had the time then he could spend a couple of hours driving around the towns and villages of the immediate area to re-familiarise himself with the whole of this part of east Lancashire. He took his mobile phone from the inside pocket of his jacket which hung on the hook behind him and called Maxwell's office. Joanne answered the phone and handed it to Maxwell.

'Hi, boss. I'm here in Lancashire. What I'm looking at through the car windscreen is almost the same as one of the images from Quinn's flat. The photo was taken here.' Maxwell was excited with the news and put the phone on speaker so that Joanne could hear it.

'That's great news, Alan, well done. Are you sure of it? I've put you on speaker so Jo can hear as well.'

'Quite sure boss. If you or DS Baker can get onto Google Maps I can tell you exactly where to look.' Joanne turned back to her computer and fired up the maps programme.

'Ready when you are Alan' she called out for the speaker phone.

'Search for Pendle Hill Joanne, and look to the south for a small village called Sabden, then follow the minor road out of the village towards a place called Padiham.' He paused for Joanne and Google to catch up.

'Got it, Alan,' she said, after a few seconds.

'OK. Follow that road until you see the first road crossing that minor road. Turn to the southwest and there's a car park there near the junction. That's where the photo was taken from.' There was silence on his end of the phone as Joanne manipulated the software.

'Got it, Alan,' she said.

'OK. Now hold down the control key and use your mouse to manipulate the map image. Do you see it?' he said. There was a few seconds break as Joanne did as he asked then a brief yelp of delight as she brought the image into almost the same perspective as the images. Her voice excited as she recognised roughly the images she had spent the past few days looking at. Maxwell broke in.

'Good man Alan. This is brilliant. I remember the photo you meant. It's the one with the big hill on the left then in the distance is a range of hills with some smaller ones in the foreground.'

'That's the one sir,' Alan broke in excitedly. 'Sir. I want to spend the next couple of hours having a look around the towns and villages in this area, just to see if I can perhaps match up any of the other photos we have. In addition, I want to see if I can find the address in Burnley you gave me. Then I'll make my way back to Edinburgh.'

'That sounds good Alan, go ahead. But don't go snooping or asking questions of the local Police though. OK?'

'Fine sir. OK. See you in the morning.' He pushed the disconnect button and sat back in the car seat, satisfied and pleased with himself. Starting up the car he continued along the road to Padiham, and spent until mid-afternoon driving on and off the links from the M65, looking at the small villages and townships which made up the almost continuous stretch of buildings of that part of Lancashire. The one thing he did not find was the address they had been given for the army colleague of Quinn. The address in the town of Burnley had been pulled down in a demolition spree in the 1970s. It was a dead end.

Finally, when he saw the first of the school crossing patrols dive out into the road to stop him outside a school, he turned northwards back to the M6 and the A74M to Edinburgh. The weather maintained its kind attitude to him, and the drive home was as good as the one south that morning.

Later that evening, exhausted and hungry he settled down in front of the television in his small house in Edinburgh and enjoyed a 12' pizza and the contents of four bottles of beer. He slept well that night.

CHAPTER 15

B
rian Jones was one of the first in the team to arrive in the incident room the following morning. Maxwell and Joanne came through to catch up on what exactly he had found the previous day. It all appeared to be good news. As they stood chatting the room filled behind them with the rest of the team, and soon they had a full compliment. Maxwell called them to order to start the morning briefing.

'Good morning all. First some good news. The cost of recruitment and advertising for Police Scotland has been recouped during the past twenty-four hours.' There was a puzzled buzz from the room. He carried on.

'DC Jones, our new incomer from England, went back home yesterday and found the placing for some of the photos we have been working on from Quinn's flat.' There were a couple of rounds of brief applause from Jones's colleagues. Maxwell continued.

'It seems likely therefore that the friend of Quinn, who might or might not be involved with the child molestation, was from Lancashire, more specifically, perhaps from a town called Burnley. This is good news.' He looked across the group before him until he found the man who had found the army records. Pointing at him he said,

'Jack, I want you to start digging to try and find where this guy lived, did he have family, what sort of records he had, if any. You can work with Brian Jones here.' He nodded in Brian's direction who turned to look around at the man he would be working with.

'So we have good news then. Who has more good news for me from yesterday?' He caught a hand raised at the back.

'Yes Mac, what do you have for us?' A grey-haired detective in the back row glanced down at his notes before speaking.

'I've been looking at what sort of a life he had after moving from Glasgow sir.' Maxwell nodded in encouragement for Mac to continue.

'Obviously, lived alone. Seems he divorced his wife about ten years ago when he was in his early or mid-sixties. Moved into the flat then. Rent and council tax were all paid for by the city. He was on an old age pension and mobility allowance and some other benefits. The only source of his income, judging by his bank statements, was benefits. Came to just under a thousand pounds a month.'

'Fucking hell!' exclaimed a voice from the middle of the room. Maxwell glared in the direction of the outraged voice which made no further outburst.

'Carry on Mac.'

'Right. A thousand pounds a month income. Spent about a hundred and fifty a month on groceries, about eighty on booze, and some cash withdrawals.' He held up his hand for silence as the level of muttering from the others in the team started to rise.

'Three or four cash withdrawals seem to coincide with his visits to the bookies on the Plaza, but apart from that he spent very little. Had a balance of about fifteen thousand pounds in his current account.' Again protests rose from the team but fell again as Maxwell raised his hand for silence. Mac carried on,

'He had no savings account and he had been on benefits for over fifteen years, so this fifteen thousand was the result of him spending very little and saving what he never spent.' He paused for breath before starting again.

'It appears that the neighbour was the only person in recent years who had access to his bank card. I believe she said as much to Jack Dwyer.' He looked around for Jack, who nodded in agreement.

'That's right sir. She said she used to go every week or so to draw £200-300 pounds a time. Used it for groceries, Buckie, Booze and newspapers.' He said.

Maxwell paced slowly before the table for a few moments before finally taking a deep breath and saying,

'OK. So, what we have is an old man, living by himself, bets on the horses from time to time, spends little on food, drinks a little, and saves the rest, apart from, obviously, the heroin. We don't yet know how much he used or where it came from. My bet the person who provided him with it was

Mrs Cullen. But where did she buy it from?' He paused again for any response, but there was none. He carried on.

'He was killed by someone who he let into the flat, in view of there being no forced entry, killed after having drunk a little Irn Bru, Buckie and whisky. The place was wiped clean with vinegar to get rid of any DNA traces or fingerprints, and no bugger sees anything. Am I about right so far?' He looked up at the people in front of him who were now silent. A few heads nodded in agreement. He continued,

'Brian Jones has been down to Lancashire and confirms that the photos of some of the landscapes are definitely from there. So it would seem that Quinn's associate, whoever he was, lived or came from that area.' He looked up. 'Any thoughts?'

'Maybe his mate from the army, the one who took the photos was the man from Lancashire. Came up to see Quinn and family from time to time and then went back home after a wee holiday.' A voice from the back row. Maxwell paced again, glancing up at the officer from time to time.

'I think what you say makes a lot of sense. It fits the bits of information we have anyway. The next step is to take a trip to England, or at least start to make enquiries there with the local CID to see if our man is known.' He paused as a hand was raised from the second row. It was a young woman detective who had not been on the MIT all that long.

'Sir. You know in the pathologist report it says he had whisky, Irn Bru, Viagra and Quinine in his stomach and blood?'

'Aye, along with Buckie and traces of heroin. Go on.'

'Quinine is used in the making of Irn Bru, it's used as a flavouring.' A voice behind her called out,

'So he overdosed on Irn Bru then?' The team collapsed in laughter. The young woman reddened and half turned to face her colleague. The place fell silent as she slowly lifted her left-fisted hand and extended her middle finger, then silently closed it into her fist again. She turned back and carried on,

'If someone gave him Quinine in his whisky and Irn Bru then that might mask the taste of an overdose of Quinine. An overdose could cause him to pass out, or even kill him, sir.' She turned back to the joker behind and slowly stuck out her tongue at him, then smiled.

Maxwell perched himself back on the edge of the desk and smiled broadly. 'So, now we have someone, who is welcomed into the flat, or lets himself in, manages to slip some Quinine in his whisky and Irn Bru. The Quinine is disguised by the taste of the Irn Bru and causes him to pass out. The assailant then slits his femoral artery in the left leg, and blood starts to gush out, he flips the covers over and when Quinn is dead pulls back the covers, places the knife between his thighs, fixes his hands across his chest, pulls over the eiderdown, wipes down the whole place and buggers off, not leaving a trace. Oh yes. And gives him a quick wank before killing him.' A murmur rose from the room again. Maxwell waited until it had subsided before carrying on.

'This is so far-fetched it really cannot be true, can it?' he continued. A mixed murmur of agreement and disbelief rose from the room. Maxwell paced the front of the room once more. He looked up at the detectives in the room.

'Some of it could well be correct. We might be able to find out which bits, or on the other hand it might continue to be a mystery. The bit about the Irn Bru is interesting though. Might be the only reason for his having Quinine in his blood and stomach.' He paused again before carrying on.

'So, we may be looking for a woman with quite a lot of medical knowledge wearing a red duffle coat and who owns a cat. She is also partial to giving hand relief to old age pensioners and has access to Quinine, and the knowledge that this drug is a flavouring constituent part of Scotland's second most favourite drink. Not only that, she has access to a surgeon's scalpel or a cutthroat razor, and the knowledge of anatomy to correctly use it. Quinn trusts her enough to let her in the flat and give him some quick hand relief, so not a stranger. When he passes out she finishes him off by slitting the femoral artery, then cleans the place up before silently disappearing into the night like a ghost. Oh aye, cleans up everything except traces of seamen on his legs. Do I have this right at last then?' He sat on the edge of the table shaking his head.

'So it could still be Dr Mansoor then sir?' said a voice well hidden in the back row.

'Go home!' he called out in frustration. 'Go home the lot of you! I will see you all in the morning when hopefully this pile of shite will have started to make sense.' He gathered up his file and started to leave the room. Joanne caught him by the elbow.

'It could be right sir.' She said.

'I need a drink, Jo. Fancy one?' she shook her head as the room emptied around them. 'No thanks, sir. I'm off for an early night.' The room emptied and after locking up her files, Joanne left the office and drove home, quietly, thinking of all that had come to light that day.

CHAPTER 16

The following morning should not have happened, not according to the restless nights' sleep which DCI Maxwell had endured. He lay awake for ages after his ritual of reading with the light on and then turning over into his duvet and disturbing his wife. She grunted once and he tried hard to relax, but sleep was not coming, not remotely. He slept for a little over an hour and woke, wide awake. He went to the toilet and then crept silently back into the bedroom, stubbing his toe against the wardrobe by the bed. Back in bed, he lay awake for another hour and then fell asleep and slept for another hour. At 5.30 am he gave up, and wrapping his dressing gown around him went downstairs and into the kitchen where he made the first of his day's coffee. It was not normal behaviour, he thought to himself. Normally he slept through the night no matter what the day had brought him. Why was this so different? The answer failed to materialise in his mind. He dressed and drove to the office in the centre of Leith.

Though it was only shortly before 8 o'clock when he arrived there he had been beaten by Joanne. She was sitting in front of the photos and parts of the file from his desk with a mug of coffee in front of her. Maxwell grunted a greeting, hung his coat behind the door and walked over to the coffee machine. Joanne had prepared a mug for him, it simply required filling from the coffee percolator standing on the desk. He carried the mug to his side of the desk and sat back in his seat.

'You alright Jo?' he asked.

'Fine sir. Rubbish night's sleep though.' Maxwell grunted in agreement as he tried to sip the hot coffee in his hand.

'We need to get a grip of this lot Jo. We are grinding to a halt here. The house to house have shown up nothing. The only potential lead is this rather tenuous link to the army guy in Lancashire. Do we have his name somewhere Jo?' He shuffled through the files on his desk to try and find the information.

'Hawkins sir. Coleman Hawkins.' She said, beating him to find the information.

'According to Brian Jones the house he had recorded against his army record has been pulled down. Bit of a dead end.' Maxwell sat quietly for a few minutes first thinking then looking at the mine of information in front of him.

'Is that his real name, Coleman Hawkins? You're not pulling my leg are you?' Joanne looked at him quizzically.

'No, it's real sir. Why should it be strange?' Maxwell shook his head absently.

'Wonder if his parents were jazz fans. No matter,' he said.

'Right. Back in a minute Jo.' He said, and rising from his desk he left the room. Jo looked around wondering where he had gone. He had gone to the small incident room which housed the HOLMES2 computer system. Two officers sat in front of terminals and looked around as he entered then waited expectantly. He paused for a moment thinking, then asked them to give him a view of the suggestions that HOLMES had come up with as possible leads to be followed up and the relation of Quinn to others who had been involved in the investigation. With the help of one of the input officers he quickly found his way to a Graphical Markup screen which showed him the relationships and connections the system had made with Quinn.

The visual representation that the screen gave him of the people and places where Quinn had been and which were mentioned in the statements taken by the officers in the investigation reassured Maxwell. He sometimes worked better with a visual representation or some physical evidence he could see. Whilst not immediately pointing to one person or another as being a potential suspect for his murder, it became clear that many people over the years had had dealings with Quinn for one reason or another, many of them not very healthy or legal.

A picture appeared before his eyes that painted Quinn's long history. One in which the name of Coleman Hawkins had figured regularly over many years, starting with their time together doing their National Service. Maxwell spent some time switching back and forth between the Markup screen to related documents on the system. The more he saw, it seemed, the more Hawkins was somehow involved, together with their wives and possibly their children. He finally sat up in his seat and grunted before closing up the documents he had been reading.

'Thanks, lad, good work,' he said to the operator, rose from the chair and returned to his office.

The coffee machine had just come to a boil, so he poured two mugs for himself and Joanne, placing one on the desk by her side without saying anything before going back to his seat. Joanne sat working silently and waiting for him to say something. Over the time she had worked with him, she had come to recognise his thinking process and knew it best not to interfere just yet. Give him time, she thought, just a bit of time. After a few minutes thought he sipped from the mug and replaced it on the desk.

'Right, need to get something moving don't we Jo?' She swivelled around on her chair and faced him across his desk.

'Anything particular you had in mind sir?' she asked. He felt in his pocket for the pipe and gave up at the disapproving glance from her across his desk.

'You're worse than my wife,' he said. Joanne bent down to the bottom drawer in her desk and took from it a brown paper-wrapped parcel, oblong, about ten inches by eight by four, placed it on his desk and pushed it towards him. Maxwell looked at her quizzically.

'What's that?' he asked.

'Take a look and you won't die curious,' she replied grinning. Maxwell pulled the parcel towards him, it was heavier than it looked. He lifted the plain brown wrapped box and shook it, it rattled mutely. He made a great play of sniffing it and listening to it until she lost her rag and said,

'Oh get the bloody thing opened, sir.' She said grinning. Maxwell took a small black-handled smoker's knife from his right-hand pocket and opened the blade, inserting it into a small gap at one end of the parcel. He very slowly slid the knife blade along the length of the parcel slitting the parcel tape fastening it together, and then along its width until the brown paper was flapping open. He bent his head down towards the desk to see what was inside.

'Give it to me you child!' Joanne snapped and reached across the desk to take the parcel from him. He picked it up and lifted it out of her reach.

'Temper Joanne, temper,' he teased. Unwrapping the paper from the box he discovered a two-kilogramme box of Lion Midget Gems, the sort he had been scrounging off Joanne for months now. She had bought him his supply. He laughed loudly.

'You are something else, Detective Sergeant Baker,' he said and tore the lid of the box open revealing a stout polythene bag inside containing at least a month's supply for him, and possibly less if he shared them. He sat back and grinned as he opened the bag and handed it to Joanne to take some. She lifted just one sweet daintily with two fingers from the bag and returned the box across the desk.

'Notice I did not take the black ones,' she said holding up the sweet before popping it into her mouth. He grunted as he took three of them and pushed them into his mouth, then sat back in his chair.

'Let's assume that Hawkins is the connection we are looking for. And let's assume he has kept in touch all these years and was involved in some way with his paedophile activities and got tired of what he was up to and killed him. If that's not jumping to too many conclusions in one go,' he said chewing on the gums in his mouth and swishing them from side to side. Joanne was silent and just looked at him.

'What?' he asked after enduring her stare for a minute.

'And came up to Wester Hailes just to give him a wank before killing him?' she said quietly. She screwed up her face in disbelief.

'I can't see that sir, I just can't see it' she said.

'No, you're probably right. Though, if he was interested in kids then would he not also be interested in sex with men or sex with women in a kinky way?' he mused. Joanne considered this for a moment before replying.

'Unlikely sir,' she said, 'Though not impossible. Generally, paedophiles are attracted to children because they are unable to make normal, or even abnormal, sexual relationships with adults. Quite often they come from a family where abuse for them was the norm, where kids were brought up to play with each other sexually because their first sexual activity was by their closest adult relations. If they came from a large family then they might even be witness to, or certainly aware of sexual activity taking place with their siblings. It's a scenario which normally brought up people who develop what are termed normal sexual activities and attractions, find hard to understand or accept. You and I would find it difficult to understand why a grown adult would be attracted to sexually abuse a child, but if it was the norm in your upbringing, then it could have been the norm as an adult. So, it could be a possibility, but it's a thin one.'

'And you got all this from your psychology degree? 'Maxwell asked, smiling.

'A lot of it sir.' She replied. Maxwell thought in silence for a moment again then said,

'So we're no further forward then? It still looks like a woman who killed him, just because of the masturbation?'

'Unless he did it himself.' Joanne said.

'No. Can't see that. Someone gets into the flat, he masturbates and then takes an overdose of drugs and whisky and then she kills him by slitting his leg open.' He shook his head in disbelief and frustration.

'It's not making any bloody sense Jo, none at all.' He rose from his seat, 'I'm off to the yard for a pipe,' he said. She watched him leave the office and rose to refill her coffee mug from the percolator.

CHAPTER 17

Down in the yard behind the station, surrounded by high stone walls of the station and its neighbours, Maxwell lit his pipe and blew clouds of smoke into the cold air, walking slowly from one side of the yard to the other, avoiding cars coming in and out of the station. Nothing appeared to be adding up. Nothing was falling into place. The investigation had gone on way beyond the first forty-eight hours when murders were often cleared up, now they were into the hard slog of digging and sifting. The laborious grind of detective work. He took out the smoker's knife from his pocket and cleared off some of the ash from the top of the pipe bowl and tapped it into a small drain in the centre of the yard, then relit it again with his Zippo. After ten minutes he went back into his office where Joanne was working on her computer.

'Well Jo,' he asked. 'Any thoughts?' Joanne turned round in her seat to face him, her back neatly concealing what she had been doing on her computer.

'Coleman Hawkins. Born 1929 Burnley, died 2003 in Burnley, last address in Burnley.' She said with a triumphant grin on her face. Maxwell did not attempt to see what was on her computer screen but went to take his seat.

'How the bloody hell did you find that out then?' he asked.

'Ancestry website sir.' She said. 'Easy when you know how. We're not the only ones with access to records you know. Sadly the address at the time of his death appears to be the one we already have, the one demolished during the ''70s.'

Maxwell sat back in his chair looking blankly at Joanne before he finally spoke. 'Well now. It looks like we need to be talking to the police in Burnley then, doesn't it? See if they have anything on him. By the way, what about Quinn's wife? What do we know about her?'

Joanne glanced at a file on her computer before saying, 'Living out near the M8 at Linlithgow. Interviewed two days ago and knows nothing of his life in Edinburgh since they were divorced. Could be an idea to see her again you think?' she asked.

'I think so, Jo. You and me this time. What's she like?'

'The officers who visited said she is,' she paused and turned back to her screen to read from the document she had up there. 'An evil little shrunken witch of a German cow. To quote from the side notes made by the reporting officers.' she said.

'Not biased then' Maxwell quipped. 'Wonder what in particular she said to upset them?' Joanne continued to read from the notes.

'Seems she tried to get shut of him back in the 70's when she suspected him of interfering with one of their kids. Swore he wouldn't do it again and there was nothing to it, so she let him stay. Divorced when the last of the kids left home and she could put up with him no longer. Seems to be a feeling that our Jimmy reciprocated. Happy families eh?' Maxwell nodded his head silently.

'You think the child abuse was at the centre of it all, she got rid of him when it became too much, you think?' he asked eventually.

'Don't think so sir, the kids were well away and married or at least grown up by then. Maybe he might have been starting to cast his evil little eyes on the grandchildren by that time and that's why she got shut of him.'

'And of course, she is a woman. Might she have gone round for old times sake, had a drink or two, given him the drugs, he falls asleep and she slits his leg open?' He sat back and thought for a moment about what they had both said and eventually moved forward to touch some of the things on his desk absentmindedly. 'We're not getting far at all are we Jo?' he said, more to himself than Joanne. 'Not very far at all.'

The two of them sat back again in their seats having exhausted, they thought, the possibilities and scenarios. Maxwell reached into the bag of Midget Gems which he now kept in the top right-hand drawer of his desk and popped two into his mouth. 'Jo,' he said, 'Do you think you can find me a copy of the Police Almanac please?' She nodded and got up from her seat. Almost at the door she stopped and turned to him,

'If it's just a phone number you need then you can get it online sir,' she said.

'No, not just the phone number, I want a name as well. Sometimes you get more by flicking through the pages.' Jo came back in a couple of minutes carrying the yellow book which listed all the Police forces in the UK and Ireland. Maxwell took it from her and after checking the index found the page he was looking for.

'Right. Favour please young lady,' he said. Jo looked around from her desk. 'Can you call Burnley CID and ask for DI Moore?'

'Sir?' she asked.

'Method in my madness Jo. If you put on your most pleasing voice then you have far more chance of getting through to him than if I rang up, you know what men are like.' Joanne grinned picked up the phone on her desk and dialled the number. It was answered in three rings.

'Good afternoon,' she said, her voice dropping half an octave. Maxwell choked on his sweets at the soft polite Scottish sultry voice she was performing. 'May I speak to Detective Inspector Moore please, I have a call from Detective Chief Inspector Maxwell from the Major Investigation Team at Leith in Scotland?' She flicked a button on her receiver and the hone on Maxwell's desk rang. He picked up the receiver.

'DCI Maxwell here. Am I speaking to DI Moore?' It was confirmed he was indeed talking to the right man.

'DI Moore, we have a murder investigation ongoing at the moment and I want to find out some background on a man who might have been involved with the victim at some time in the past. The man I'm looking for background on came from your area, he's dead now I believe, but I wanted to know if you knew anything about him. Maybe his name rings a bell with you.' He listened to the reply for a few seconds and then continued.

'His name was Coleman Hawkins and he lived in Burnley at the time of his death in 2002. Ring any bells.' Maxwell pulled an A4 pad from the corner of his desk towards him and made notes during the conversation, occasionally nodding his head and smiling from time to time. After a few minutes, he sat back in the chair, a look of disbelief on his face as he listened to the information the detective continued to give him. As the detective from Burnley came to the end of his story he said, 'That is great Inspector. One last thing, if we come down to Lancashire do you think you or your lads would be in a position to help us out should the need arise?' Another pause. Joanne was becoming frustrated at hearing only one side of the conversation. Finally, Maxwell gave his thanks to the other officer and replaced the handset on the receiver. He sat back in his chair beaming but said nothing. Joanne gave him ten seconds then burst out,

'Come on sir, What does he say?' Maxwell grinned and fished again into the bag of sweets in the top drawer. He took out the bag and held it out for Joanne to take one.

'Sweetie?' he said. She shook her head in frustration and grimaced at him. He grinned back.

'It appears that our Detective Inspector Moore knows Hawkins, or knew him when he was still alive.' He held up a hand to stop Joanne from interrupting and continued.

'Appears that Moore knew him from way back, came across him when he got married and Hawkins did his wedding photographs. He was a keen amateur photographer. Did all sorts of stuff and belonged to a camera club locally. From then on Hawkins managed to get himself a lot of work with various Bobbies who got married. He was cheap and he was always available. Then, and this is interesting, seems our Detective Inspector became a member of the local Masons Lodge some years ago on his way up the pole, and guess who he bumped into in amongst the apron-waving antics? No less than Coleman Hawkins!' Maxwell sat back beaming.

'And there's more?' Jo asked. Maxwell glanced up at her across the desk and grinned. 'What makes you think that?' he asked.

'You wrote an awful lot of notes whilst listening for all that length of time unless you were making your supermarket list for the week, that is.' He smiled broadly at her and tapped his pen on the notepad a couple of times.

'You're right of course. Got most of his life story. Seems he had a bit of a rough time during his life before finally dying in 2002.' Maxwell pushed back his chair and got up from his desk, picking up the pad in his hand and walking over towards the window. Once there he turned and faced back towards Joanne, leaning against the wall by the side of the window.

'Had two kids. The first one went off the rails a bit and was sent away to a boarding school.' He glanced down at the notes,

'Three boarding schools over several years, she was very difficult and nobody wanted her for long once she started to kick off. From what he said it looks like the Masons might have helped fund the school fees, not one of the top class schools in any case. There was some suggestion that the girl spent time in a reform school, but went on to boarding school later. Anyway, when the second girl was born everything looked like it was going well, then the wife died when the second girl was only a baby, not sure what age. But it left Hawkins to hold down a full-time job and look after the bairn at the same time. Couldn't manage it and got the second girl fostered out with a series of foster carers until the child was about five or six.' Maxwell bent over to his desk and took out the sweets again, popping three into his mouth. He chewed on them as he attempted to speak, and eventually stopped to finish them off, then started again.

'The DI says that there were times when he went off to Scotland to see a mate of his who he met in the army, sounds like our Jimmy, and took the young girl with him for the breaks. Happened a couple or three times a year, then the girl started school and he started to come up here on a more regular basis, in each of the school holidays. DI Moore was a good drinking mate of Hawkins and they used to meet up now and again apart from the Masons thing. Anyway, Moore and he kept in touch over the years, probably for eight or nine years until he was promoted and moved out of the area. Then they lost touch until he was promoted again and moved back to Burnley. By that time Hawkins was living by himself, the younger girl had grown to be a young woman and got herself married, so Moore lost touch with her, but kept spasmodic contact with the father from time to time until he died. Went to the funeral he said. Most of the Masons turned up for the planting he said. And that's about it.' Maxwell tossed the pad onto the desk and folded his arms across his chest, looking across the room at Joanne.

'What do we think?' he asked eventually.

'What did he say about Quinn sir?' she asked.

'Nothing. Said the name didn't ring any bells. Didn't know who he went to see up here, Hawkins never mentioned the friend's name, just said it was a bloke he met in the army whilst they were doing National Service. Sounds like we've found the man in the photos doesn't it?'

'I think you're right sir, fits the bill completely. So was he involved with the abuse, then you think?' Maxwell thought for a moment before replying.

'There's nothing the DI said to tie him in with Quinn. What we do have though is the photos, no doubt in my mind that Hawkins and his family were involved. Wonder what Mrs Quinn would have to say about it.'

'We could go and have another word with her. The guys who went said she was a bit weird, but maybe that was just the fact she is getting on a bit now and hated Jimmy by the time they came to a divorce.' Maxwell nodded his head in agreement.

'You're right. I think you and I need to speak to the good lady. See if you can fix it for us to see her tomorrow. No point in spoiling her afternoon at this point is there?' Joanne flipped through the file on her desk and found the phone number for Quinn's ex-wife. The conversation with her was difficult. Mrs Quinn was partially deaf and used a loudspeaker on her phone. It didn't help that she still had a strong German accent. But she got across quite forcefully that she could see no reason why they should be troubling her again, he was her ex-husband, he was dead, she had not seen him for some time, and what was more, as it came over loud and clear through the conversation, she hated Jimmy Quinn.

Maxwell doodled on the desk pad for some seconds before finally lifting his head to talk to Joanne.

'I think,' he finally said, 'Before we go to see the lovely former Mrs Quinn it might be good to see what else Mac has turned up on the relationship the two men had. If any.' Joanne nodded her head and lifted the phone to her desk. Five minutes later DC Douglas who had done the initial search with the Army records walked nervously into the office.

'Sit yourself down Jack' Maxwell said. The young man took a chair from near the wall brought it towards his desk and seated himself. He looked nervously from one to the other. Maxwell grinned.

'Nothing to sweat about Jack.' He paused and found a page from the notes on his desk.

'Give me what you have on Quinn and his mate Hawkins. A4 sheet, one page. No more. Keep it simple.' Douglas settled back in the chair and opened the brown file he had with him. He cleared his throat.

'It seems that the two of them met when they started national service. Went through the basics together and then both were posted to The Signals Regiment. Both posted to Germany together as part of the BAOR.' Joanne raised her hand like a child in class.

'Please sir what's the BAOR?' she asked with a grin. Maxwell returned the grin looking from Joanne to DC Douglas, 'For the ignorant amongst us, the BAOR stand for the British Army of the Rhine. In effect one of four occupying forces in Germany following the Second World War. OK?' She nodded her head and made a note on her pad. Maxwell nodded at Douglas to continue.

'So. They were in the same mob for the whole of their service. Always in Germany and always in the Sigs. During their time there they met a pair of sweet German girls, a bit younger than them apparently, and married them. Hawkins had a child in Germany and then they were demobbed back to the UK. Quinn came back to Scotland and Hawkins to England. And that is where their records end." He looked up at his boss. 'Is that OK sir?' he asked.

'More than OK Jack. Well done. Dare I ask how you managed to get so much information from the tight-lipped buggers at Army Records?'

'No problem sir. Remember I said most of the records were held in England? Well, it turns out a mate of mine in the job in Lancashire has a friend,' he made air quotes with his fingers and carried out.

'Well, the friend works in the records office and for the cost of a few gin and tonics was persuaded to dig around a bit. It's not as though it was state secrets or anything like that. So the friend came up trumps sir.' He sat back satisfied and smiled broadly.

'Bloody good work Jack. Bloody good.' He turned to Joanne.

'See all that money wasn't wasted was it?' She grinned but had the sense to keep quiet.

'Right. Thank you, Jack. Let me have the details and make sure HOLMES is kept up to date as well will you?' The young DC nodded his head and rose from his seat.

'That all sir?' he asked.

'That's more than enough Jack. Good work. On you go.' As Douglas left the office Maxwell turned to Joanne.

'I think we need to pay a visit to the lovely Mrs Quinn.' He looked down at his notes.

'Renate by name if I'm not mistaken. He rose as Joanne reached for her jacket and shoulder bag, stuffing pen and mobile phone into her pockets. 'Come on young lady. Let's be off.'

CHAPTER 18

Renate Quinn, the former wife of Jimmy Quinn, lived alone in a two-bedroomed bungalow on a small estate close to the Linlithgow canal and not far from Linlithgow Loch. Though she no longer had a car, the dwelling had a small garage with a driveway. A small garden at the front appeared to need care, a fact that both Maxwell and Joanne noted as they pulled up outside the house later that day.

Joanne turned off the car engine as Maxwell started to climb out of the car, Renate Quinn was opening the front door to the house as Jo got out. A small grey-haired old woman with obvious signs of arthritis in her slight, bent form, stood in the open doorway supporting herself on a wooden walking stick in one hand whilst the other held onto the door jamb. In the time it had taken the car to stop and its occupants to exit the car Mrs Quinn had spotted them from inside the net curtains of the living room and hobbled through into the hallway and opened the front door. She did not wish for her neighbours to see more than was necessary for any visitors to her house.

It was no affair of theirs. She was a very private woman and was generally disliked by all of her neighbours. The feeling was reciprocated, and she made no secret of her dislike of them. Although she had lived amongst them for much of her life she still considered herself to be German, and superior to the working class people which circumstances now forced her to live amongst.

Her life had started to end with a bomb jettisoned by a British aircraft on its way back from the Ruhr during the war. Her parents had been keen to evacuate from the city out to the countryside away from the industrial areas of the Ruhr valley, only to have both of them and the house they lived in flattened by the determination of the bomber pilot not to return home with a full load. She had viewed Jimmy as a passport out of the wreckage of Germany and leapt at it with both hands when he had presented himself. The truth came home later in Scotland over the years when she saw the blossoming new Germany she had left behind for the slums of Edinburgh and the low-wage life she had endured with the bus driver that Jimmy Quinn had become.

The life was sucked out of her by the three children she bore and the life she came to lead, withdrawing more and more into her thoughts and memories of what life had been and might have been. Life with the man she married was bearable only because of the time he was away from home working. She became narrow and twisted in mind and as the years wore on her body followed along, until now she was a small thin, bitter person who clung onto life whilst despising her children who had left her alone, and lived mainly on the drugs her doctor gave her to pacify her belief in her illnesses over the years. She had outlived most of the neighbours she had known over the years and many of the scattered family she had left behind in Germany. Her perpetual cause, and her only reason for living on, was her ill health and the feeling, she would tell anyone trapped into conversation with her, that she was sure to die soon. But still, she lived, and for the past close to twenty years since divorcing Jimmy had lived in the small bungalow in Linlithgow, alone and twisted.

She left the door open for the two officers to enter and shuffled through into the living room. By the time Joanne and Maxwell had stepped into the house and down the small corridor to the door of the living room, she was already ensconced in her upright armchair by the side of the fireplace. As they appeared at the doorway she pointed with her walking stick for them to take a seat on the sofa along the back wall of the room. Maxwell stepped in front of her and held out his hand in greeting. She took it and held it for a second like the frail bones of a bird, then let his hand drop when she pointed again to the sofa. Maxwell took his seat by the side of Joanne who was sitting forward with her knees together holding onto a thin file of papers she had put together from the large collection in the office.

She looked at them silently waiting for one of them to speak. Maxwell glanced sideways at Joanne and then back at Mrs Quinn.

'Mrs Quinn,' he began, 'We wanted to try and find out a little more about your former husband Jimmy.' She nodded her head and opened her mouth as though to reply then allowed her lips to close without saying anything. Maxwell continued.

'When you were living together Mrs Quinn, did he ever make any sort of advances to children in the area, can you remember if any of the neighbours said anything to him about that sort of thing?' He paused for her to reply. She looked down at the carpet beneath her feet for a few seconds and then glanced out of the window across the room from her.

'He was a bastard. A nasty dirty bastard.' She said eventually, her voice thin and reedy, her accent still German.

'He beat me you know, when we lived in the city. The police were involved. I threw him out, but stupid that I was I took him back.' Joanne nodded her head encouragingly and she continued.

'Twice I throw him out. Should have killed him, the bastard.' Though the voice was thin the accent was strange, a mixture of Scottish and German, but mainly German.

'If not for Coleman then I would leave him sooner you know. Coleman and his little girl. They come to see me and they keep me sane!' Her voice rose as she recalled their visits as the girl had grown older. Joanne leaned forward on the sofa.

'Do you remember anything about the visits Mrs Quinn?' she asked softly. Mrs Quinn looked sideways towards her and smiled, a warm smile which faded quickly. Some memory had flitted through her mind and had been quickly pushed to one side.

'They came to see us when Erika died. Later, when the girl was growing up, not a baby any more. She was at school and Cole came during the school holidays. The English holidays were different than ours, so when they came Jimmy was working. That was nice. Coleman took me for a drive, with the child as well.' A hint of warmth came into her voice as she recalled the times. Joanne said,

'But Mrs Quinn, can you tell us about the girl on the bus who complained when he touched her?' The old woman fired a cold dart of hatred at her.

'That girl was a little cow, she went with men, only little girl, but not Jimmy's fault.' She sat back in her chair and took in deep breaths to calm herself.

'Her mother reported it to the Police though didn't she?' Joanne said.

'Yes, she did, the bitch. That girl was a little cow. No good. My Jimmy never touched her. Police did nothing.' Joanne looked at Maxwell who nodded for her to continue asking the questions.

'The Police spoke to him though didn't they?'

'Yes, but did nothing.' She relaxed back in the chair again, almost relieved to have opened the gates to a field closed for so many years.

'Another time a man came to the house. Said he kill Jimmy if he touched his daughter again. Jimmy was scared, oh yes, he was scared. Cowardly little man. If he were a real man then he beat up the father for saying things like that, but not Jimmy. He coward, frightened. He would run a mile.' She smiled proudly at the use of the phrase, forgetting for the moment that she was admitting her ex-husband had been interfering with young girls whilst still married to her, and she had tolerated it. Maxwell coughed to clear his throat.

'Can we talk about your children Mrs Quinn? Do you think Jimmy ever interfered sexually with them? Did you ever catch him doing anything?' She gazed sadly out of the window for a moment, her shoulders slumping down. Finally, she spoke.

'Yes. I catch him.' she said.

'He played with all three when they were little. We argue about it, I threaten him, but he says it ok, that it was the way he was brought up by his father. I do not know if this is true or if this is how Scottish parents bring up children. I was young you know. I did not know about life then. I fought him, but he hit me and I did nothing.' Her head dropped down towards her lap and she sat looking sadly at the floor.

'I not know anything. I was an only child when I met him.' She gulped a sob in her throat and wiped beneath her eye with the end of the arm of her cardigan. All three sat for a moment in silence before she spoke again.

'I went back to Germany once you know. I hated it. So changed. Better than here, much better. I felt cheated. Life was not fair. I live with that bastard and Germany became a nice place. Rich and clean, but Scotland was dirty and wet and we were poor.' She fell into silence again keeping the sobs in her voice under control.

'My children left me.' She said quietly. 'Leave me because of him. He interferes with them all. Bastard. Now they are drunken and druggie and live in America.' Finally, she could hold back the tears no longer and her meagre skeletal shoulders heaved with the sobs as she searched in her cardigan pocket for a handkerchief. Joanne pulled a pack of paper hankies from her coat pocket and leaning across, pressed them gently into her hand. Taking one from the packet she wiped her eyes, then screwed up the damp paper in her hand as she sat back to continue her story.

'One year he came up with Wartburg car, from the Ost, the east of Germany. It was ugly. We called it the Warthog. For many years he had this car.' Maxwell and Joanne exchanged questioning looks. Maxwell said,

'Who came up with the Wartburg Mrs Quinn?'

'Coleman. He wanted a German car but could not afford a Mercedes so he buy this ugly thing. Lasted for many years then he buy Skoda.' She shook her head sadly at the memory before carrying on.

'First year he come with the Warthog was summer time in holidays for one week, two weeks. Jimmy was working night shift for extra money for some of the time.' She stopped suddenly and looked up at Joanne.

'I do nothing against the law you know. It was him.' Joanne nodded her head encouragingly, and she continued her story. 'Coleman take me to pictures and we go to the pub after for a drink. Jimmy is still at work when we get home so we go to bed together.' The memory from forty or fifty years earlier came back to her warmly for a second then was wiped off her face. 'Jimmy, he started to play with Coleman's daughter then. The little one. Not sure how long this went on for, but each summer Cole came to Scotland with the little one and she slept in the bedroom with my daughter, and if Jimmy was on nights, I slept with Cole in our bed.' Her voice dropped to nothing and she slowly lifted her head to look at the two of them, the look on her face defiant as though daring to criticise her for finding some happiness in the pitiful soulless marriage. Maxwell let the silence hang for a moment then quietly said,

'So whilst you were having an affair with Coleman Hawkins, his daughter was being sexually assaulted in the next bedroom?' he said. She fired a look at him which should have killed him on the spot.

'Not while a child is in the next room!' she spat out, the colour rising rapidly in her cheeks. 'I do not see anything, I think what was happening but I do not see anything. He doing it to my daughter at the same time!' She poked her walking stick heavily into the carpet in anger.

Joanne quietly opened the file on her knee and took from it the photo of the small girl that they had taken from Quinn's flat. She held it out to Mrs Quinn.

'Was this the little girl Mrs Quinn?' she asked. Mrs Quinn glanced at the photo for a second and nodded her head.

'Yes, Yvette. Very pretty girl, very pretty.' Her head fell again. Maxwell looked silently at Joanne as she replaced the photo in the file and nodded to her.

'When did you last speak to Yvette, the daughter, of Mrs Quinn?' Joanne asked. The old woman lifted her head and thought for a moment.

'Maybe two months ago. I telephone her. She, not a nice woman now.' Maxwell paused silently for a moment then slapped his hands on his knees and started to rise.

'Thanks for your time, Mrs Quinn. We'll be going now. If there is anything else you can think of to tell, then get in touch will you?' he said. Joanne got up, and the two of them left Mrs Quinn, sitting in her high back armchair, by the side of the fireplace, clutching a damp paper handkerchief in her skeletal thin hands. Joanne closed the front door quietly behind them as they left the house.

Outside Joanne clicked the key fob for the Volvo. Maxwell strode round the car to the passenger side and settled quietly into his seat. He pulled the seat belt down and clicked it in place. Joanne started the car and was about to pull away from the front of the house when she spotted a young girl, about five or six years old. She was riding a scooter in the quiet roadway towards them. She wore a light-coloured flower-patterned dress and a pink quilted hooded coat on top. The coat was unfastened and flapped in the breeze as the young girl pushed with her foot on the floor to scoot herself towards them. Joanne watched in silence.

'That lass would have been the right age for Quinn', she said quietly as the girl went past them. Maxwell nodded his head in silence. Joanne felt her eyes welling up. She sniffed and felt in her coat pocket for a tissue. And dapped her eye. 'It reminds me of something, this.' she said. Maxwell looked sideways at her but said nothing.

'It's like the day after my mum died. I was only a couple of years older than the girl.' She paused to dab again.

'I remember going out after she had died and wondered why nobody else felt that the earth was still going round. Why does nobody else feel like me? I found it hard to understand.'

'Aye, well. It's harder for children when a parent dies. Different when you are older.' Maxwell said quietly. He waited a few moments then gently patted her knee.

'Come on Jo. Time to get back.' Joanne nodded her head silently and started up the car engine.

The drive back to MIT took close to an hour. Joanne drove slowly and carefully, aware that she could have an accident if she failed to concentrate fully on the road. The story they had heard, and its implications, had stunned them into an abnormal sickened silence during the journey. On their arrival at Leith Police Station, they made their way without speaking into Maxwell's office. Joanne closed the door behind them quietly and without taking off her coat sat at her desk. Maxwell walked to the side table and silently held up an empty coffee mug for her. Joanne nodded her head and he turned to make them a mug each. What they had heard was beyond either of their experience, and for the time being wanted to have nothing to do with any of the remainder of the team. In silence, they drank their coffee and considered what they had heard. Outside the windows, the trees across the street waved their branches gently, and the odd Sparrow flicked from branch to branch. The world was still spinning on its axis, though for both of them, it would be a long time before life felt anything like normal again.

CHAPTER 19

Shortly after ten-thirty the following morning Joanne walked into Maxwell's office, very quietly. She was suffering badly and wanted nothing more than to simply go back to bed and die. She closed the door behind her and went to stand contritely before Maxwell's desk. He looked up and smiled warmly at her.

'You alright Jo?' he asked. 'You look like shite.'

'Feel like it, sir. Sorry about being late. I'll work on it tonight if that's alright.' She replied quietly.

'Don't be daft lass. We all work more hours than we should. Want a coffee?' he asked.

'Please, sir.' She replied quietly.

'Make one for me while you're at it then will you?' he grinned. Jo smiled and made her way to the coffee machine and made up two mugs for them. Placing one in front of her boss she went to take her seat by her desk opposite and tried to sip from the hot coffee.

'Want to tell me about it Jo?' he asked. Jo swung round in her seat to face him, holding the mug between her two hands.

'Had a rough night sir. Couldn't sleep. Drank too much.'

'Mm. How much?' he asked kindly.

'Bottle of red wine,' she murmured, then added, 'And a few drams after that.'

'How many drams was it?'

'Half a bottle.' She looked up over her mug at him and smiled guiltily.

'Shit Jo, that's too much. Are you sure you're fit to drive this morning? Never mind, don't answer that. You made it in without killing anyone. Just keep the coffee topped up during the day. So, was it just the visit yesterday?' he asked, leaning back in his chair. She raised her head and nodded towards him.

'Aye, sir.' She paused to try and remember what it was like the night before, then continued.

'Couldn't stop thinking about what she said. Then the wine kicked in and I was restless as hell, did a load of washing then dusted the house down. Must have used half a tin of furniture polish.' She grinned at him.

'Couldn't settle so went for a walk about half twelve. Nowhere special, just on the streets. Got back about two thirty and went to bed. After, I finished off the whisky.'

Maxwell thought for a minute, and she didn't interrupt until finally, he said,

'Look Jo. If you want the day off then take it, or perhaps you might feel a bit better if you went to headquarters and tried to get a chat with the psychologist there. It might do you some good to talk to someone. I know it helped me last night.' She looked at him in silence, and he continued.

'Thank God I've got Anne. If it weren't for her last night there would have been two of us sitting here in the same condition this morning. We sat down to eat about seven last night and I could hardly eat anything. She knew immediately something was wrong and turned the screws until I opened up.' He paused to drink from his coffee before continuing.

'We must have sat there 'til after midnight, me just talking and her just listening. In the end, we went to bed and I fell fast asleep, exhausted I suppose. Like I said, thank God for Anne.'

Jo replaced her mug on the edge of his desk and for a second or two tapped the edge of the wooden desk nervously, glancing down at her feet and then her knees. Eventually, she looked up across the desk at him.

'Thanks, sir. I appreciate what you said, and the offer to go to HQ, but I think I'll be alright now. And I will bear it in mind though.' He smiled at her, rather a fatherly smile, though he knew it was not what she needed.

'If you do need to speak to anyone then do it, Jo. Don't want you dropping out because of the pressure.' She nodded her head and swung back to her desk.

For the next hour the two of them filled in forms, either paper ones in front of them or on the HOLMES 2 system to record all they had done and the people they had seen.

By now the enquiry had been scaled back a bit, only two of the uniform computer operators were working in the other small incident room, and the team of detectives had been reduced to just four, including themselves. Maxwell glanced at his watch and tapped the desk. Joanne looked around at him.

'Fancy lunch Jo?' he asked. She grimaced at the prospect of yet another canteen fry-up or sandwich.

'I'm paying,' he continued, and then when she failed to signal any real enthusiasm added, 'We'll go out this time, promise.'

'Aye. You're on, but only if I can choose where we go.' She said.

'On your bike lady. We're going to Credo across the road or nothing.' She nodded her head and stood up from her chair, arching her back to take out the aches of sitting for so long, and a disturbed night's sleep. They grabbed their coats and walked out of the station and across the road to one of two or three watering and eating places frequented regularly by the officers from the MIT in Leith. The restaurant had only four or five people sitting in and eating when they arrived. Maxwell chose a table and a young waiter came for their order and drinks. Jo chose a long iced glass of Orange juice. Maxwell did not comment, other than to make the same decision. By mutual agreement, neither of them talked about the case or anything connected with the job whilst they ate. It was a useful break for both of them and as they later made their way back to the office, both felt the benefit.

'So what do we have now do you think Jo?' Maxwell asked as he settled himself back behind his desk. She paused for a moment and then held out the fingers of her left hand, ticking them off with the index finger of her right hand.

'One' she said, and paused, then dropped her hand. 'Fuck knows.' She finally said. Maxwell grinned at her.

'I can't get my head working today sir, sorry.' He held up his left hand, mimicking her actions, fingers extended and started to fold them down with his right index finger.

'OK. One.' He began. 'Forget Quinn's children as suspects. The eldest son is in Bermuda. The daughter is around the bend and too drunk. Youngest son should be in the State Hospital and frightened to death to leave his flat by himself, and probably completely incapable of putting together a scenario we found at the flat.' He waited for her agreement and got it with a nod of her head.

'Two. The ex-wife. Certainly hates him well enough. Especially since she found out what he was doing whilst she was doing what she was doing, but I can't see her making it thirty-odd miles on public transport in her condition to finish him off. I suppose she could have paid someone to do it, but how would she have found that person? She doesn't fit into the normal criminal scene in Edinburgh does she?' Jo shook her head in agreement again.

'Three. Dr Mansoor, his GP. The red coat seen going into the flat on the Friday before he was found is probably her, but she has no motive unless she knows about his past. But, no. Not the good doctor.' He paused for a moment then said,

'Four,' and stopped again after folding down the index finger of the left hand and looked silently across the desk at her thinking.

'Do you remember Gunther's reaction in the corridor when I asked him if Jimmy had been molesting him? He was immediately right up the wall wasn't he?' She nodded her head in agreement. Maxwell carried on.

'In retrospect, having spoken to all the family, and especially yesterday after talking to Mrs Q, it seems like all the family were fair game for him, and all the kids knew about it. She said the daughter used to share her room with Hawkins's girl, didn't she?'

'Whilst she was having it off with Hawkins, Quinn was in the daughter's bedroom having it off with Hawkins's daughter. You think that's how it was sir?'

'It makes sense doesn't it?' he asked. Joanne sat looking at him in silence, then said.

'School holidays in England are different than in Scotland. Hawkins comes up from Lancashire with his wee girl, Quinn's kids are back at school leaving him alone in the flat from time to time when he isn't working, and his wife is out on the razzle in the afternoons with Hawkins. He has the opportunity to have a go at the girl without anyone knowing. She is too young or knows too few people in the area to complain, and is too frightened to talk to her dad when she gets home in case she is sent off to boarding school like her sister. I think it might be worthwhile speaking to her if we can find her. If the molesting went on for any number of years then she might remember about other kids in the neighbourhood at the time who he was having a go at. Might be able to pinpoint other victims who still live in the Edinburgh area who could be up for killing him.' She sat back in her seat and waited for Maxwell to comment. It was not long coming.

'I feel that this is possibly the best lead we have at the moment, Jo. There is nothing which forensics have come up with, nobody witnessing anyone coming in or out of the flat, just a history of child abuse involving his kids, a girl off one of the buses he drove, a Police involvement with another child, and maybe this daughter of the Hawkins bloke. Let's see if we can find out who she is now and where she lives and get someone to have a word with her. It's worth a try if nothing else. Otherwise, we have bugger all else at the moment.'

Joanne stood up from her desk,

'I'm going to have a good look at what we have on HOLMES, sir.' Maxwell nodded in silent reply and concentrated on the file before him on the desk.

Joanne spent most of the remainder of the afternoon perched uncomfortably before one of the HOLMES terminals and found nothing to help her identify the daughter of Coleman Hawkins. The name Yvette Hawkins appears a couple of times but only in connection with her father, and then there is nothing further to help her identify her. In desperation, she turned to the Ancestry website, and using her account started a search again for the woman. Moving from one site to another then one search engine to another she gradually pulled together enough information to be able to go back to Maxwell. He had not moved from his desk and was still making notes on his computer terminal. He looked up and grunted as she entered the room.

'I think I might have her sir,' Joanne said. He turned from his screen and looked at her.

'Go on' he said, 'I'm listening'.

'I started with Coleman Hawkins and found his date of birth and death, it was 2002 as we've been told. Remember we were told his wife died two years after the second girl was born? Well, I searched for deaths for surnames in the area and came up with the surname of Hawkins but with a German-sounding name, who died in the late 50's. Then did a search on births with the German name and came up with Yvette Hawkins, daughter of Coleman Hawkins and Renate Hawkins.' She paused to see if her boss was following her. He motioned her to carry on.

'Next, I searched for the possible marriage name for the girl, just in case, and found one for a man called Brookes. So, I went on Dogpile and DuckDuckgo.com..'

'What the bloody hell are you talking about Jo!' Maxwell burst out. 'Dog pile, duck duck, what the hell are those?' She smiled at his confusion.

'You've heard of Google and Yahoo and Bing haven't you?' he nodded his head. 'Same sort of thing but better. Search engines. Lots of them.' She continued. 'Did a search for Yvette Brookes, and guess what I found?' Maxwell shook his head but said nothing.

'Yvette Brookes lives in Maryland USA, Florida, and Tennessee. So probably not who we're looking for is it?'

'Not unless she has done and gone and emigrated I don't suppose.' He groaned.

'So, I did another search for her maiden name, Yvette Hawkins. Guess what I found?' He dropped his pen onto the desk and leaned back in his chair.

'No doubt at some time today you are going to tell me Detective Sergeant, but I fear I might die first before you get around to telling me.'

'My word we are touchy today aren't we?' she quipped, and before he could retaliate said,

'Dr Yvette Hawkins is living and working in the area Brian Jones went to see the other day.' Maxwell sat upright in his chair.

'Is that right?' he asked. 'Go on, more, tell me there is more?' He said.

'Indeed there is sir. Seems she was married and then after seven years or so got herself divorced and reverted to her maiden name of Hawkins. Which is why I found her. She is a Clinical Psychologist who works for a company which has a dozen or so Mental Health residential homes in the northwest and midlands parts of England.' With a self-satisfied grin on her face, she sat back in her seat and looked him in the eye. 'Want to know more?

'Aye go on with you.' He said shortly.

'There is no more. Not been able to find her home address, yet,' she said. 'But I dare say I will in time.' Maxwell was interrupted by what he was about to say by the telephone ringing beside him. He raised his hand to motion to Jo to stay where she was and picked up the phone.

'DCI Maxwell,' he said. The voice on the other end spoke for a couple of minutes, during which Maxwell made notes on the pad in front of him. Finally, he said,

'I'm very grateful Alex. Many thanks. I'll be in touch soon.' Replacing the phone on its receiver he looked briefly at the notes he had made before turning to Joanne and said,

'Go on Jo, you were saying'

'Yes sir, at the moment I don't know where she lives, but no doubt can find it in time. Just give me an hour or so.' She started to rise from her seat, Maxwell motioned her to remain seated.

'Wouldn't be 230 Southfield Lane, Near Burnley, Lancashire, now would it?' he said, grinning sheepishly at her. Joanne pushed herself back from his desk.

'How did you do that?' she demanded. 'Who was that phone call from?' Maxwell laughed and rose from his desk to stretch his legs. He walked to the window and on the way flicked on the coffee machine.

'We need to get some more stuff for this machine,' he said, pointing to the percolator. Joanne stood and went to the desk with the machine and selected two of the less dirty mugs and spooned sugar into both, then stood there with her arms folded waiting for the machine to explode and watching him.

'Go on sir, spill the beans.' She said. Maxwell half turned and went back to his desk and consulted the A4 pad once more.

'That was the DI from Burnley I spoke to a couple of days ago. He was talking to one of his colleagues after my phone call, simply because most of the Police there knew Hawkins from his wedding photography job. One thing led to another and the other detective knew the daughter from some work she had done with him on a case several years ago. So, being the very helpful Detective Inspector that he is, he did some basic digging around and has come up with this address and the place she is based at, out in the country somewhere not far from where Brian Jones was digging last week.' He turned to the coffee machine and flicked it off, then picking up the glass jug poured two mugs full for him and Jo. They took the drinks back to their desks and sat for a moment thinking, then Maxwell said,

'So I think you and me are due to take the low road down to England to try and have a word with Dr Hawkins. If nothing else, she might be able to pinpoint some other potential victims of Quinn' to find his killer.' Joanne nodded her head,

'Sounds like a good idea to me sir.' She said and drank deeply from the sweet almost black liquid in her mug.

CHAPTER 20

Dr Yvette Hawkins replaced the cordless telephone receiver on its black holder standing on the corner of the marble work surface in her kitchen. She moved the stand back into the corner an inch and idly rested her hand on the cold grey surface then walked slowly around the kitchen, absently touching implements and tools as she went. Her cat joined her, jumping up onto the surface and walking alongside her, purring and making scratchy sounds from deep inside her throat. Yvette stretched out a hand and the cat walked into it, allowing her to stroke her and scratch behind her ears, rewarding her with the same deep-throated scratchy sound.

'Don't you think the floor is a more suitable place for a cat?' she said quietly to the cat. The cat replied with a scratchy noise. 'Well, I can tell you that you are a cat. No question, and you should be on the floor.' She reached for the cat who deftly slid out of her grasp and jumped down to the kitchen floor with a dull thud. Yvette came to the knife rack and stopped, checking that the line of knives were all in perfect alignment and all facing the same direction in size order. The phone call from DCI Maxwell from Scotland had disconcerted her, more than that, she was very worried. Not so much for the reason that he and his colleague wanted to come and talk to her this coming weekend, but how had they found her so quickly?

It couldn't have been fingerprints or DNA, she thought. She had been meticulous in wearing surgical gloves during the visit to Jimmy's flat and had then carefully wiped over every surface she had touched whilst in the flat with Surgical Gel, the acetic acid it contained would have cleaned away any sign of DNA. Then the sudden thought struck her that it could not have been either of those two signs which had led them to contact her, she did not have a criminal record and therefore they would not have had a record of anything about her. So what had led them to consider her as a suspect? She walked listlessly around the kitchen, touching things on work surfaces, and looking out of the window into the garden. A Thrush and a Blackbird were disputing something on the lawn. The Blackbird appeared to be winning. Several miles away, far beyond the garden was the dark outline of Pendle Hill. Clouds scudded along its ridge and were being blown towards where she lived by a westerly wind. 'Wonder how far it is to Pendle?' she thought to herself. 'Eight, nine miles? Bet a crow would know.' Between her and the hill lay the old former cotton town of Burnley, new industries pockmarked the former farmland on the outskirts of the town. In the town itself, she could make out the roofs of houses and the occasional tall chimney of long-demolished cotton mills.

Like most Lancashire towns the past half century had not been kind, but Burnley was now starting to thrive with new industries tied to aerospace and defence. And pies, she thought with a grin. A recent television programme had extolled the fame of the local pie maker, only to be followed some weeks later by a similar article about a pie maker in Wigan.

Moving items out of place and then absently replacing them in their original position, nothing immediately came to mind about the Police investigation and their visit to Jimmy's flat. Could Jimmy Quinn have left a note somewhere giving details of her or her father? Had they found her by tracing him or her from that? Had Jimmy told a friend or neighbour about the cards she had sent to him? She doubted it. Knowing Jimmy he had probably thrown them out almost as soon as they had arrived. Certainly, she had found none of them on her visit to the flat, he had disposed of them. That was a dead end. Jimmy had few friends, which didn't surprise her at all. Miserable evil sod had probably kept his head down for the past few years. Too many skeletons for him to potentially disturb. Too many children are now grown up who might be more than happy to talk over old times with him. Maybe that is what the Police were after talking to her about. Just a thought.

From her infrequent contacts with Gunther, it seemed that nobody kept in touch with him, or his family. The family was truly dysfunctional and disjointed. Nobody was ever in regular touch with each of the others, living scattered around the UK and Europe. The thoughts ran through her mind until she eventually sat down by the work surface and tried to recall exactly what the detective had said during the phone call.

He had told her that Jimmy Quinn had been found dead and did the name mean anything to her? When she had replied that he did, from years ago, he had gone on to say that their visit to her was to try and establish if she could help to throw any light on possible offences Jimmy had committed whilst she had been visiting him and his wife, or since then since she had had contact with Gunther. Then she recalled that the detective had used Gunther's current name, Graham, so did that mean they had spoken to Graham? More than likely they had, so what had Gunther said to them? She needed to call him and find out what they had pumped him for and what he had given away during the conversation. Knowing him as she did, it was more than likely that he had told them all about life as a child, but equally likely that he had denied any possible molestation carried out by Quinn on him. Calling Gunther was not a good idea, she thought. If she called suddenly out of the blue it might trigger him to call the detective back again. Better to leave him.

She remembered Gunther's reaction when she had broached the subject in the past. He would have denied everything. So how had they found her? For over an hour, she wandered around the kitchen then other parts of the house mulling over in her mind the conversation with the detective and the forthcoming visit from them. She needed to keep herself in control during the visit and make certain she gave nothing away.

She went upstairs to the small bedroom she had converted to an office and looked again through the files on her computer and the paper files in the boxes she kept. There was nothing there to tie her to Quinn which was a recent incident, what there was seemed to her to be limited to old photographs taken by her father during the visits to Scotland when she had been a child, visits which had finished when she was thirteen or fourteen, by which time Jimmy had turned his attention from her and Margaretha to younger girls in the neighbourhood. She had few memories of the times after that simply because Jimmy never bothered her once she had started puberty. He liked small children, and she was too big for him, mentally and physically.

Yvette was five foot six inches tall and was starting to put on weight for the first time in many years. Her figure was still good enough to attract the attention of her male colleagues and that pleased her. She had short thick light brown hair which was starting to go grey, but the occasional visit to an expensive hairdresser had managed to hide the grey and keep it attractive. She wore expensive designer prescription glasses which enhanced her face and looks.

From her early to late teens she had been fit and active and that only now was that fitness starting to leave her. Age was beginning to tell. Although now in her early sixties, she looked some fifteen years younger and felt thirty years younger. Though much of her life had been a struggle, it was now being good to her.

Going downstairs into the kitchen she picked a mug decorated with cats from a cupboard above the sink and flicked on the electric kettle. Taking a jar of instant coffee from the same cupboard she started to unscrew the lid, then paused and tightened the lid again. Replacing the jar in the cupboard she took a tea bag from an opened packet on the shelf and dropped it into the mug. From now on, she thought, I will stick to Green Tea. Don't need any real caffeine stimulation on the day the police are due to arrive, but they can have one. She made the tea fished out the bag from the mug and dumped the bag into a stainless steel kitchen bin, then took the drink through to the living room and had a look around at the layout.

She needed to control as much of this interview as she possibly could, and that would start with the positioning of the two people visiting her. The lumpy three-seater sofa opposite the window would be where she would seat them, she would take the armchair in the bay window so that the afternoon sun coming in from the window would make it hard for them to see any telltale giveaways she might make. At the same time by seating them on the sofa they would not be able to see each other without looking directly at each other. She would be able clearly to see any eye contact and other nonverbal signs they might give to each other.

She looked at the sofa with its scatter cushions. She had used them on the furniture because the cushions making up the sofa had become well-worn and sagged badly. She removed the cushions and left them by the door to put them out of sight before Saturday when the officers were going to arrive. The sofa would now be quite uncomfortable to sit on for any length of time. The main window of the room was wide, almost the width of the room, and was furnished with floor-to-ceiling curtains over net curtains which afforded her the potential for maximum privacy during the evening. She walked over to the nets and unhooked them from the side fastenings on the window frame, folding them carefully and placing them near the cushions on the floor by the door, ready to be removed upstairs and out of the way along with the cushions. The room was instantly a lot brighter, and the sun flooded in. Come Saturday afternoon, provided it was a fine day, the room would be unbearably bright for them, sitting directly facing the sun through the window. She lifted a small round wooden antique table from the side of her armchair and placed it at the end of the sofa, giving the impression that it was there for one or other of them to use to make notes upon if they wished. The table was old, somewhat battered had uneven legs and was too small to use properly as a desk, but they would have to use it to find that out. At either end of the sofa stood a standard lamp, each with a forty-watt bulb in it. She unscrewed the bulbs and removed them and made a mental note to replace them with at least a sixty-watt bulb or larger before they arrived. If they stayed long enough and the light started to fade then turning on the two lamps would keep her in darkness and them in bright light. Psychologically they were all effective things to do to ensure they were as uncomfortable as possible and that she was as comfortable as possible, and in control.

As she stood in the middle of the room looking around at the effect she had created her cat, a long haired multi coloured cat she had called Catkins, sidled into the room and brushed itself against her legs. She looked down and collected it in her arms, scratching behind its ears. The cat purred for a moment then stretched itself free and dropped to the floor. The room would not look unusual to someone who had never seen the room before, of that she was sure, yet at the same time would make life difficult for anyone attempting to interview her. They would arrive tired from their three or four-hour drive down from Leith during the morning, and by the time they had found somewhere to eat and then driven to her home, they would have the food on their bellies and that would cause them to become more fatigued and maybe not as bright as they would have liked. If she offered them a coffee or maybe a cold drink on their arrival then this, on top of the food and drink they had eaten would add to the pressure on their digestive system and make them more uncomfortable. She smiled to herself and opened the living room door to the corridor.

As she went to move the cushions and curtains from the room the telephone rang. The cat rushed to her and leapt up into her arms. She picked up the receiver on the hall table as she went out of the living room. It was a work colleague, Nigel, suggesting that they meet up over the weekend for a meal. She pondered the suggestion for a moment in silence then said, 'Sorry Nigel. I can't. My aunt Maggie is not too good and it's been on my mind a bit this last week. I promised to go and see her again. Can we leave it for a few days? You know I wouldn't put you off unless it was something important don't you?' Since he had arrived at her place of work some months ago she had made a determined but subtle effort to attract him. Giving him a lift home from work from time to time and occasionally accepting his offer of a cup of tea. She would have him in bed soon, she thought. She smiled at his reply and replaced the phone on its stand, then walked through to the kitchen to hide the cushions and curtains from the living room.

Saturday, she said to herself, was going to be an interesting day, providing that the weather held out and it was fine and sunny.

CHAPTER 21

The following day, Friday, Maxwell and Joanne set off from Leith Police Station in the mid-morning in Joanne's car. It was a bright sunny day and both of them anticipated an untroubled drive down through the hills to the border with England, then on to Burnley along the M6 and M65.

As they sat in the car outside the station Joanne switched on the inbuilt sat nav system in the car. Maxwell looked at it with interest.

'Not used one of these before' he said. 'Looks pretty smart. Is it as good as people say?' Joanne punched buttons on the face of the instrument as she spoke.

'Well, it works well enough for me, though when I bought the car I had to download and update the latest version of the mapping. So it should get us to Burnley ok.' They sat for a few moments looking at the map of Leith as it appeared on the small inbuilt screen in front of them. Joanne flicked various buttons on the screen to show her boss the map of where they were due to go. He was impressed. 'Pretty good eh?' he said.

'I like it,' she replied. 'One of the good things about it is that if I want to go somewhere I've been before I just need to find the destination and it works out the new route from wherever I happen to be at that time. Pretty good eh?' Maxwell grunted. 'Prefer paper maps myself.'

'I agree sir. I like maps, but if you want to go somewhere in a hurry and you don't know the way this is pretty bloody good.' She grinned pushed the car into gear and started from the kerb.

The journey went as they had anticipated, without incident and with not much traffic, despite it being a Friday. Shortly after mid-day, they arrived at the rather grim old stone Victorian building which housed the Lancashire CID in the centre of Burnley. Neither had been to the area before and Joanne in particular was happy that she had added the Sensus Navigation system to the spec when she had bought the Volvo. They found the building on a side street just off the centre of town without any problems, and despite the local Friday traffic, felt quite at ease and comfortable when they introduced themselves to Detective Inspector Alex Moore in his office in the old building.

DI Moore's office was small and cramped and in need of decorating. Years of previous cheap decorating made the office feel even bleaker than it might have been. One window faced a stone wall of the building next door. Two hardback chairs were placed in front of his desk which he invited his visitors to occupy. They settled in and looked around. Despite its decor, the office was light and airy. A small desk to the side of his main desk was occupied by a computer terminal, whilst against two of the walls were three drawer filing cabinets, piled high with files on top of them, doubtless inside as well. The introductions and offers of refreshments were made and refused, DI Moore started the conversation.

'Have you found your hotel yet? Is it up to scratch? We don't have many decent places in Burnley, which is why I had to get you a room out in the sticks a bit. But it's alright for getting around, not all that far from the motorway, and only ten or fifteen minutes drive from Dr Hawkins's place,' he said. Maxwell shook his head,

'We've come straight here, thought it best to come and make our introductions first before stamping around.' He grinned and glanced sideways at Joanne who was nursing a file on her lap. She smiled broadly at the young Detective Inspector who returned it.

'I appreciate that, thanks very much. Now. How can I help you?'

DCI Maxwell began.

'I told you about Quinn and what we feel his background was before he was killed. Spent most of his life abusing kids from what we have found so far, including all of his children.' Moore nodded his head but said nothing. Maxwell continued.

'We are struggling to get a handle on who might have killed him. His wife and two children living in Scotland are out of the frame for one reason or another, and nobody around where he lives seems to have anything to say about it. He kept himself pretty much to himself and even when we dug further back when he lived in the centre of the city, well, nobody there can recall him. So, you see we are struggling. We think that Dr Hawkins might be one of the children he abused when she was a kid.' He paused for his Lancashire opposite number to take it all in. Moore used the break to ask,

'So you think her father, Coleman Hawkins, might have been involved in the child abuse in some way?' Maxwell shook his head.

'No, not exactly. He and Quinn met in the army when they were both doing National Service, kept in touch when they finished and came back to the UK. They were posted to Germany together and met a couple of young women who they married. So there was a link between the two girls, who were friends in Germany when they were growing up during the war. Although Hawkins came up to Scotland many times to see Quinn it seems that the main attraction, after Hawkins's wife died, was Mrs Quinn. They were having an on-off affair whenever he came to see them. She and Hawkins would go off for the afternoon or evening leaving Quinn in charge of his children and Hawkins's daughter. We are fairly sure that when they were out the house Quinn was abusing the kids, probably both boys and the girl and Hawkins's daughter.' He settled back in his chair to allow Moore to take it all in.

Moore shook his head in silent disgust.

'What did the children say? I suppose they are middle-aged adults by now?' Moore asked. Joanne sat forward in her chair to answer.

'The eldest boy is living abroad,' she said. 'Has done for several years. We think that he left the UK to get away from his father. The girl is an alcoholic and severely disturbed and the other son is up to his eyes in drugs, has a mental health history and is almost agoraphobic. Probably never leaves his flat from one month's end to the next. Gets his fix of drugs brought in for him. He has lots of connections.' She paused for a moment to consult the file on her knee.

'Mentally, he isn't capable of carrying out what is quite a sophisticated killing. If he did kill someone it would be in the heat of the moment and he would do a runner, not stay behind and clean up.' Moore nodded his head, sitting in silence thinking for a moment. Joanne continued.

'There's nothing to indicate that it was one of the locals who did it, it's a rough area with its share of drunks, druggies and neds, but again, nobody with enough nouse to carry out this sort of crime.' She sat back to allow Moore to digest this. 'It's quite a sophisticated murder' she said. DI Moore was silent in thought for a moment.

'Neds? You meaning yobbos?' he asked. Joanne nodded her head and smiled.

'Local name for our own yobs,' she said returning the smile.

'Right. Seems we have a lot in common.'

'What about the wife and Dr Hawkins then? You think they may know some of the other kids from way back who were abused by him? Seems a long shout don't you think?' He paused for a second and grinned.

'Sorry. I'm not telling you how to suck eggs, but as a fresh pair of ears, sometimes it helps.' Maxwell waved his hand to brush away the apology.

'You're right Alex, you don't mind me being familiar do you?' Moore shook his head and smiled. Maxwell continued.

'It could be that she is the only person from those days who are not drugged up or alcoholically fuelled at this time, or so screwed mentally to be unable or unwilling to remember anything, so we have to give it a try. We're clutching at straws a bit, as you can see. The wife, by the way, well, she's as much a fan of him as their kids hate his guts. But again, she isn't capable of physically killing him, not even getting herself from her home to where he lives. She's in her eighties and has real health problems, and some imagined ones as well.' Moore nodded his head in agreement and thought silently for a moment before speaking.

'What about Dr Hawkins as a suspect then?' he asked. Maxwell looked at Joanne who lifted her shoulders in acceptance of the suggestion.

'I suppose it's a possibility at that. It's a thought which went through our minds a few days ago when we first heard about her, but I think it was easier to discount all the other suspects first before coming to her.' she said. She looked at Maxwell who confirmed what she said with a silent nod. Joanne carried on.

'The long-term effects of child abuse are well documented.' She paused for a moment before continuing.

'However, although the effects are well documented it is not always the case that the kids carry on abusing their own children. It's not like it's an automatic reaction to abuse in every case.' She settled back and Alex nodded at her to continue.

'Just because it happened years ago doesn't mean the child forgets it, on the contrary, they can remember many things quite vividly.' She held up the file in her hand and nodded at it.

'There is a lot of supposition in here, and we know the memories of children can become altered and warped over the years. But there is still often a large kernel of truth there, it just needs teasing out, and the truth separating from the memories of long ago, and the alterations the mind can make to those memories during those long years.' The three of them sat in silence mulling over what had been said, until Maxwell broke the silence.

'What we have with her is this, she visited Edinburgh regularly over several years when she was a child. During that time Quinn was abusing his daughter and the younger boy, and during that time had probably stopped abusing the older boy only because the boy had become too old. The Hawkins girl comes on the scene, whilst her father and Mrs Quinn are carrying on an affair whenever he comes up to see them. It would be illogical that Quinn did not abuse the Hawkins girl when she became the right age, say five or six. The abuse likely carried on until she was eleven or twelve, especially if he was left alone with her, or the other girl together.' He turned to look first at Joanne, who nodded her head in agreement, and then DI Moore who nodded as well.

Maxwell sat back in his chair and fidgeted in his pocket for Midget Gems. He had none. Joanne bent down to the floor and fished a bag out her of handbag, offering it to him, and then reached across the table to DI Moore who smiled and accepted the offer.

'Not seen these for years,' he said smiling, popping a couple in his mouth.

'Jo buys them for me to stop me smoking in her car.' Maxwell quipped.

'Then she pinches all the black ones for herself.' Moore laughed and glanced at Joanne who was blushing.

'That's not quite how it goes,' she said, stuffing the sweets back into her handbag. 'And it's also the last time I bring them out in company.'

DI Moore smiled and continued.

'So how are we going to play this interview tomorrow then, or would you prefer not to have me tagging along? It might make it easier if a 'local' was not around.' Maxwell looked between the other two for suggestions. Joanne was the first to respond.

'I think we go alone and early sir, catch her off guard. She's expecting us at one o'clock, so let's get there about noon. That might also give us time to work out if she is telling the whole story truthfully or if she is hiding something. If she is not telling us the full truth then we have time to detain her and bring her back here.' She paused and looked at Maxwell,

'Or take her straight back to Leith.' Moore coughed gently and smiled at Maxwell.

'You know how Scottish law operates far better than I do Joanne. My knowledge is almost non-existent. I know the law allows you to arrest someone here in England and take them back to Scotland, but how about a search warrant, how does that work? You would either use our lads or bring your own down for the job.' Maxwell thought for a moment and looked across at Jo.

'What do you think Jo?' he asked. She grinned and looked down at her knees for a moment. She guessed he was struggling to remember what the cross-border law enforcement law regulations were, and looked to her for illumination. The three of them looked silently from one to the other until Joanne broke the silence.

'If we need to detain her then we can take her straight back to Leith. That then gives us 12 hours to bring her before the court in Leith from the time we arrive at the station. We can pre-warn our office that we are going to need a search warrant and that you and I are going to be due back in Leith sometime on Saturday night with a prisoner. Sunday morning we see the Procurator for a Search Warrant who will then have to approach the local Sheriff in Wester Hailes. The Sheriff grants the warrant and then we bring it back down here to get it backed by one of your local Sheriffs, sorry Magistrates, and we can then execute the warrant and search her home and even her office where she works.' Maxwell smiled at her, as did DI Moore.

'Alright. I'm impressed,' said DI Moore, smiling at Jo after a moment's silence.

'Quite obviously one of us has mugged up on the different legislation.'

'You're impressed?' Maxwell exclaimed,

'I'm bloody flabbergasted. Never knew you knew so much Jo. Well done!' Joanne settled back in her seat and folded her arms, tossing her hair back.

'You see sir,' she said, 'not just a pretty face.' The three of them relaxed and mentally went over once more the routine that Maxwell and Joanne would have to go through to obtain the Search Warrant should there be enough evidence to warrant detaining Dr Hawkins.

'Why not bring her back here to the station in Burnley?' Moore asked. 'I'm not being awkward, just want to know what your reasoning is.' Maxwell nodded his head.

'No problem. She'll have to go back to Scotland at some point, so for me, it makes more sense to get her straight back up there. Apart from anything else, it might disorientate her a bit and also cause her problems in getting her solicitor up to Leith. The physical evidence at her home and office could be taken straight to Scotland when the warrants are executed. There's no real point in bringing her in here, and then having to take her off up the road later. It just complicates things a bit. There isn't anyone here involved with the investigation who could question her properly is there?'

'No, you're right there,' said Moore.

'So you'll want my lads to execute the warrant, or just assist in the search of the premises?' Maxwell nodded his head in agreement.

'We'll need to ensure a couple of our lads are in on the search from a continuity point of view, that's going to be essential to prove the warrant in court. If we could have some of your lads to guard her home and office until the day after her arrest, when we get the warrant down here, that should be fine.' Maxwell paused for a moment, thinking.

'So, we lift her Saturday afternoon, get back to Leith late that night and get her bedded down.' He turned to Jo and said,

'We need to get someone from the Procurator's office forewarned we are going to spoil their Saturday night, same with the Sheriff as well.' He looked at her for confirmation. She nodded,

'If we have them both lined up and ready in Leith, we could have the warrant by one or two o'clock on Sunday morning, come down here for six or seven and execute the warrants with your guys then. How does that sound to you, Alex?' He smiled warmly at her.

'That sounds good to me.' He said. 'I think what we need to do now is organise some troops just in case you do push the button tomorrow lunchtime. One last thing though, what about her car? If she did drive up to Scotland to kill Quinn, then there has to be some forensic evidence of some sort in her car. I'll arrange for it to be lifted as well, but it should be taken back to Leith for a forensic examination. Just for continuity, I think.' He sat back in his seat and regarded the other two officers for a moment.

'This is going to cost a fortune isn't it?' he said quietly. Maxwell nodded his head in agreement.

'Cheaper than bringing a whole team down from Scotland to do it though. Anyway, just send me the bill!.' He said. Joanne, injecting a note of caution commented,

'We do need to keep an eye on the costs though. I can see our bosses going ape over this.'

'Nothing to be done about it Jo,' Maxwell said. 'Quinn's up there in Wester Hailes, the killer could be here in England. We have to abide by the rules, she has to be taken back. End of story.' He glanced at the other two for approval and received it through their nods.

CHAPTER 22

That night they slept well in the Higher Trapp Hotel a few miles from Burnley. Set in a beautiful wooded area it was a pleasant, quiet hotel with a good restaurant which both of them enjoyed a good dinner before retiring for the night. The following morning over a heavy breakfast they discussed the finer points of the day ahead of them. Out of the large dining room window old green-leafed trees of various varieties provided a degree of seclusion they had not anticipated. In Edinburgh, visitors normally were relegated to small three stars full of tourists. This was something different.

'What do we do if we feel she is a suspect sir?' Jo asked, licking a dribble of marmalade from her lip and making it disappear the same way the toast went. Maxwell sipped from his third cup of coffee, pushing away the paltry remains of the full English he had demolished.

'There's going to come a point when we both feel she is the one. That's the point where normally we would arrest her. Because we are down here we need to ensure that she can't get away or call anyone.' He stopped to carry the thought forward in his mind.

'At that point, I think that you make some excuse to go outside and call DI Moore. We'll give him a call before we are due to start knocking on her door and forewarn him to get the troops ready. That way, we arrest her and keep her in the house until the uniforms turn up and then whisk her away to Scotland, leaving Alex to take care of things here.' Jo nodded her head and reached for her coffee.

'I'll give Alex a call now,' he said, looking at his watch. 'Should be out of bed by this time.'

He rose from the breakfast table and walked out into the hotel foyer to make his call. DI Moore was on his way to the Burnley CID office and confirmed the arrangements for later on that day. Maxwell went to re-join Joanne who was still making the pile of toast perform a disappearing act.

'You've a hell of an appetite Jo,' he said pointing at the almost empty toast rack on the table. She tried to speak between mouthfuls, but failed and just raised her shoulders in resignation. He sat back in his chair helped himself to another cup of coffee and sat looking for a moment out of the dining room window at the trees coming into bloom in the hotel gardens. There were few people in the hotel, and the place was quiet. Better than the average place they were forced to stay in occasionally, he thought.

'Alex says he's told a uniform inspector pal of his about the arrest and search. Didn't tell him where or who, just in case it got out. Sounds like they might have a leak problem, not by themselves though are they? He'll be waiting for your call. Though he's going to have two teams on standby from eleven o'clock this morning to secure the house and her office. Then when we come back with the warrant and our guys, they will come in with us.'

'Sounds like all the 'Is' are dotted and the 'Ts' are crossed, sir.' Jo managed to say between bites of toast.' Maxwell nodded and glanced again at his watch.

'Ten o'clock' he said. 'Time we were checking out don't you think?' Jo wiped the crumbs from her mouth and with a wistful sigh pushed herself from the table.

'If you insist sir,' she grinned.

Thirty minutes later they sat in Jo's car whilst she punched the address of Dr Hawkins into the sat nav of her Volvo. They were a little over five miles and ten minutes away. Jo told Maxwell this.

'Shit. That's too early, even for us Jo.' He said. She nodded her head in agreement, and they sat in the car for a further half hour before leaving, watching the clouds blowing across the landscape they could see in the distance from the hotel car park. It was a fine day, clear and without the chance of rain. A good day to pull a killer, Jo thought to herself.

A few minutes before twelve the car with both of them on board pulled into the short driveway of Yvette's house. The car wheels crunched on the gravel drive, causing Yvette to dash to the window of the bedroom and look down on the two officers as they climbed out of the car.

'Shit!' she cried out in desperation.

'Shit, shit, shit. They're early!' She stepped back from the window and pulled a blouse from its hanger on the wardrobe door, forcing her arms into it as she listened to the footsteps approaching her front door. 'Keep calm,' she told herself. 'They're only early, nothing sinister in that.' As she tried to force herself to be calm she fastened the buttons on the dark blue blouse and tugged at the cuffs to make them lie on her arms more neatly. The doorbell rang, twice. Taking two deep breaths she went down the staircase to the front door and opened it. Maxwell and Joanne were standing back from the door side by side.

'Hello, Dr Hawkins. I'm Detective Chief Inspector Maxwell from Leith Police, and this is my colleague Detective Sergeant Baker. I telephoned to see you today if you remember, sorry if we are a bit early.' He smiled warmly at her. She smiled back and stood away from the door for them to walk into the hallway.

'Come in please,' she said. 'Go through into the living room,' she indicated with her hand the door to take. They walked past her in silence and into the well-lit room. The sun had not yet come over the roof of the house so although it was bright, the sun was not shining into it as Yvette had anticipated.

Joanne moved to one side as Dr Hawkins came into the room and stood with her back to the sofa against the back wall. Maxwell stood by her side. They both held out their warrant cards as identification to her. She examined them both, nodded and invited them to sit on the sofa. She sat in the armchair in front of the window opposite them. She had gained no advantage from the light because they had arrived early.

'Not to worry,' she thought. 'They only want to know what Jimmy was up to'.

Maxwell glanced sideways at Joanne, who flicked her eyes closed for an instant indicating she was ready for him to begin.

'I'm sorry we are a little early Dr Hawkins. We arrived yesterday so that we could talk to the local police, to see if there was anything they could connect Jimmy Quinn with to your father.' Yvette stared at him speechless for a moment before replying.

'He had nothing to do with that man.' She said finally and coldly. Maxwell glanced sideways at Joanne and then back at Dr Hawkins.

'Do I understand you to mean that your father did not know Jimmy Quinn? He said.

'Of course, they knew each other. That's not what I meant and you know it.' Yvette snapped, the colour rising in her pale face. 'I mean he had nothing to do with what Quinn was doing to his kids, and you disgust me even by suggesting that.' She sat upright in her chair, her eyes wide open and lips pursed in anger. So this is what they are trying to do, she thought, tie dad and Quinn together. They couldn't be more wrong, the stupid sods. Maxwell looked sideways at Joanne and paused for a moment before continuing.

'That isn't what I mean to imply Dr Hawkins. I don't think for one moment that your father and Jimmy Quinn were involved in child abuse at all. It was all Quinn. Nothing to do with your father, nothing at all. What I wanted to know is, what was your father's involvement with Quinn once they left the army, for example.' He watched her reaction and could tell little or nothing of what she was thinking. From the look on her face, she was trying to compose a story which would exclude her father from Quinn and his activity but knew she had to be very careful in how she produced the story.

The only thing which came to Maxwell's mind was that she was hiding something, why else would she immediately become defensive and twist what he had asked, denying at first that the two men even knew each other? He watched her shoulders relax and drop a little as she mentally scored herself a point. She settled back in the chair and smiled at the two detectives. The sun was just starting to make an appearance in the top corner of the window, but still not enough to distract Maxwell from his questioning. He returned her smile and she continued.

'Yes, of course they knew each other. They served in the army together from what my father told me. They married two German girls and brought them back to England with them. I don't think they kept in touch very much, though I think their wives did, they were good friends in Germany and probably had no friends here in England when they first arrived.' She leaned further back in her chair and continued,

'The first time I met them would have been after my mother died, that was when I was two. I do remember being taken to see them when I was four or five. I might have been taken there before then, but it's not easy to remember things from when you were only two or three years old, is it? Up to then, I knew them as Uncle Jimmy and Aunty Renate. It was probably around that age that I realised, or might have been told, that they weren't my real uncle or aunt. Possibly my father told me how they had come to meet. Certainly, I knew that my sister was born in a British army hospital in Germany around that time before they came back to England' She paused and straightened out the skirt over her knees. Her original thought to distract the male detective when she was planning the visit, was to try and throw him a little by displaying her legs. She quickly realised this was not going to work and settled herself more demurely in her chair. She looked from one to the other to try and estimate what they were thinking at that moment. Maxwell, she thought, was still digging. DS Baker had so far said nothing, simply sat there in the corner of the sofa clutching her brown cardboard file, her handbag at her foot.

'Dr Hawkins. As I explained during our phone conversation the other day, we are here simply to try and build a picture of James Quinn, his life and his habits. How he approached and selected children which he later went on to abuse. We are doing this to see if there was any one person, or family, in Scotland who might have borne a hatred of him all these years to such an extent that they would wish to murder him.' He paused to allow all this to sink in. She nodded her head silently. After several seconds of silence, he continued,

'So, whatever you can tell us about the times you went there, your contact with him or his family since then, would help us to that end.' He nodded his head again at her, and she nodded her head back in acceptance but still did not make any comment. Maxwell glanced sideways at Joanne who made no expression with her eyes, nor said anything. He carried on.

'When was the last time you saw him or his wife Renate Quinn?' Yvette looked to one side and then up at the ceiling searching her memory for the answers, though they were on the tip of her tongue, and had been for years.

'The last time I saw either of them would be, what? over forty years ago. I'm sure it would have been when I was about twelve. My father and I had been to see them together, and I think that would have been the last time. Forty-plus years ago.' Maxwell stared at her for a second or two, his brow furrowed.

'You said, 'together', with your father. Does that mean there were times when you went by yourself to see them?' She flushed red instantly and quickly added,

'Well, no. Well, yes. There was once when I went by myself. I remember it well because I was mad with my father.' The colour left her face and regained its normal hue. She settled back in the chair and carried on.

'I must have been about seven years old. It was during the summer holidays. I had measles or something, anyway, I wasn't well. Dad put me on the train and told me to get off at Glasgow where Uncle Jimmy would be waiting for me. He was. My father came up a couple of days later. I don't know why he insisted on me going alone, but I remember being mad with him. I didn't want to go. That was the only time. The other visits dad and I went, we went together. He had a small car then, later bought a German car, it was a slow cold thing, then he got a Skoda.'

She turned slightly to one side and then back to Maxwell, 'I probably stopped going there at that age because I started to go off out with a hiking club. I used to go all over the place. That's where I met my husband, in the hiking club, when I was about nineteen.' She paused for a moment then continued,

'About that time my dad started to see another woman, and I was a bit left out of things. It went on for some time.' She looked at him with an even gaze, trying to give nothing away. Maxwell nodded silently and looked down at his notepad for a second then said,

'During the times you went there how often would Jimmy Quinn have molested you, can you remember?' Maxwell asked the question calmly and in quite a low voice. Yvette thought at first she had misheard him.

'What did you say?' she asked quickly.

'How many times did he molest you sexually Dr Hawkins? We have spoken to Gunther, to Margaretha and Mrs Quinn and have a fairly broad picture of what Jimmy Quinn was up to all his married life.' She flushed red again and drew in a quick deep breath. 'How much do they know'? She thought to herself. 'What the hell has Renate told them'? She felt fairly certain that Gunther would have told them nothing. On the few occasions she had brought up the subject with him he had always vociferously and strenuously denied that anything had happened with his father. It had always thrown him into a panic.

From the strength of his protestations then she knew Gunther had been lying, and after all, why would Jimmy not have abused his sons whilst he was also abusing his daughter and herself at that time?

They were digging, she thought, then just as quickly realised that they would not have made such accusations about Quinn if they did not know what he had done. She sat back in her seat again, her hands folded on her lap in front of her.

'I don't know that he did. Perhaps when I was a baby he might have done something, but certainly nothing when I grew older. I always had Margaretha with me then, she made sure of it.' She stopped suddenly, aware that she had made a slip. Maxwell paused to consider what she had just said.

'Why would she always make sure she was always with you if nothing had happened to you?' he asked gently.

'Was it perhaps that she was protecting you from him? Margaretha started to protect you because she did not want to you what had happened to her, isn't that how it happened?' Yvette blinked three or four times and looked again from one to the other. Still, Joanne had said nothing. Yvette sat in silence, refusing to answer the question. 'Let them make of it what they could', she thought. 'I'm just helping them, not obliged to answer any of their questions'. Joanne spoke for the first time.

'Dr Hawkins, if I may. How long have you been a psychologist?' she asked. Yvette looked closely at her for the first time for a few seconds before answering.

'Over twenty years now. Hospitals, clinics, homes. That sort of thing. Never in private practice, always in the NHS or private organisations, like now.' She said.

'Where did you qualify to become a psychologist?' she asked.

'I did my final degree at St Andrews in Scotland. I have six degrees in all. Never able to stop studying. One went onto another.' She said smiling. 'Why do you ask?'

'When you are studying to become a clinical psychologist there is a part of the training called, well loosely it's an introspective examination of your own life up to that point. A time when you are paired with a fellow student to investigate and talk about all that has happened in your life. Do you remember it? Navel examination!' She laughed lightly at the last phrase. Yvette joined in the laughter.

'Oh yes. Remember that well. Hated it. Refused to do it, it was too private, I didn't want anyone to know what was going on in my head.'

'But it's more about what has happened in your life up to that point which goes on to make you the person you are now, isn't it?' Joanne asked.

'Well, in lay terms, yes, that's it.'

'Well, not so much lay terms. That's what St Andrews psychology department terms it.'

'Oh? How do you know that Detective Sergeant? You have been doing your homework?' she said with a superior grin on her face.

'I'm doing my second degree there at the moment, in Criminal Psychology.' Yvette went quiet and blanched a little. She regained her composure and smiled at Joanne.

'I hope it goes well for you. Not an easy course. I'm sure you will do well,' she said without any feeling and settled back in the seat once more.

Maxwell was concerned. This woman had nothing to hide, yet she was hiding something. She was refusing to accept she had been abused, which was understandable in many respects, but she was being very difficult in her general answers about times, and visits. No doubt the sexual abuse was a terrible thing for her to have to recall, but he hadn't asked her to recall anything which happened during the occasions Quinn had abused her, he simply asked her if it had happened. Surely, she must realise that from talking to the Quinn family someone must have given away something. Why was she refusing even to acknowledge that she had been a victim of Quinn? Joanne sat forward in her corner.

'Dr Hawkins. We're not asking for any details of what he did. We know he was a persistent child abuser, over many years. It seems he started well before he even met your father, possibly when he was in his late teens. We're just trying to link him to other potential offenders in Scotland he might have known, or children he might have abused. For example. When he was abusing his sons or daughter, were there other men in the flat at the time?' She smiled gently at Yvette. This one is a clever woman, Yvette thought. She dropped her eyes down to her knees for a second then raised them to look Joanne in the eye.

'Not that I can remember.' She said with a smile.

Joanne looked around the room. On the wall opposite her were two of the pictures she had first seen on the wall in Quinn's flat. She pointed to the one of Yvette's mother, it was next to the one of the two men in army uniform.

'When was that taken, Dr Hawkins? Do you know?' Yvette turned around to look at where she was pointing.

'Not sure,' she said after a moment's hesitation. 'Maybe in Germany when they were in the army.'

'Quinn had one on the wall of his flat.' Joanne said offhandedly.

'Yes,' Yvette said, 'Both of them.' She went very quiet for a moment, before regaining her self composure, hoping the two detectives had not noticed or understood the implications of what she had said. Rising quickly to her feet she said,

'Look. Can I offer you some coffee or tea or something?' Joanne looked at Maxwell who looked at his watch. Time was getting on and he felt justified in sending Joanne out to make her phone call. Dr Hawkins was hiding too much which did not add up, the slip-up with the pictures together with the comment about Margaretha making certain she was always there and then dodging the question Jo put to her. He felt there was enough there to question her further. She was hiding too much for no apparent reason.

'Coffee would be fine for me thanks Dr Hawkins. Joanne?' He turned to Jo who had already guessed that what was coming next was an excuse to get her out of the house so she could make the phone call to DI Moore. Jo suddenly rose to her feet.

'Coffee is fine with me thanks Dr Hawkins.' She turned to Maxwell. 'Sir, I've just remembered a phone call I need to make about my mother, she had her operation yesterday. I should have phoned the hospital last night but forgot. If it's alright I'll nip outside and make it from the car whilst Dr Hawkins is making some coffee. Won't be two minutes.' She glanced at Dr Hawkins and smiled as she made her way out of the room. Maxwell nodded his head slightly as Jo went to leave the room. At this stage, he did not feel there was sufficient evidence to arrest Dr Hawkins, although both felt in their stomachs that she was involved in some way. To call on the resources of DI Moore at this point might blow the whole thing. Jo smiled briefly at him as she left the room. She understood his concerns.

Once in the car, she telephoned the incident room in Leith. Brian Jones picked up the phone.

'Brian. It's Jo. Listen to me and don't interrupt. We're with a suspect in England. I want you to get on to ANPR and see if a Blue Mazda MX5 was anywhere on the M8 or around Wester Hailes around 7 pm onwards on the Friday or Saturday before Quinn was found. The number is PF 10 DFN. Blue MX 5. Get back to me immediately OK. No. Don't call me, just send me a text.'

'Right Jo. Give me five and I'll get back to you. Bye.' She redialled and spoke to Alex Moore who was sat by the side of the phone in his office in Burnley. She quickly explained how things were going and the ANPR search which was underway.

'If I get a text from my colleague in Scotland I'll send you one straight away and we'll be arresting her. You should get things moving, then get up to her house and her office asap. Is that possible?'

'No problem Jo. Leave it with me. I'll get the troops fired up and ready to go. I've got them all briefed. Hopefully I'll see you soon.' He replaced the phone and picked up his mobile to call his uniform inspector colleague to get his finger hovering above the starting button.

For a moment Joanne sat in the car thinking. There was nothing more she could do at this stage. Now, it all depended upon ANPR coming back quickly with a positive sighting of Dr Hawkins's car. She got out of her Volvo and went back into the house, taking a good look as she walked past the blue convertible standing in the driveway.

In the living room, Dr Hawkins had brought in a tray laden with three mugs of coffee a delicate cut glass bowl of sugar and two spoons. The tray was resting on a small leather poof which now stood on the rug in the middle of the room between them.

'There you are,' she said, 'Help yourself to milk and sugar if you take it.' She said. Maxwell lifted his head as Jo came back into the room. She shook her head briefly as their eyes met, then looked at the tray with coffee.

She smiled at Dr Hawkins and turned to Maxwell as she regained her seat on the sofa next to him.

'She had a good night's sleep thank goodness. Everything seems to have gone well,' she said. She turned to Yvette and added,

'Taken in a few days ago after a stroke. Seems she is starting to pull out of it.'

'I hope she'll be alright.' Yvette answered solicitously as she bent to pick one of the mugs of coffee from the tray.

The three of them used the hot coffee as a blind and a decoy to stop from resuming the interrogation, fussing over sugar and milk and stirring the hot drinks before settling back in the sofa.

'I needed this,' said Jo eventually. 'Seems ages since we had breakfast.'

'Where did you stay?' Yvette asked.

'It was a Best Western place about ten minutes drive from here.' Maxwell answered.

'Oh, that would be the Higher Trapp wouldn't it?' Yvette said. Maxwell looked at Joanne, who nodded her head in agreement,

'Yes, that's the one. Nice place. Very comfortable. Lovely area.' she said.

The two of them felt that time was beginning to drag and that sooner or later Dr Hawkins would demand the interview be brought to an end, and that was something neither of them could do at the moment, not until the results of the ANPR search had been sent to them. Joanne took a sheet from her notepad and scribbled on it, *'ANPR Leith. Brian Jones checking.* Then handed it to Maxwell. He glanced at it and stuffed it into his jacket pocket. Joanne looked through the window behind Yvette.

'That view is beautiful isn't it?' nodded towards the fields beyond the house. Yvette half turned and looked through the window, nodding her head.

'Yes. It is. Good to watch it through the seasons. To see how the colours on the trees change.' Joanne nodded her head in agreement and jumped as the phone in her inside pocket vibrated.

'Oh!' She said, 'Excuse me.' She took the phone from the inside pocket and hit the text message app. It was from Brian, in the ANPR monitoring centre in Edinburgh. He had telephoned ahead to the operations supervisor to tell her what to search for and then shot down the road from Leith Police Station to the centre. On his arrival, the supervisor was standing in the centre of a double desk full of monitors with a very smug and yet pleased look on her face. She then showed Brian what they had found and as a result, Brian sent the following text to Joanne, who beamed with delight on reading it.

From: Jones, Brian. DC Leith. MX5 blue, PF09DFN soft top, seen 7.50 pm Saturday turning from A720 - bypass - into Babberton Mains View and Wester Hailes estate. Driver - alone, female, top-down, wearing a red hooded coat.

She handed the phone to Maxwell who was sipping his coffee. He read the text and spluttered his coffee over the phone as Jo hastily pulled it out of range of the spraying coffee. He leaned forward to place the mug on the tray and reached into his trouser pocket to find his handkerchief, wiping the coffee from his hand and face. Replacing the handkerchief he turned to Jo who looked him directly in the eye and nodded imperceptibly.

'You think?' she asked quietly.

'I think.' He answered softly, nodding his head. He stood up from the sofa and Joanne followed suit. Tugging at the bottom of his jacket he brought himself to his full height.

'Yvette Hawkins. I am arresting you under Section 1 of the Criminal Justice Scotland Act 2016 for an offence of murder. The reason for your arrest is that I suspect that you have committed an offence and I believe that keeping you in custody is necessary and proportionate to bring you before a court or otherwise deal with you by the law. Do you understand? You are not obliged to say anything but anything you do say will be noted and may be used in evidence. Do you understand?' Yvette flushed red and said nothing.

'The reasons for my suspicions are your answers under questioning and the fact your car was seen in the vicinity of the crime before the offence was committed. You will be detained to enable further investigations to be carried out regarding the offence. You will be taken to a Police Station where you will be informed of your further rights in respect of Detention. I require you to give me your name, address, date of birth and nationality. You are not obliged to answer any further questions but anything you do say will be recorded and may be given in evidence

Yvette remained seated on her chair and said nothing. Her face drained of colour, and she slumped back in the chair. Eventually, she managed to speak.

'I don't know what to say. This is ridiculous. You have no evidence. What evidence do you have?' she ended up saying loudly, and angrily. She got to her feet and stood with her hands clasped dramatically in front of her as though waiting for handcuffs to be placed around them, They said nothing for a moment, then Maxwell began.

'You will be taken from here to Leith police station where you will be questioned. In the meantime, your house and your office will be searched under a warrant I will arrange to have granted. Your car will also be taken to Leith.' Her head whirled as she tried to understand what was happening and how she could get out of the situation in which she now found herself. Everything she had planned had been meticulous. She hadn't made any mistakes. She hadn't left any fingerprints or DNA traces. There were no witnesses she was sure, but what was that he had said about her car being seen in Edinburgh? Nobody there knew her or her car. They were bluffing!

'I want to phone my solicitor.' Yvette said sharply.

'You will be afforded a phone call when we arrive at Leith Police Station.' Maxwell replied.

'That's going to be hours off. I need my solicitor now!' she retorted.

'When we get to the station you can make a phone call, and we will call your solicitor for you.' He replied quietly and turned to Joanne, nodded his head at her then in the direction of the door. Joanne knew what he wanted and left the house to make the phone call to DI Moore from the driveway of the house.

'She's under arrest Alex,' she said when Moore answered the phone.

'Good. Right, I'll get two men to you immediately and two to the office. I guess the officers there will need some sort of explanation in case the press start to turn up,' he said.

'Tell them she is helping with enquiries. The usual bullshit.' Jo replied.

'OK Jo. I'll get that lot organised, and inform our press office as well. Meantime I suppose you and DCI Maxwell are off to Scotland now?' he said.

'As soon as your lads arrive we'll be off. We'll wait until they arrive here.'

'I'll come with them, make sure you two have everything you need before leaving and that the two uniforms know exactly what is happening. I'll have the uniform Inspector with me as well.'

Within fifteen minutes DI Moore together with his uniform Inspector colleague and two of his uniform officers arrived at the house. Maxwell briefed them all on what had happened and what they hoped would happen during the next twelve hours or so. They now had a fast drive to Leith Police Station and a hurried meeting with Procurators and Sheriff, followed by an equally fast return trip back down to Lancashire and a meeting with the local Magistrate to look forward to.

Maxwell cast an eye over the two constables tasked with guarding the house and was pleased to see that they were full Constables and not the PCSOs so disparagingly referred to as Plastic Policemen. In any case, he was glad that the two officers looked to have a few years of service under their belts and looked quite capable of dealing with anything cropping up during the coming hours. He walked to the two officers with DI Moore and their inspector listened to the briefing they were given and added his thanks to them for the boring task they had ahead of them. He went back into the house to find Joanne with Dr Hawkins standing awkwardly in the living room in silence.

Yvette turned to Joanne and Maxwell.

'I need to get some clean underwear and toiletries.' She said, looking coldly at Joanne. Joanne replied equally coldly.

'You won't. You'll get all you need up there.' Yvette sniffed and glared at her.

'You will now be required to be searched Dr Hawkins,' he said, nodding to Joanne to commence searching her. Nothing was found in her clothing.

'I need your mobile phone, Dr Hawkins.' He said. Yvette said nothing and simply gave him an icy look. Maxwell paused for a moment. 'If you won't hand it over then I will find it tomorrow when I return with a search warrant. It could be a messy search.' She remained silent. Maxwell knew that unless she handed it over he had no authority to search for it without the warrant, not yet even granted.

Hawkins turned to Maxwell.

'If you won't let me take clean underwear with me can I at least change into something more comfortable for a long journey?' she demanded. Maxwell looked at Jo.

'Go with her Sergeant would you?' he said. Joanne nodded and followed as Dr Hawkins left the living room and walked across the hallway to the stairs. The two women climbed the stairs, Joanne dogging Dr Hawkins's footsteps. They entered a large bedroom at the front of the house. Along one wall was a large double-fitted wardrobe. One of the doors was half open. Dr Hawkins reached in and took out a pair of faded light blue jeans from a hanger. Standing in front of the double bed she unfastened the skirt she had on and allowed it to drop to the floor, kicking off the shoes she was wearing as well. Stepping from the garment she stooped to pull on the jeans.

DS Barker stood silently watching close to the bedroom door. On the wall between the two large front windows was a square oil painting, or it could have been a photograph, thought Joanne. It was of a wild meadow in summer chock full of wildflowers. She thought the painting was beautiful. She nodded towards the painting.

'That's beautiful' she said quietly to Dr Hawkins. Dr Hawkins looked up from her jeans and glanced at the painting.

'Yes. It's called Star's Garden. Named after a cat I had, but it died.'

Fuck me! thought Jo. She names a field after a dead cat! What sort of sicko is this? She took her eyes off the painting and looked to another door in the bedroom. The door was slightly open and she could see that it led through to an en suite bathroom. Dr Hawkins fastened the top of the jeans and started to walk towards the bathroom.

'Where are you going?' DS Barker asked.

'I need a wee' was the peevish reply.

'Make it quick, and leave the door open.' Joanne replied equally peevishly and waited patiently.

Coming from the bathroom a few minutes later Dr Hawkins picked up a medium-sized soft leather shoulder bag from the floor close to the door. Joanne held out her hand for it.

'I'll take that' she said. Dr Hawkins glared at her and reluctantly handed over the bag. They walked down the stairs to the front door.

A small table by the door had two bunches of keys on it. Maxwell pointed to them.

'Which are the keys for your house Dr Hawkins? We need to secure it after we have searched it.' She nodded down at the two bunches.

'The one with the cat on them. The others are my car keys.' She said. Joanne picked up the set with a small metal cat fob attached and put them in her pocket.

'Can I take a coat?' she asked Jo. Jo nodded and stood to one side whilst Dr Hawkins picked a short leather jacket from a line of ornate hooks on the wall to the side of the door. She put the coat around her shoulders.

Joanne held open the door and the two women stepped towards the front door where DCI Maxwell stood holding a pair of stainless steel handcuffs in one hand. Dr Hawkins blanched when she saw them.

'Oh come on. Not handcuffs!' she exclaimed.

'It's not like I am going to run anywhere is it, not with you two here and others outside.' She glared from one to the other of the two officers. DCI Maxwell held out the cuffs towards her.

'You walk down the drive alongside me. You get in the car and when we are ready for off, you get these on. Understand?'

he said coldly. She nodded her head in silent acquiescence and stepped towards the door, Joanne held the door open for her.

As she stepped out onto the drive from the front door her eyes swept out towards the few other houses on the road. Three of them had neighbours out in the front garden, ostensibly gardening, but more intent on the excitement of what was happening at Dr Hawkins' house. She groaned.

'Oh god.' she moaned. 'Look at them. Having a field day aren't they?' Joanne flicked the key fob and the doors on the light blue Volvo unlocked. She walked to the rear passenger door and held it open for Dr Hawkins to get in. She slid in and settled down, trying to make herself as small as possible from the curious nosey eyes of the neighbours.

DCI Maxwell closed the door once she was inside and stepped around to the other passenger door. Joanne slid into the driver's seat. Inside the car, Maxwell leaned across and slipped the handcuffs around Dr Hawkins's wrists and pulled the seat belt from behind her into the securing slot between them. Her coat was around her shoulders, her bag on her lap. Maxwell took the bag and placed it on his seat away from her hands. 'Oh god, you are pathetic aren't you?' Dr Hawkins said.

'Don't want anything to happen to you en route do we?' he said. 'It won't be for long though, will it? Not like Edinburgh is at the end of the earth is it? Four hours at the most.'

'I suppose so. Depends how you drive though doesn't it?' Dr Hawkins replied. Maxwell paused for a moment.

'Thought you said you hadn't been there.' he said softly. She made no reply and simply looked out of her side of the car.

'One further thing Dr Hawkins.' he said. She looked back at him. 'Your phone. Where is it?'

'In the bag.' she answered shortly. Maxwell opened the clasp on the bag and looked inside.

'This the only one?' he asked holding up the smartphone she had placed there.

'Of course it is. Think I'm a drug dealer or something do you?' she snapped. He closed the bag.

'No accounting for anything these days doctor.' he replied quietly.

'Are we ready to go then Jo?' he asked.

'In a moment boss.' she said. Two constables and an Inspector were standing by the pavement. Maxwell got out of the car to speak to them. He turned to one of the Constables standing to one side of his boss, the Inspector.

'Keep a good eye on both doors please officer.' He said and turned to the Inspector.

'Thank you for your help, Inspector. I hope we are going to be back this time tomorrow.' He paused on the drive and turned back to the inspector.

'One other thing Inspector, he said.

'Can you get someone to feed the bloody cat? Don't want a pesticide complaint coming our way.' The Inspector nodded and smiled.

'Don't worry sir, we'll take good care of it. Nobody in and nobody out until you come back with a warrant. Then we'll get cracking with the SOCO guys.'

'This should keep the neighbours in gossiping topics for a few weeks to come,' Joanne thought to herself as she closed the driver's door. Maxwell opened up the rear passenger door on Dr Hawkins's side and deftly flicked the child-proof lock switch on the edge door. Shutting the back door he walked around to the other passenger side and slid in alongside Yvette and behind Joanne. Joanne turned on the engine as Alex Moore stepped over to speak to her. He tapped the window sill of the driver's door. Joanne hit the window winder. As the window slid down he said,

'Drive safely. I've had a word with the North West Motorway group. They'll probably pick you up on the M61 to give you some sort of escort. Keep your eyes open for them. See you tomorrow. Keep in touch will you?'

'Will do,' she said and gave him a broad smile.

'Thanks for your help, Alex. See you tomorrow.' She let off the handbrake and pulled away from the curbside into the road. What the hell did he mean by that, she wondered. North West Motorway patrol group?

Joanne flicked on the sat nav which spent a few seconds finding out where she was. Whilst she waited she picked up a paper map from the front passenger seat to give her a general sense of where she was in relation to the M65. By the time she had found it the sat nav was ready and waiting for her instructions. She typed in the destination and the young lady in the machine asked her kindly to wait whilst she worked out the route. Joanne waited. Tapping her fingers on the rim of the steering wheel. Eventually, the lady was ready and told Jo to take the first left at the end of the road. She knocked the car into drive and started. The neighbours swivelled their heads to watch the car depart.

'That should keep them going for a bit.' she thought.

The motorway was a few miles from the house on the outskirts of Brierfield and Joanne had to battle her way through Saturday afternoon shopper traffic before she reached the M65.

'Thank God for that' she said as she accelerated along the slip road onto the main carriageway, then had to immediately ease off the accelerator as she saw two lines of slow-moving traffic.

'Oh bloody hell. Hope it's not like this all the way through,' she exclaimed. Maxwell looked forward through the windscreen.

'Not looking good is it?' he said quietly. Joanne joined the main carriageway and quickly slid over to the outside of the two-lane.

'Is it like this all the way to Preston Dr Hawkins?' she asked. She glanced in the rearview mirror. Dr Hawkins said nothing and turned her head away to look out of the side window.

After a few miles, the carriageway became three lanes and their speed picked up a bit until they hit another slow-down close to Blackburn. There they hit what was football traffic, cars full of men, mostly, scarves streaming from side windows and hands waving out the side. Joanne groaned again. By now she was seeing the signs for the M61 and M6 so turned off the annoying woman on the sat nav.

'Do without her for the next few hours' she commented, glancing into the mirror again. Maxwell nodded in agreement.

'Bit of an annoying type wasn't she?' he agreed.

Soon, but not soon enough, she picked up her speed and was heading in the direction of the M61 and M6 north, keeping to a shade over 70 mph. Not long after joining the M61, she spotted a Police car stationary on the hard shoulder and instinctively checked her speed, okay, it was only 72 mph. As she came close to the liveried vehicle, a Range Rover, it started to accelerate along the hard shoulder and then pull into the left-hand lane of three. As Jo watched it the blue lights were turned on and the vehicle accelerated hard to overtake her. It came alongside her Volvo and slowed down. The front seat passenger wound down his window and indicated for her to pull off onto the hard shoulder. Her heart raced as she complied with the instruction wondering what on earth it was she had done wrong.

The two cars pulled up, and the passenger immediately jumped from the Range Rover and made his way to Joanne's driver's door. She turned off her engine and got out to join the officer who now stood by the car bonnet. He was a young, tall-looking officer wearing a hi-vis jacket over his uniform.

'DS Baker?' he asked. 'Police Scotland?' She nodded her head and brought out her identification from her inside pocket. The young man smiled and said,

'It's OK. DI Moore from Burnley CID asked us to escort you through the traffic. Believe you have a prisoner onboard?' She nodded her head and glanced back to the rear passenger who was now leaning forward to watch the interaction.

'That's right. Going to Edinburgh with her. You're not coming all the way are you?' she asked. He shook his head.

'No. Sadly. It's a long time since I visited that beautiful city. Could do with another holiday there. We'll not be taking you all the way, we'll be with you to the Scottish border when one of your motorway cars takes over.' He nodded to the Volvo.

'Is 90mph about right for your car? We couldn't justify going much faster.' Joanne was a bit nonplussed but nodded her head.

'90 will be fine. I'm alright for petrol.' She said.

'If it looks like I'm running out I'll try and flash you before we get to a service area.' she added.

'You can flash me whenever you need to Sergeant' the young officer said grinning.

'Oi. You're too bloody young!' she grinned.

'OK. Let's get moving shall we?' he said smiling, and without waiting for a reply he turned and got back into the Range Rover which almost immediately started again on the hard shoulder. Jo followed until both cars reached 50 mph on the hard shoulder then slowly merged with the traffic on the main carriageway. Then the Range Rover driver turned on the blue lights and headlights on the car and accelerated up to 90 mph. Joanne followed, a broad grin spreading over her face. They made the M6 and swung into the fourth lane going north, still at a steady 90.

'There are real bonuses in being in the Police' Jo thought to herself. 'I might have to have this grin surgically removed from my face at some time.'

The two cars swept north at speed. Once they had gone past Preston the traffic eased, then eased again as they drove past the junction for the M55 exit to Blackpool. The traffic was thankfully light with little or no heavy good vehicles, with it being the weekend.

On through the southern Lake District, she had time to glance occasionally at the hills bordering the motorway. 'Not a bad job' she thought. 'Getting paid to drive a decent car at speed through the Lakes. Have to try this again.'

Finally, they met up with a Police Scotland car close to the border at Gretna where the M6 changed to the M74. Again they stopped on the hard shoulder whilst Joanne discussed the route she wanted to take back to Leith with the Scots driver, then they were off again. There was little time for her to enjoy, or even observe, the beautiful rolling countryside and hills of the Scottish borders as the two cars flew along the roads towards the Pentland Hills.

A little over two and a half hours after leaving Lancashire, they pulled into the station at Leith. Maxwell escorted his prisoner to the station charge room, whilst Joanne shot off to use the first toilet she could find.

The charge office was ready for them. Dr Hawkins was allowed her solicitor call and was settled into a cell for the night. It was going to be a long night for her. Joanne and Maxwell filled in some paperwork and then left for their respective homes. Tomorrow would be interesting.

CHAPTER 23

The following morning, Joanne drove slowly around the corner of Queen Charlotte Street into Constitution Street and what she saw made her smile. The left-hand side of the street was empty of traffic and parked cars. She pulled into the left-hand kerb opposite the old church, pushed the handbrake button on and the gear selector into park. She sat back for a moment and stowed her seat belt then turned off the engine. Looking far ahead over Baltic Street Ocean Way she imagined the view over the docks and onto the Firth of Forth. 'Be nice to pop out to North Berwick today,' she thought. 'Perhaps sit on the beach road and have a coffee and a thick bacon roll. No chance.'

'Sunday' she said to herself. 'Just like Saturday except not as many drunks on the streets or the roads.' She peered forward to look at the sky. 'Blue skies, just like yesterday.' As it was Sunday, and quite early on, she was dressed in blue jeans, a thin v-necked lightweight woollen sweater and trainers. She reached over and collected her mobile phone, shoulder bag and leather jacket from the passenger seat and got out of the car. Closing the driver's door behind her she flicked the fob, closed the doors on the car and strode across the street to the nondescript blue door in the side wall of the police station. Fiddling in her shoulder bag she pulled out her warrant card holder and held the accompanying swipe card to the machine in the door. It noiselessly clicked open a few inches. She pushed on it and stepped up the steps and into the building.

As she made her way up the stairs and along the corridors to the boss's office she glanced at the large stainless steel wristwatch on her left wrist. Shortly before seven. 'Should have the place to myself,' she thought. 'Boss won't be in just yet.'

She stopped in front of the door to DCI Maxwell's office and saw that it was slightly open. Pushing it open she saw that Maxwell was sitting at his desk, head down reading a report in front of him.

'Morning sir' she said. 'Bright and early aren't we?' Maxwell glanced up and reached for an empty mug on his right-hand side, holding it out to Joanne.

'Black, please. The usual.' he said. Joanne slipped off her jacket and hung it on a wooden coat stood behind the door and took the empty mug from his hand.

As she went to start bringing the coffee machine to life he looked up from his desk and admired the view of the blue jeans.

'Could say the same thing to you Jo.' he said. 'Couldn't sleep?'

'No problem sir. I think the four hundred-odd miles did for me.' she paused.

'Which reminds me that I need to put in my mileage claim for the month soon. Doing it for the Queen is one thing, but Police Scotland can afford to pay me.' Maxwell grunted and resumed reading.

Joanne placed a mug in front of him and took her seat at the desk she used. As she sat down she swivelled around, mug in hand.

'Fancy a trip out to North Berwick this morning sir. Looks like it could be a nice day. Blue skies and all.' She grinned as he looked out of the window.

'Aye, not a bad-looking day is it? Sad we are going to be here all day though. Never mind Jo. Think of the overtime.' Joanne choked on a mouthful of coffee which then dribbled down her chin.

'Sloppy Jo, sloppy.' Maxwell said smiling at her as she reached in her pocket for a tissue to wipe away the coffee. Having wiped the coffee from her chin and a drop of two from her sweater she sat back and tried to drink again. Maxwell gave her a second or two then said,

'Right Jo. The situation is this. Dr Hawkins contacted her solicitor last night. He is an old friend of hers, and her father before. He's on his way up here now.' He glanced at his watch.

'Well, if he's anything about him he will be on his way now. If he has just left he should be with us by mid-day at the latest.' He took a sip from his mug and carried on.

'I checked on her when I arrived. She was still asleep. She should be having her breakfast soon, then we'll go and have a chat when the solicitor arrives.' Jo nodded in agreement.

'Sir' she said, 'When we spoke to her yesterday it was strange. At first, we just wanted to ask her about other kids Quinn might have had a go at, but she was on the defensive so quickly.' she paused. 'Right from the start. I am sure we did the right thing in arresting her. She has to be the one who killed him, but how? And with what?' She thought for a moment sipping again at the coffee. Maxwell said nothing, just sat back in his chair and allowed her to get on with the thought process churning through her mind. He left her to think for a few moments. She turned to her desk picked up a copy of the pathologist and the toxicology reports and tapped them with her finger.

'Pathology says he had remains of potatoes, carrot and meat together with what he thought might be Weetabix in his stomach, together with liquid which contained whisky and some traces of quinine and heroin.' She flicked the edge of another sheet in her hand.

'The tox report confirms the presence of a small amount of quinine and a good dose of heroin, but neither were in sufficient quantity to suggest cause of death. Though the heroin in his system showed he had been a user for some time. So maybe we have Death by Weetabix and Stovies sir.' She grinned at Maxwell. Now it was his turn to choke on his coffee.

'Jo you have a cruel streak in you do you know that?' he grinned at her. 'So.' he continued, 'Cereal and Stovie for a last meal, but that doesn't answer how he got the heroin in him does it?'

'No sir, you're right.' She paused again.

'How about this for a theory? Mrs Cullen the neighbour does his errands for him. Gets his groceries from time to time along with whisky and Irn Bru. She occasionally draws money from his bank through the Hole In The Wall, and sometimes places the odd bet.' She glanced out the window for a second or two to compose her thoughts again before continuing.

'Now and again he gets out of the flat to do the shopping and placing bets for himself and also picks up a deal or two of heroin whilst he's at it. When he can't manage to do this himself he gets the good lady neighbour to do it.'

Maxwell grunted. 'Sounds good so far Jo. Any more thoughts?' She placed the reports on the edge of his desk and folded her arms.

'Well, sir. If you remember when we went to the flat. There was an ashtray half under the bed. He used it regularly, but there was no trace of heroin there or in the flat, nor were there any packs of cigarettes or a lighter in the flat. However, when we paid a visit to the good Lady Cullen, she had two different packs of ciggies on the go and two disposable lighters. That's strange, isn't it? Normally folk who smoke stick to one brand don't they?'

Maxwell nodded his head in agreement. 'You're right there Jo. They do. I noticed that when we spoke to her. So if we search her flat we will probably find traces of his last lot of heroin and perhaps a pipe or needle in there as well.' He paused and looked down at the desk and idly nudged the edge of a report until it was flush with the edge of the desk.

'I'm not sure at this stage that that is going to be profitable Jo. It could well be exactly as you suggest, that she is the errand boy for the heroin and has moved it out of the way to either use it herself or maybe flog it back to the dealer for a few quid.' He rose from his seat and walked the few paces to the coffee machine with his empty mug. Jo held out her mug as he walked by. He took it from her hand.

'Perhaps we let that lie for the time being. We can turn her place over in the next few days when we've got madam downstairs sorted out. I don't want to forget her, but she isn't a priority at the moment. Do you agree?' Joanne stared at him thoughtfully.

'I'm not sure sir. Molly Cullen says she did some errands on Sunday morning and then went in to see him later that evening. By that time she said the second doctor had been. Perhaps if Molly had taken him some heroin then the doctor's prints could be on some of the stuff.' Maxwell nodded his head in agreement.

'You're right Jo. Dr Hawkins could have left her prints on the heroin pack or a pipe or needle. Depends on what he uses.' He paused again for a second before carrying on.

'I think we need to get one of the lads to swear out a search warrant and go through dear Molly's flat and try to find his fixings'. Joanne picked up the phone on her desk and rang through to the incident room. When she put down the phone she turned to Maxwell.

'Sorted sir. Some of the team are going round there later, soon as they've got a warrant sworn out.'

'Good. Let's hope she hasn't got rid of the fixings yet. So. What about the good doctor? Is it my imagination, or did she deny that her car had been seen on the ring road? If nothing else, that was strange, to say the least.' he added.

The door to Maxwell's office opened and Brian Jones's head appeared around it.

'OK to come in sir?' he asked. Maxwell waved his hand at the young detective.

'Aye, come on in Brian. You did some good work yesterday getting the sighting of her so quickly. Come on in and pull up a mug of coffee.' He grinned at the young man, who was not smiling half as much as Maxwell or Joanne. Maxwell sensed something was wrong. He sat back in his chair and nodded for Brian to take the seat in front of his desk.

'What's the problem then?' he asked eventually.

DC Jones inched to the front of his seat nervously. He cleared his throat and began.

'I'm sorry sir, but it's bad news. Well at least not good news.' he paused to sip from the coffee. Maxwell urged him on impatiently.

'Get on with it Brian. What's so bad?' Brian placed the mug on the desk in front of him and took a deep breath.

'When I had a closer look at the ANPR images of her car it isn't at all clear that it is her car. The number plate isn't recognisable.'

'What the fuck!' Maxwell yelled. 'What d'you mean it isn't recognisable? Do you know what this means lad?' Brian had no time to answer before Maxwell jumped in again.

'It means we don't have a proper reason for having arrested her. It means we are going to be sued from hell to high heaven if this ever gets out.' Brian held up his hand to try and interject, but Maxwell was already at a cruising height of thirty-six thousand feet and would take a lot to bring him back down. Joanne rose from her seat and came around the side of the desk to face Brian, the unfortunate harbinger of bad tidings.

'What exactly do we have Brian?' she asked as steadily as she was able. Brian looked thankfully at Joanne for potentially saving him from the wrath of Maxwell. He jumped in quickly at the life-saving hand extended to him.

'The car we have on the ANPR is the same make and colour, but the number plate is not completely visible. It could be her, or someone else. It is definitely a woman driver and she is by herself in the car, with the top down. She's wearing what appears to be a red coat with a hood.' Maxwell shot out of his seat.

'A what? A red hooded coat. Not that again' he smacked his forehead with his hand and slumped back down into his seat. 'How many women have we got in the Edinburgh area driving around in a blue Mazda MX5 and wearing a red duffel coat?' He raised his eyes to the ceiling.

'For pity's sake, you'll be telling me next that Dr Mansoor has a blue Mazda?' he said. Brian jumped in quickly before his boss could start again.

'No. No sir,' he said, 'We do have another ANPR image of Dr Hawkins's car, the right car, colour and registration plate with her driving, wearing her red duffel coat.' Maxwell leaned forward in his seat and pointed his finger at Brian.

'This had better be good Brian or you'll be responsible for me having a bloody seizure.' Brian continued.

'It's her car sir, about seven hours later and on the ring road, but heading away from Wester Hailes and south towards England. She is still wearing the duffel coat or something like that, maybe an anorak sort of thing, but the hood on the car is down, it's a fine night, and even though it's dark you can make her out. She's by herself in the car. If you compare the two images, the one from earlier and the later one it looks like the same driver. A woman, definitely.' He relaxed back in his seat, as did Maxwell. He closed his eyes for a moment in relief and then opened them and smiled at Brian.

'Give me a shock like that again and I'll have your nationality papers rescinded young man.' Maxwell said, with more than a little relief in his voice and a slight grin on his face. As he relaxed a little to consider this latest information Joanne leaned on the side of the desk and looked down at her boss.

'So why did she deny she had been here and that the images of the ANPR could not have been her? To me, it smacks that she knew damn well that there was a good chance of her being picked up by the ANPR and that's why she said nothing.' Maxwell grinned up at her.

'You're right Jo. Of course. If she had not been here then she would have immediately denied being anywhere near

Scotland. We have her by the short and curlies.' he sat back and grinned at Brian.

'Your bacon is well and truly saved young man. Well done.' Brian got to his feet and pushed the chair back to the side table.

'Thanks, sir. I'll get off back to the incident room if that's all right.' Maxwell waved him away.

'Off you go Brian, and thanks again. Good work.' He sat down heavily in his chair and looked across at Joanne.

'That was too bloody close' he said.

'We need to check if her car has a sat nav sir' she said quickly.

'What? Why?' he replied.

'If she has a sat nav and it was used to get her to Wester Hailes then it will show up in the history on the machine'

'What history?'

'A sat nav is a computer sir. Whatever she has programmed into it will still be there unless she has wiped it clean, and even then I suspect it will still be traceable if we get our computer whizz kids on it.' Maxwell breathed a sigh of relief.

As Brian closed the office door behind him Maxwell blew out a long sigh of relief and grinned at Joanne.

'That was too bloody close' he said again. Joanne nodded her head looking down at the files on his desk and wondering what came next, though she knew what it was. A trip south to England again, but hopefully, not at the same breakneck speed as the one the previous afternoon. She glanced down at her watch, it was mid-morning, and they had an appointment with the Procurator and Sheriff to swear out a search warrant.

'Shit sir. I've just remembered. 12 hours' she said.

'Not to worry Joanne. I sorted it last night before I went home. Had a word with the Chief Super and he's granted a 12-hour extension. Also had a word with the DI in the incident room. Soon as the 24 hours is up he is going to bail her to come back in a week or so. Give us time to get the forensics done and dusted.' He grinned at her discomfort. 'Good job one of us has their wits around them isn't it?' Joanne blew out a sigh of relief.

'Sorry sir. I was so tired last night it went right out of my mind.' she said.

Maxwell leaned back in his chair and raised his hands behind his head. 'So. How are you fixed for the trip south? Fancy going along the A7 instead of thrashing along the M74? Should be a nice drive on a sunny day like today?' he asked.

'Suits me fine sir.' she said. 'We could stop off in North Berwick and pick up some sandwiches and a brew to make a stop along the way if you want.'

'Sounds like a good idea.' he replied. He swung his arms down and stood up. 'Let me grab my coat and pay a visit and I'll meet you outside. Need to have a quick word with the DI upstairs first then I'll be with you soonest.' Joanne rose from her seat and picked her jacket from the hook by the door as Maxwell opened the door for her. 'Thank you kindly sir' she said.

'Pon my word it's my pleasure, my dear.' Maxwell said in a very bad imitation of W C Fields. Joanne looked at him quizzically and strode past into the corridor.

As Maxwell peeled off to go to the incident room Joanne left the station and out onto Constitution Way and into her car. She sat with the engine running as she waited for the DCI to arrive. He opened the door and slid in, tossing his overcoat onto the back seat. Strapping himself in he glanced towards her. 'All set?' he said.

'Good to go sir.' she replied and flicked the gear lever into drive and pulled out into the empty street.

'Looks like a good day for it doesn't it?' she said looking up to the still blue sky.

'Yes it does' he replied. Joanne said nothing more and concentrated on her driving through to the coast road and then onto the A7 towards England.

CHAPTER 24

B y late morning they were well down the road again in Joanne's Volvo, with the search warrant tucked safely in Maxwell's inside jacket pocket. The journey was almost as fast as the previous day but without the befit of a stripey car escort. In three hours they were back in Brierfield Lancashire. Despite it being a Sunday the traffic was fairly free of traffic apart from the odd daydreaming driver intent on sightseeing.

When they arrived at Yvette's house they were greeted by two uniformed officers from Lancashire police who, though warned of their arrival, still asked to see their identification. Maxwell was pleased with this, as it was a good indication that everything appeared to be going by the book. Within ten minutes of their arrival at the house, they were joined by Alex Moore and a team of search detectives who proceeded to go through the house and its contents with a toothcomb, gathering several large evidence bags full of documents, clothing and a computer from the office.

Maxwell and Joanne stood close to where the teams were searching but kept well out of their way. After the search had been progressing well for half an hour DI Moore came into the hallway holding a paper evidence bag in his hand. It was unsealed.

'Thought that you might like to see this before I sealed it. Might bring a smile to your faces.' He held out the bag for them to peer into. Maxwell leaned forward and looked in.

'Jesus!' now that's something I didn't expect to see.' he exclaimed. Joanne edged forward to look into the bag.

'Hells teeth,' she said. 'Fingers crossed it has some DNA on it.' Lying gleaming at the bottom of the brown evidence bag was a surgeon's scalpel.

'Has to have' said Maxwell. 'Bloody well has to.' He turned to Moore with a broad grin. 'That it?' he asked. 'Nothing else is there?' DI Moore returned the grin.

'We've got a computer from the house here and one from her office. There are other bits and bobs but I don't think there's anything of real significance, apart from this. We're keeping on looking sir, let you know what else turns up.' He turned to go back into the living room where a constable was guarding the bags of evidence that had been collected and was busy writing down a chain of evidence cards for signatures.

A similar search team was carrying out an equally detailed search of Dr Hawkins's office some miles away in the next town, under the very surprised concerned watch of the duty shift supervisor. He had taken the opportunity to call Yvette's immediate boss, a director of the company, who arrived in a hurry and completely flustered. Naturally, the director was full of questions about the arrest of one of the company's senior managers and tried hard to find out what the cause of the arrest was. The rather terse reply she received of 'On suspicion of murder,' threw the director into a total spin and she had to be taken from Yvette's office to sit and recover in the staff restroom. The only topic of discussion was the events taking place along the corridor. Nobody knew anything, not even Nigel, who it was widely believed by the other members of staff was having some sort of relationship with Yvette. So much for trying to keep under wraps what she had tried so hard to do with Nigel. It seemed all the staff had some sort of suspicion about what was going on between the two of them. Nigel kept silent and refused to be drawn into any conversation with the other staff.

During the search team's visit to the home, other detectives were busy taking statements from the staff to try and pin down the movements of Dr Hawkins during the previous week. As the search was completed the file of statements were collated for the information of the visiting Scottish detectives. The case was systematically and carefully being built against the good doctor, and the more they regarded the content of the statements, the smaller the opportunity seemed for her to escape.

By 4 p.m. both the search teams had completed their work. The various bags of potential evidence had been loaded into the boot of Joanne's Volvo which stood outside the doctor's house. DI Moore stood in the hallway with Maxwell and Joanne as constables walked past them loaded with the evidence bags. When the last of them had been taken out of the house the sergeant came back into the doorway. He was a small wiry man with a short grey beard.

'That's the lot now sir,' he said to Moore.

'Thanks Alex, your lads have done a good job here today, and at the office. Not left anything behind have they?' he asked.

'Nothing sir. All loaded up and ready to go. OK if I get the lads off to the nick for a brew?' he asked.

'Course it is Alan. Give 'em my thanks too will you,' Moore said. The sergeant turned and left the three of them standing in a small group in the hall. Maxwell extended his hand to the DI.

'Many thanks for your efforts over the weekend Inspector. You and your lads have done a grand job.' They shook hands all around and Joanne gave him a wide smile.

'Thank you, sir. It's been a pleasure meeting you. She said.

'You too sergeant. You too. His eyes were saying something his voice didn't and Joanne registered the look, a feint lingering as they shook hands too. Maxwell rubbed his hands together as they walked through the front door.

'If you get the chance to come up to Edinburgh Inspector I hope you will remember us and come for a drink.' he said.

'No problem sir. Be glad to.' he grinned again at Joanne as he turned to push a key into the door lock. Turning it he pulled hard on the handle to ensure it was fully safely closed and walked down the driveway to Joanne's car parked close to the end of the drive. She opened the car up and the two of them got in. As she started up the engine she flicked the window switch and her window fell to the sill. Pulling away from the kerb she waved her hand through the open window at the figure stood by the driveway.

'A good man isn't he?' she commented to Maxwell.

'He seemed to be a bit stuck on you Jo. Need to watch these English you know.' he grinned.

'Oh, I can handle them, sir. No different than Scotsmen really. Perhaps a bit more refined that's all.' She turned the car sharply at the end of the road and Maxwell bumped his head on the side window.

'Sorry about that sir. You alright?' she asked smiling. Maxwell grunted as he pulled himself back into a comfortable position.

'Just drive' he said and pulled a bag of Midget Gems from his jacket pocket.

CHAPTER 25

They made good progress on the motorway, the miles churning away quickly. North of Preston on the M6 Joanne flicked a finger towards the windshield.

'Traffic eased after the Blackpool junction going our way, but it seems to be quite heavy coming south. Wonder why that is.' she said. Maxwell looked up from the file on his lap and studied the southbound flow for a moment or two.

'People going back home after a day trip or weekend in the Lakes or southern Scotland. Popular places you know.' he said. She nodded her head.

'Suppose so. Hadn't really thought about it much, come to think of it I've not driven along this route much before.' She was keeping her speed down to just under 80 mph. The other traffic seemed to be doing much the same. Maxwell lurched over to take his mobile phone from his pocket. Joanne glanced towards him. 'Work call sir?'

'Aye. Wanted to give DI McMillan some instructions for tomorrow.' he replied.

'Hang on sir. I've got Bluetooth set up for my phone. Use that.' she said and pushed a button on the steering wheel. She spoke towards a small microphone fixed discretely into the car roof just above her head and in front of her.

'Call DI McMillan' she said. A disembodied female repeated, 'Calling D I McMillan.' The sound of the dialling tone rang through the car. Maxwell muttered,

'Bloody hell. Technology!' The voice of DI MacMillan came through the car. 'Hi, Jo. Are you ok? Where are you?' he asked.

'Coming up the M6 through the Lake District at the moment sir. Should be coming off at Gretna in twenty minutes or so. You're on speakerphone in my car, so watch what you are saying. The boss wants a word.'

'OK. Thanks, Jo. Afternoon Sir. Good trip?' he asked.

'Very good thanks,' replied Maxwell.

'Got some good evidence and a couple of computers which need raking through, see what we can get off them.' He paused to unstick a Midget Gem from the roof of his mouth.

'Sorry about that. Got a sweet stuck in my teeth. Listen. I'm sure you and the lads have been hard at it over the weekend same as Jo and myself, so I want you to give everyone a couple of days off. I just need one person in the office on Monday and Tuesday. You can make it half days for four or one day for two. It's up to you. Got it so far?'

'Aye got it, sir. Lads'll be pleased about that. Starting to flag a bit. Some of the married ones are getting divorce papers served on them in the office from what I've heard.'

'Get off with you man, it's only been a week or so. Nothing at all. Anyway, one person a day in the office. They can start trawling through the home computer we snatched, and see what she's been looking for. See if there's anything in the search history for Jimmy Quinn and anything related to the family.'

'Will do sir. I'll sort out a couple of bodies for the two days. What time are we starting on Wednesday?'

'Make it 9 o'clock, will you? The panic is over now. We can start living normal lives again. There's one other thing though. The Chief Super granted a 12-hour extension for the good doctor. Should be back up early this evening. If we're not back in time can you make sure she's bailed for at least ten days, longer if possible? I think that we might need that for the forensics to come back to us.' He was about to end the call when he remembered a vital instruction.

'One final thing Mac. We'll be leaving this load of evidence in my office when we get back. Can you ensure SOCO get onto examining it first thing in the morning? I would like as many results as possible when I get in on Wednesday?'

'Right, you are sir. I'll see if there is anyone in SOCO at the moment and ask them to get on with it first thing. Drive safely, Jo.' Joanne ended the call with a further flick on the steering wheel button. Maxwell looked across to try and see which button she had pressed. She indicated one on the right hand spoke of the steering wheel.

'Bloody marvellous isn't it?' he said. 'My mother wouldn't recognise the world we live in. She never had a fridge, electric cooker, freezer, television or a phone.' Joanne snorted.

'Your mother sir?' she said. 'How about my mother? She never had them either. A lot of changes in the past twenty years or so. Unrecognisable now. Just think about how computers have altered our lives in the past twenty years.'

Maxwell looked out of the window at the hills flashing by, green and verdant. Wordsworth's Daffodils show in large clumps on the hill bottoms. The first blue signs for Gretna were appearing at the side of the motorway.

'Which way were you thinking of going Jo?' he asked. She waggled her head from side to side in thought for a moment.

'Well, we could do either the straight run on the A7 or dogleg across at Selkirk to the A68. That will take us directly into Leith without having to fight our way through the city centre. What do you think?' Before he could answer she added,

'We could stop along the A68 for a coffee if you like. I remember a nice little place I stopped at once.' He looked sideways at her.

'Why did I bother to ask?' he muttered aloud to Joanne. 'That's that sorted then. A7 and then the A68 at Selkirk it is.'

CHAPTER 26

Shortly after 10 am on the Monday morning following the trip to Lancashire, Joanne woke in her flat on the reclaimed docks demolished some years ago. New port facilities had left a lot of development land, and her flat was on the third, and top floor, of a small block. She opened her eyes and stared at the ceiling trying to remember what day it was and what she had to do. Moving her head sideways she glanced at the digital alarm clock by the side of her bed and panicked when she saw the time. But only for a second or two, then she relaxed back and remembered that DCI Maxwell had given her and the rest of the murder team two days off. Today was hers.

Turning her head away from the clock and towards the window on the other wall, she tried to work out what the weather was like outside. The sound of rain falling was the answer. She groaned and pulled the duvet up around her neck, but the insistent pressure of water in her bladder made her sadly throw off the covers and leave the bedroom for the bathroom along the corridor.

Fifteen minutes later, showered and dressed she crossed the corridor into the living/dining/kitchen room and looked in amazement as the rain falling outside turned to a vicious hail downpour. She stepped to the window and watched as the hail blotted out most of the cloud-shrouded sky. The storm lasted for no more than four or five minutes and stopped as quickly as it had started. It left lines of white painted in the roof tiles of the nearby buildings she could see, and a carpet on the roadside grass verges. As soon as it had arrived it left, leaving puddles of water in dips and potholes in the roadway.

She turned back to the grey fake granite work surface of the kitchen area and flicked on the electric kettle. Taking a mug from an old-fashioned mug tree by the kitchen wall she opened a metal container of instant coffee and spooned two teaspoonsful into the mug, followed by two teaspoonsful of brown sugar from another container. As the kettle came to the boil she looked again at the weather. Clouds were clearing over the Firth of Forth and the Kingdom of Fife was becoming visible once more. 'Scotland' she thought. 'Don't like the weather, then hang around for a half hour. Something else will turn up.' She smiled ruefully at the well-known complaint about the weather in her home country.

She poured water into the mug and stirred it, then walked across the room again to the window. More of Fife was becoming visible. She imagined she could see Aberdour on the north side of the Forth, the place where her parents had bought her dog, Reg. He was one of a pair which had been for sale when she had been in her last year at high school. She grinned as she remembered the day they bought it, as she sat herself down at the circular wooden dining room table.

The people selling the two dogs had lived in a fairly small three-bedroomed semi and already had three small dogs. When Jo and her parents had been invited into the living room of the house Reg had come bounding in from the kitchen at the back of the house. He had bounced up to her, stood on his hind legs, placed his front paws on her shoulders and given her face a good licking. She had turned smiling to her father,

'I think this is the one dad,' she said. The owner apologised for the dog's behaviour and explained that there were two of them, Ronnie and Reggie, named after the Kray twins. Ronnie had been sold to someone in the Highlands last week, she had explained and they were having to sell Reggie because the house was too small for such big dogs. Reg was big. A cross between a Deer Hound and a Labradoodle. He had tan-coloured hair and a short scruffy beard. Deep brown eyes and straggly ears endeared himself to Joanne in seconds. Already at nine months old, he was the size of a full-grown German Shepherd dog. No wonder they were selling him. The lady owner went on to say that when the puppies were bought they were small and at fourteen weeks old. 'As big as a West Highland White', she had explained. Now he was enormous and the two dogs were causing havoc in the house just by breathing. They had to go.

She and Reg had fallen deeply in love with each other immediately and she had gladly taken on the responsibility of feeding, teaching, walking and loving him. He was a fine dog and returned the love and affection every day. When she had left home to join the Police her parents took over responsibility for the dog, but Joanne still saw him every day and he was always the first to greet her through the front door on her return from work, no matter what time of day or night that was. Then, several years later at age 13, he died. As all dogs do. And Joanne was heartbroken. She never had another dog, and her new post with MIT made it completely wrong for her to have a dog. Any dog would be home alone for most of the time. She couldn't do that. It was just wrong.

So now she lived alone in her third-floor flat and enjoyed the joys of the odd takeaway and the odd bottle of single malt, all by herself, content to concentrate on making the best of the career choice she had made. She sipped at the coffee and watched as the clouds continued to slide away to reveal a clear blue sky underneath.

Finishing her drink she went over to the sink and started to wash the leftover dishes from the Chinese takeaway she had picked up late last night on her way home. It had taken Maxwell and herself some time to empty the search items from the boot of her car into the property store and then complete the paperwork for the items. After her Chinese, she settled in to watch some television, but with it being Sunday night there was little of interest to see. Soon she felt her eyes closing and knew if she didn't move off the sofa and into bed she would wake sometime in the middle of the night with an aching neck and gummed-up mouth. She went to bed.

The two days off were something of a luxury and Joanne made the most of them. She caught up on some housework, which wasn't a big deal and didn't take long, then sorted out the small pile of mail which had arrived during the previous week. A couple of circulars from The Alzheimer's Society, a dog rescue charity in the south of England, Shelter, and the local SNP, Conservatives and Labour parties had wasted their money on sending her letters extolling the undoubted value of her vote in the forthcoming local elections. 'I don't think so' she muttered to herself as she dropped them in the waste paper box in the corner of the kitchen, mentally promising herself she would read the charity circulars later.

The rest of the day and the following day were spent in valuable expenditure of time, she walked around the centre of Edinburgh like a tourist and did touristy things and saw touristy trash in touristy shops. 'How much tartan do these shops sell?' she asked herself as she walked past the fifth or sixth tartan shop on the Royal Mile. She treated herself to lunch on Tuesday in The World's End pub and remembered what she had read of the horrific story of the two girls taken from there, raped and then dumped after being raped. The length of time it had taken the police to convict the man responsible, and the fact he had died in Glenochil prison near Stirling after serving only five years imprisonment, started to come back to her. Only a change in the double jeopardy law allowed him to be tried. He had already been tried in 2007, but the trial had been thrown out. Changes and developments in forensic and DNA science allowed him to be tried a second time, and convicted.

The memories brought back to Joanne the current investigation she was involved in. What would the boss come up with tomorrow, and what would forensic and fingerprints reveal?

CHAPTER 27

Shortly after 7.30 am on Wednesday Joanne left her flat near the docks. The foul weather of yesterday had gone, replaced by the clear blue but chill skies of Sunday. She glanced up at the cloudless sky as she closed the door to the block of flats and shook her head in wonderment at the vagaries of the Scottish weather. Walking across the pavement she saw where she had left her car the previous evening. As she came closer she groaned aloud.

'Bloody lousy seagulls' she said. The closer she came to the car the more she could see splashes of white on the bonnet and front screen of the car.

'Bloody foul bastards' she exclaimed, and looked around to check that there was nobody around to hear her words. There were no pedestrians around and what few cars there were could not hear her. She flicked the fob and the doors unlocked. She slung her shoulder bag onto the front passenger seat and got in, starting the engine quickly. The front screen was liberally splattered with several large liquid dollops of seagull shit. She flicked the washers and doused the screen, then switched on the wipers. After half a minute most of the white stuff had smeared itself over most of the screen. Muttering more obscenities to herself she squirted more water onto the screen. Most of it was removed. She selected drive and moved out of the car park reminding herself to run the car through a car wash at the first opportunity she had.

Shortly before 8 o'clock, she walked into DCI Maxwell's office. 'Morning boss' she said. Maxwell lifted his head from the four stacks of reports in front of him on his desk.

'Morning Jo. Had a good weekend?' he asked looking back to the stacks. Joanne hung her bag over the back of her chair and her jacket on the coat stand by the door. As she unwrapped a brown and yellow patterned Pashmina from around her neck she half turned to him.

'Not bad really. Ended up in the World's End pub in town.' Maxwell looked up in surprise.

'Bit of a strange place to go isn't it?' he asked.

'Yes. I suppose so. Made me realise just how much science has come to our help these days in finding out who has done what and to whom.' She hung the scarf on top of the leather jacket and glanced over her shoulder.

'You alright for a coffee boss?' she asked pointing towards the kettle and mugs on the small table.

'Fine thanks Jo.' he replied, lifting a white mug from the desk top and sipping from it. Joanne made one for herself and placed it on her desk.

'Jo. I want us to be in the incident room by nine. No later.' Maxwell said. She glanced around.

'No problem sir. I think I've got all I need,' she replied. Maxwell lifted the mug towards her.

'I want to try and get this sorted today if possible. I think we should have everything we need to nail Dr Hawkins, what with all the forensics and stuff.' Joanne nodded her head silently and took a drink from her mug. It was too hot and she winced.

'Bugger' she said. Maxwell grinned.

'Bit warm Jo?' he asked.

'Just a bit' she replied, replacing the mug on the desk. She glanced at her wristwatch. Forty-five minutes to go before they were due along the corridor to meet up with the rest of the team.

Both of them worked silently for a few minutes on the files they had on their respective desks before them, then Jo heard a soft tapping noise. She stopped working, lifted her head and turned towards her boss. He was tapping his index finger on the file in front of him and looking distractedly at the wall close to Jo's desk. His eyes were unfocused.

'You alright sir?' she asked. He came to and looked at her smiling.

'Sorry Jo. Yes. Miles away,' he said. 'Jo, can you get hold of Jack Dwyer out at Wester Hailes? See if he can make it to the briefing at nine o'clock, will you? I'd like to know what went on at Molly Cullen's place. I'm sure he'd be certain to be there when they turned the place over.' She nodded her head and picked up the phone on her desk.

*   *   *

A minute before nine in the morning Maxwell and Joanne walked into the incident room. It was only half full, four men and two women, so with Joanne and Maxwell it was five and three. Maxwell made his way to the head of the large oblong desk which dominated the room. Jo snagged a chair by his side. The buzz of conversation carried on until Maxwell tapped the desk and turned to one of the detectives seated to his right halfway down the table.

'Billy, can you open one of the windows a bit? Getting to be a bit warm in here.' The young detective rose and opened the large window immediately behind him a few inches.

'Better. Thanks,' Maxwell said.

'OK ladies and gentlemen, let's get started shall we?' He ran his eyes over the small group and stopped when he spotted Jack Dwyer seated near the far end of the table.

'Jack!' he exclaimed. 'How the hell did you get here so quickly? Thanks for coming.' Dwyer, almost the same age as Maxwell and like him one or two years away from retirement grinned.

'Well you know how it is sir, small minds think alike. Felt you might like to hear about Lady Cullen, so sort of drifted down this way for a brew.'

'Glad you did Jack. Did you get your brew?' Maxwell said.

'Aye, I did sir. Thanks very much.' Dwyer grinned.

'Alright Jack seeing you are here and full of it, I think you can kick off with your visit to Molly then. On you go.' Maxwell sat back in his seat allowing Dwyer to start.

'So' he began. 'Search team in full assault regalia, myself and warrant arrived at Cullen's flat about ten-thirty the other morning. I knocked on the door, she asked who it was, I told her it was me and I wanted a word. She opened the door and invited us in, and in we went.' He paused as Maxwell and the rest of the team burst into laughter.

'Bloody hell Jack! As simple as that? No hassle, no bother, no screaming blue murder?' Maxwell asked.

'Well, none to speak of sir,' he replied. The laughter died down.

'So, carry on Jack.' Maxwell said. Dwyer cleared his throat.

'Found a scrunched-up empty pack of Quinn's cigarettes in the kitchen bin sir. The only prints were hers. There were some fragments of prints but not enough to match up with Quinn, but it was a fairly new pack. Circumstantial, but enough to worry Molly when I pointed out they were not her normal brand, but were the same as matched the dog ends in Quinn's ashtray.' He paused and took a sip from the mug of coffee in front of him.

'So she admitted lifting them from his flat before she left.'

'Good Jack. Did she admit to anything else? Maxwell interrupted.

'Only when we found the pipe he used to smoke his heroin, sir. Then she admitted she had taken it, the cigs and the matches. Denied she had taken any money from his wallet, and honestly sir, it wasn't worth pushing it any further' he said. 'Be a bit difficult to prove any money she had came from Quinn's wallet.'

'So did you not find the wrap of heroin then?' Maxwell asked.

'No sir. No trace. When I pushed her a bit she admitted she had sold it back to the ned on the estate she had been buying it from for Quinn.'

'How long had she been buying it then?' Maxwell asked.

'Seems like quite a long time. Many months, if not a couple of years. He'd started on grass which his son Graham gave him and then went onto the strong stuff. I've passed on the details of the heroin to the drugs team. Seems like there's been a County Lines gang going for some time now in that part of Wester Hailes. They were aware of the ned selling Quinn his stuff but seems like this is a new outlet for their knowledge. He was selling it to Quinn, and then Cullen, right outside the bookies by appointment, the cheeky buggers.' He stopped talking and settled back in his chair.

'Good. That's good Jack.' Maxwell said, looking around for the next speaker.

'OK. Andrea.' he lifted his index finger towards a young DC on his left of the table.

'You were involved with Dr Hawkins when she left us, weren't you? Tell us all about it.' Andrea Salt was young, one of the youngest at MIT, but had gained her place on the team because she was bright, very bright. Bright enough to replace

Joanne if and when Joanne was ever promoted. She inched forward to the edge of the table pushing the file in front of her away a little with a dainty hand.

'Right sir.' she began. 'Her solicitor was not too happy that she had been detained for twenty-four hours. Seemed not to realise that the normal twelve hours could be extended on the authorisation of a Chief Super. Anyway. He's probably got over it by now.' She flashed a grin at Maxwell who returned it.

'Get on with you Andrea.' he said 'Don't keep us in suspense.'

'Right, sir. As I was saying, she was released and allowed to go home in her lovely Mazda sports car. We interviewed her twice in the time she was here. We also made a copy of the hard drive from the sat nav and the vehicle telematics software in her car. All that has been looked at by the computer people. When they had a look at it sure enough they found that the address in Wester Hailes had appeared in the history. That was first entered on the Saturday before he was killed. Another use of the same destination appears on the Sunday evening. Then there is a destination set for her home address later that same evening. She appears to have stopped for a short time on the A7 on her way home. She made a No Comment reply to everything in the two interviews we had with her. I think you've got the hard copy with the file before you sir.' she concluded.

A low hum of conversation rose from the group. Maxwell turned to Joanne.

'That's about it isn't it?' He said quietly to her. Joanne thought for a moment then said,

'I think so, sir. Heroin, ciggies, pipe, sat nav. Ties her into the time of death. If we can have a look at and find where she stopped on the road home we might be able to find the scalpel she used in a dustbin on the A7. It's worth a try sir. I'm sure that the no comment answers will reveal a lot when it gets to court,' she said nodding her head as she ticked off the items on her fingers.

'Perhaps the only thing missing so far is the knife she used to open the vein in his leg. Though that might turn up in the search results from Lancashire or the stop on the A7. It's interesting to see what's on the scalpel we turn up. If we can turn it up' Maxwell nodded in agreement.

'You're right Jo,' he said. Maxwell tapped lightly on the table and the conversation dropped to nothing.

'Right people. A lot of good results. My thanks to you all. As Joanne just reminded me, the only thing missing now is the knife or other implement, she used to open his femoral artery, and that might turn up from one of the searches in Lancashire if the one we did find shows nothing. I hope to have that report tomorrow.' He leaned back in his chair and appeared pensive for a moment or two then leaned forward and said,

'Let's get someone to have a run down the A7 and see if we can find the dustbin she might have ditched the knife in. Worth a try.'

He turned to one of the junior detectives and said,

'Andy, I think that might be a job for you please young man,' he said. The young man inwardly groaned but nodded his head.

'Anything anyone else has to add. Have we forgotten anything so far, or have we got it all?' There were whispered questions and shaken heads around the table as the group considered what he had said.

'Good. Right. Off you go, and once again, my thanks for some really good work. Take the rest of the day off.' He paused.

'That was a joke. Bugger off and get some work done.' The group pushed away from the table and made their way out of the room. When it was empty, Joanne gathered her files and together with her boss made her way back to their office.

CHAPTER 28

As Joanne settled in at her desk and a mug of coffee, she went to pick up the telephone when it rang. 'Mm.' she muttered, 'Psychic.' and picked up the phone from its cradle. 'DS Barker' she said and listened to the voice on the other end of the call.

'Right. OK. Two o'clock should be fine. Many thanks.' Maxwell looked across his desk. 'Well?' he said.

'That was the pathologist's secretary sir. He would like to see us at two today. I said it should be alright.' Maxwell nodded.

'Yes ok. Wonder what Andrew wants.' He pondered for a moment. 'Any thoughts Jo?' he asked. She shook her head.

'Can't think of anything. Unless there is something else which has shown up in the tox reports. They should be back by now.' Maxwell nodded his head.

'That's about all it could be, isn't it? Unless they've found something in his body which wasn't immediately obvious.' he paused, 'Like a bullet.' he grinned.

Joanne grinned back. 'Away with you.' she said. 'Even I couldn't miss something that obvious.'

After they had caught a sandwich at their desks later that morning they drove to the city mortuary off Cowgate in Edinburgh. As she drove along Canongate Maxwell tapped her on her knee.

'Pull in here will you Jo,' he said. 'Want to get some tobacco.' She said nothing but did as her boss requested, once again keeping a judicious eye out for the parking wardens.

He was no more than four minutes, the shop was empty.

'Thanks, Jo. The shop was empty. Lucky that.' She grunted a reply. A few minutes later she turned off Cowgate into High School Wynd and parked behind the mortuary building, flanked as it was by trees in an attempt to disguise the nature of the building from the inhabitants of the city. Though most people knew what it was.

Jo pushed her finger on the doorbell and spoke into the microphone positioned just above it. A mature female voice answered. Jo said who they were and who they had come to see.

'Right you are' said the disembodied voice and a click announced the silent opening of the left hand of two doors. They walked inside. Jo shivered by habit and the two of them walked through the double doors into a reception area where a woman in her late forties wearing a white lab coat was waiting for them. As Jo approached the woman held out her hand.

'Moira Jackson, Dr Douglas's secretary,' she said by way of introduction. She smiled at Maxwell.

'Good afternoon Chief Inspector. Well, today are we?' she asked.

'Fine thank you, Moira. Keeping busy?' he asked.

'As always sir, as always.' she replied with a smile and turned to take them through into a further reception area. Jo could see a curtained-off window which she knew was the viewing area where the dead were put on display for grieving relatives.

'Can you hold on here for a second please,' she said, waving towards a line of foam-backed plastic chairs against the wall opposite the window.

'I'll tell the doctor you're here.' She turned and pushed open a door into a further office.

The pathologist came through and beamed a wide friendly smile at Maxwell.

'Good to see you Lewis,' he said holding out his hand. The two men shook hands. Maxwell turned to Joanne and indicated her to the pathologist.

'Dr Douglas this is my new detective sergeant, Joanne Barker.' She held out her hand and said,

'Good to meet you, Doctor.' He held onto her hand a fraction longer than was necessary and turned to look at Maxwell.

'A big improvement on the last sergeant you had Lewis. Tall, slim, bonny lass and no moustache.'

'Aye well, got her to it shave it off, especially for you,' he said. The pathologist was carrying a file in his hand. He held it up in front of him for the two detectives to see. 'Well, come along into the office and let's go through what we have found shall we?' he said, and dropping Joanne's hand he stepped back through the door into his office, holding the door open for Joanne as she stepped through.

The office was spartan. A desk with one chair behind it and two in front of it together with three metal filing cabinets against the wall behind it, was all the furniture there was. He waved them to the two chairs pulled up in front of his desk and took the one seat behind it laying the file on the desk in front of him. He opened the file and his face fell as he looked down. For a few moments, he said nothing, simply grunted once or twice. When he looked up his face was set and grave. He looked at Maxwell without speaking and then turned his gaze to Joanne. He sniffed once or twice and tapped the file in front of him. Joanne looked sideways at Maxwell, a worried look on her face. Maxwell showed nothing of any emotion, simply returned Joanne's glance and shook his head slightly. Dr Douglas coughed and looked up from the file again.

'Well Lewis, I'm afraid I have some bad news for you.' he said in a low voice. 'James Quinn. Born 1929.' he paused and looked from the file to Maxwell and then to Joanne. 'I'm afraid he's dead,' he said, a large grin flashing across his face as he saw the look on Joanne's face. He burst out laughing. Maxwell grinned and looked at Joanne's flushed face.

'I'm sorry Jo.' he said. 'He does this every time he is introduced to a new officer.' Joanne smiled and cast her eyes down.

'Everyone's a joker, aren't they?' she said smiling. They sat back in their chairs and relaxed.

'I'm sorry Sergeant Barker. I know I should know better, but I don't get many laughs in this miserable place. Can't resist it. Please accept my apologies.' he said.

'That's alright sir,' Joanne replied. 'I suppose I should have known better if you are a friend of this old reprobate.' She was smiling now and glad in a way that the joke had been played on her. It was a sign of acceptance.

Dr Douglas flipped over a few sheets in the file until he came to the one he was looking for.

'So. Blood, hair and tissue samples confirm that he was a long-time user of heroin. But, there was also evidence of small amounts of Morphine in his blood and tissues. However, I'm afraid that I cannot be any more specific than that. Don't suppose it matters though does it?' he looked at Maxwell who shook his head.

'No. The Morphine is strange though. We know he was a heroin user for some time, but Morphine? That's a bit strange. I don't suppose there is any indication of how long he had been taking the Morphine is there? It's not like somebody tried to poison him with an overdose. Did they?' he asked. Douglas shook his head.

'No. I doubt it.' he replied, looking up from the file. He paused for a moment before carrying on.

'From my observation of the body, it is obvious he had suffered from Rheumatoid Arthritis for some time. Hands were badly disfigured.' he glanced down and read from the file.

'Additionally, his medical history says he suffered from COPD.' He looked towards Joanne.

'Do we know what medications he had been prescribed by his GP?' he asked. She flipped open her notebook until she found what she was looking for.

'Well, the following drugs had been prescribed for him by the GP at the Wester Hailes surgery. Carbocisteine, Dihydrocodeine, Lansoprazole, Co-codamol, Naproxen, and a couple of inhalers, Salamol and Seretide.' She read from the list in her notebook.

'No indication of how much he had taken of the stuff I suppose?' he asked.

'No sir. Although most of the blister packs were full, only one or two had pills missing from them.' she said. Douglas sat silently thinking for a few moments before speaking.

'Right. Carbocisteine was for the COPD. Much missing from those packs?' he asked. Joanne looked again at her notebook.

'One or two sir,' she said.

'Right. He should have taken those every day. There should have been signs of a fair amount in his body. So that probably means he hadn't been taking them. What about the Dihydrocodeine and Co-codamol?'

'A fair number of those missing sir. Seems like he was taking them a lot.'

'Right. Those are painkillers, contain Morphine, took them for his arthritis. And the Lansoprazole and Naproxen were for the arthritis pain as well and the side effects of taking the Lansoprazole.' Once again he sat back and appeared deep in thought. Neither of the two detectives interrupted him. They knew he would speak when he had something to say. They waited patiently in silence. After a few moments, he looked up.

'Right. Sorry about that. Needed to get something sorted. Not sure if I've got it yet though, but here's what I'm thinking.' Joanne edged forward in her seat. Maxwell took his pipe from his pocket and started to fill it with tobacco from his pouch. Placed it between his lips and sat chewing on it until Douglas was ready to speak.

'Quinn was quite a feeble man. Undernourished for his height. Hadn't been taking much care of himself in recent times, not eating much, not taking exercise. He should have been taking the Carbocisteine to allow him to bring up mucus caused by COPD, that's what it's for. But he didn't seem to have taken any.' He paused and looked at Joanne.

'Don't suppose you made a note of when the last dose was prescribed for him did you?' he asked. Joanne looked again at the notes she had made at the flat.

'Seems to be about four or five weeks before he was found sir.' she replied.

'Right. That explains why there were only one or two missing from the blister pack.' He tapped the file before him.

'But, the lungs didn't show an awful lot of mucus in them, nor his airways. There should have been a lot more, particularly with the heroin he died of. The heroin would have been some evidence of lung congestion. But there was little or none. I have sent his fingernails and some bone away for analysis. This'll be able to tell us how long, in general, he had been using heroin, though I suspect it was quite a time.'

Joanne leaned forward.

'So although he had been a user for some time it probably didn't kill him? That leaves us with the knife in the leg doesn't it?' she said. She glanced sideways at Maxwell who gave a raised eyebrow look at the pathologist.

'Well Andrew, what say you?' he asked. Dr Douglas thought for a second and leaned forward with his elbows on the desk.

'In itself, the knife attack would not have killed him. However, if he had taken more than a normal dose of the heroin it could have made him weak enough so that he was almost comatose, unable to defend himself when someone stuck the knife in him. The cause of death was heart failure. That would have been brought on by loss of blood from the wound, which in itself was not all that big. But it wouldn't have to be big to get the blood flowing nicely out of his body.' he sat back and paused.

'And it was only a small nick.' He turned and smiled at Maxwell who barely suppressed a smile.

'Oh yes, he said, 'The semen on his loins.' he paused and looked at Joanne. 'It wasn't his.'

'What!' Joanne exclaimed. He grinned back at her.

'Joking. Course it was his. Just like to wind you up a bit.' Maxwell looked across the desk at Dr Douglas and smiled and shook his head then turned to Joanne who was once again breathing normally.

'Said he was good didn't I?' he said still smiling. He rose from his seat and held out his hand across the desk. 'Many thanks, Andrew. Let me have your full report when you can please, and the results of the hair and fingernails as well if you please.'

'My pleasure Lewis. Good to see you again.' He smiled and turned to Joanne. 'Good to meet you, Detective Sergeant. Hope you last well with this old reprobate.' Joanne shook his hand and turned to go.

As they walked across the car park to the Volvo Joanne turned to her boss.

'Bit of a character isn't he?' she said.

'Old school. Maybe I should have warned you, Jo.'

'Nothing new was there sir?' she said. Maxwell shook his head.

'No. Not really, but it does clean up a few loose ends though doesn't it? Died from heart failure caused by leaky blood and accelerated by perhaps an overdose of heroin and morphine.' He pulled the pipe from his pocket and lit it as they walked back to the car.

'Fancy a coffee Jo?' he said. 'I'm buying'

'I think so after that little performance.' she replied.

'Right let's see what Canongate has to offer shall we?' he said and led the way down the hill.

A pleasant fifteen-minute walk in the afternoon sunshine brought them to a decision. Do they take their patronage to a Cafe Nero on one side of the street or to a family-run cafe on the other side? Maxwell gave Joanne a quizzical bend of the head and she responded with a thumb in the direction of the family-run cafe.

Maxwell opened the door and let them both in. It was being well used, over half of the tables in the place were full. Mainly students but a good selection of tourists as well. Joanne closed the door behind them as Maxwell pointed towards an empty table by the far left side of the room. Inching their way through the seated patrons, past clumsily hung shoulder bags and coats on the backs of chairs they made it to their seats and sat side by side, almost, with their backs to the wall. Joanne looked around at the walls of the cafe. They were almost all covered in framed watercolour prints of various landmarks of Edinburgh and Scotland. Arthurs Seat, Edinburgh Castle, Holyrood Palace, the Royal Mile, Glencoe and Rannoch Railway Station, and what appeared to be 1950's posters of British Rail holiday destinations. All in all an old-fashioned place, but clean and neat for all that.

She picked up the menu from the table.

'Fancy anything to eat sir?' she asked. Maxwell shook his head,

'Not for me Jo. Just a black coffee.' A very thin young waitress dressed in a black skirt and white blouse with an apron over it approached the table, pen and a small writing pad in hand.

'What can I get you?' she asked in a non-happy voice. Joanne glanced up at the voice. The girl had a problem with a line of angry-looking spots across her forehead and the ointment she was using to either cure or disguise them was not working. Either it wasn't working or the ointment had been applied that morning and it was wearing off. It was not a pleasant sight for Joanne to look at.

'Two Americanos please,' she said. The girl jotted the order down on her pad.

'Do you want to milk them?' she asked. Joanne sighed.

'Americano should be black' she said, 'Just black, and no milk.' The girl gave her a puzzled scowl and turned to return to the service counter where a man and a woman were busy preparing drinks and plates of snacks. Joanne watched as the girl spoke to the woman who looked up from what she was doing and glanced over the waitress's shoulder at Joanne. She said a few brief words to the girl who tossed her head back and made a one or two-word reply.

'That's not a very happy young lady' Maxwell said as he watched the interaction. 'Wonder if she's the daughter,' he added. Joanne raised her head to look at the trio.

'Possible I suppose, but why is she not in school or college? Looks like she should be.' she said. 'Might learn some manners or customer service techniques.'

They sat back in their seats and looked around the clientele in the cafe. The usual mix for this time of year. If it had been Festival time the place would be bursting at the seams. Maxwell tapped the table with his right hand.

'What do you reckon Jo?' he asked. 'How are we going to prove the good doctor did for Jimmy?' Joanne blew a long breath of air from her cheeks.

'The pathologist had me in a bit confused with all the drugs stuff if I'm honest,' she said.

'Seems like if he had COPD then his lungs should have been showing a lot more signs of it, shouldn't they? But the drugs he had been prescribed looked as though they had never been used. So how does that work? It doesn't add up.' Maxwell looked sideways at her and considered her question for a moment.

'I think our Jimmy had conned his doctor into diagnosing him with COPD so that he could get Disability Allowance or some other state benefit. Could be a few hundred pounds a month. Not bad for him. Bet it paid for his recreational drugs, and a nice little Audi for his pusher' he said. Joanne's eyebrows shot up.

'You think sir?' she asked incredulously.

'Nothing more certain I reckon.' he replied.

'Easy enough to do if you are a busy GP and if Jimmy knew just what the symptoms were.' Perhaps if he went to see her when he had a bad cold or maybe a touch of bronchitis, then the doctor could easily have been convinced he had COPD.' He sat back as the young waitress brought them two mugs of Americano coffee and placed them down in front of them.

'Your coffees.' she said and placed a bill on the table by the side of Maxwell's mug.

'Thank you' Maxwell said. The girl glanced at them and turned away without a further word.

'Lovely lass,' Maxwell said, grinning at the back of the girl as she walked back to the counter. 'She'll go far in this company.'

'Further the better' said Joanne quietly as she tore open the two small packs of sugar the girl had dumped on the table.

'Snotty little cow.'

They sat in silence for a moment or two sipping from the mugs of coffee. Maxwell broke the silence.

'Why a Volvo Jo? Would have thought a woman of your age would have gone for something a bit sportier.' She placed her mug down on the table and folded her arms.

'What 90 miles an hour not fast enough for you? Didn't hear you complaining on the way back the other day.' He grinned.

'Aye. Suppose you have a point there. It was quite speedy, and comfortable too.'

'Well, the days of driving a Volvo that looked like a house brick on wheels have long gone. Some of the bigger ones are very luxurious. Beyond my pocket though.' she said.

'One of the other reasons was that I always felt that if I was in a smash in a Volvo I would be the one to walk away from it.' Maxwell nodded his head whilst he thought of what she had said.

'Mm. Yes, you're right.'

'Did you know Volvo invented the three-point seat belt, back in 1958, but it wasn't until 1965 car makers had to install them.' she said. She took another drink of her coffee and carried on,

'And it wasn't until Barbara Cartland introduced legislation that it became law to wear them.' Maxwell laughed out loud almost sneezing black coffee over the table.

'Castle' he said, calming himself.

'It was Barbara Castle. Barbara Cartland was the woman in pink who wrote novels aimed at women who you're thinking of. Barbara Castle was the red-haired MP for Blackburn in Lancashire who introduced this and the breathalyser law as well.' Joanne looked at him and grinned.

'I know that. Just wanted to make sure you were listening.' Maxwell put his mug down on the table.

'You ready for going then?' he asked.

'When you are sir.' She rose from the table and went to the counter to pay. Maxwell followed her and put his hand on hers as she placed the money on the counter.

'Said I would pay Jo. Put it away.'

'Oh, sir. How can I refuse?' she grinned and buttoning up her jacket stepped to the doorway.

Fifteen minutes later they were nudging their way through the city centre traffic on their way back to the office.

'Something I forgot to show you earlier sir.' she said. 'There's three pages in my bag on the back seat.' Maxwell reached back, retrieved her shoulder bag and extracted three foolscap sheets of paper clipped together. For a moment or two, he glanced from one to the other of the three sheets of paper.

'Jesus Christ!' he exclaimed. 'How the hell did he get this amount of money Jo?' She glanced sideways and grinned at him.

'Courtesy of HM Government sir. Take a look at the income side of the statements and all the income is from DSS payments. Pension, Disability Living Allowance, Pension Credit and Motability Allowance.' she said. Maxwell spluttered.

'But it shows he had over sixteen thousand in his account.'

'It was John who gave me this sir. He was the DC who came up with the original figure. Tells me he got this from some old bank statements from the living room drawer, so I got him to run off the last three months. That's what Quinn was worth.'

'Bloody hell. This is almost as much as I earn Jo.' Maxwell said searching down the list of figures in the income and outgoing sides of the statement.

'All the money coming out seems to be cash withdrawals, probably from the hole in the wall near the bookies.'

'That's right sir. Averages a little under two hundred a week. Paid for his groceries, betting at the bookies and a daily heroin purchase. Judging from the figures, he had been lying his little head off to the DSS about being married, so he gets the higher rate of pension, and claims the disability allowance and carers allowance for the care his dear neighbour Molly Cullen did for him.'

'And that's left him with over sixteen thousand in the black at the end of the day.' Maxwell grunted as he flipped from one page to the next.

'Might be worthwhile passing this info on to the DSS, do you think? They might want to claim back what they had been fraudulently paying him.'

'Too right Jo. Too bloody right. Bad enough the DSS were funding his drug use but this is going a bit too far. Let's hope they can get the money from his estate. Don't suppose he left a will did he?'

'Haven't found one sir. Which is good news. Don't want that mad bastard son Gunther getting his hands on this lot. He would never come back down to earth with what that amount of money would get him in heroin and cannabis.'

'True. The first job tomorrow for one of the troops is to get onto the DSS and tell them the good news.' Maxwell slipped the statements back into her bag and sat with it on his knee as Joanne drove onto Constitution Street in Leith.

'Suits you sir' she said, nodding at the shoulder bag.

'What?' he said, then looked down at the bag. 'Cheeky so and so. Not my style at all.' As Joanne pulled into the kerb he tossed the bag over to her.

'Get yourself off home Jo. See you bright and early in the morning.'

'Will do sir,' she said. 'Bye, sir.' Looking over her shoulder she pulled away from the kerb for the short journey home.

CHAPTER 29

As Maxwell opened up the office door the following morning the young DC who had had the unenviable task of searching the A7 for a dustbin was waiting for him. He carried a brown paper evidence bag.

'Morning sir,' he said.

'What do you have there?' Maxwell asked pointing to the bag.

'Scalpel, rubber gloves and a shopping bag from Tesco's sir,' he replied with a grin. Maxwell opened the door and walked through ushering the young DC forward.

'Pop it there on the desk for the time being, and tell me more.' he said.

'Well, did as I was told yesterday and after reading the telematics report was able to find the dustbin in a lay-by on the A7. Rooted around a bit and found the Tesco bag. Quite clear compared with the other rubbish, so picked it up, opened it and saw the gloves and a scalpel in the bottom. Thought you might like it.'

Maxwell gently opened the bag and peered in. The items were there as had been described.

'Bloody good work' he said. 'Now I want you to get these off to forensics now, never mind the morning briefing. These results are urgent. Might be just what we are looking for to tie her into the scene. Well done He looked up smiling at the detective, who collected the evidence bag and made his way out of the office just as Joanne was coming in. She held the door for him as he passed smiling.

'Morning sir,' she said, 'What was all that about? He looked pleased with himself.' Maxwell explained what had just happened and said,

'Right, we need to get along to the briefing to tell the troops about this lot. Come on.' He picked up his files from the desk and left the office with her.

At two minutes after nine the murder team briefing room was full. All the seats except one were occupied, the seat next to Joanne. The officers in the room were engaged in quiet conversations with their neighbours. Joanne included. Maxwell strode to the empty seat and slammed down the file he had carried with him. The noise brought immediate silence. Joanne jumped in her seat. 'Bloody hell' she muttered. Maxwell looked from one face to the next around the room fixing his gaze on each of the faces. Nobody spoke. Eventually, Maxwell broke into a grin and pulled back the chair from the table.

'Good morning everyone. Hope you all slept well and are raring to go.' A sigh of relief and a few chuckles broke out

QUINN

around the table. Joanne turned to the man on her right away from Maxwell.

'I'm going to kill him if he tries that again,' she muttered.

'No you won't Detective Sergeant Barker. And if you do, I have a room full of witnesses to the fact.' Maxwell said loudly, gently clipping his DS lightly on the head. She smiled up at him

'No sir. Of course not sir.' she said. Maxwell looked around the table until he found the person he was looking for.

'John.' he said smiling at the young detective who had found the bank statement in Quinn's flat.

'Good work with the bank statement. Jo showed me the last three months of Quinn's account. The bugger had over sixteen thousand in the account. Seems like he spent most of the rest on heroin.' He paused to let the facts sink in as murmurs rose around the table. The young detective watched his boss closely for anything else.

'So. It seems apart from anything else he was doing Quinn was fiddling the DSS. I want you to get onto the DSS investigation unit and put them on his trail. He might be dead, and he might not have left a will, but we don't want any of this money going to his stupid son or the crazy daughter, do we?'

'Right, sir. First thing.' replied the young detective.

'You'll find a number for them in Dundee somewhere. Give it a whirl eh?'

'Will do sir.' he replied, delighted not to have had a strip torn off him by the DCI.

Maxwell sat down at the table and shuffled forward, opening the file at another report.

'OK. The search teams in Lancashire seem to have done a good job. Didn't find an awful lot, but what they did find gives us hope. First. Her office computer shows that she did a couple of searches on Google Maps for directions to Quinn's home in Wester Hailes. That was about three weeks before he was killed. Also, she searched for the Premier Inn on Lauriston Place in the city. Again about three weeks before she paid a visit. That in itself shows quite a degree of planning.' He looked up from the report and glanced around the table. Nodded heads showed they were following him.

'Nothing else found in the place where she works, sadly.' He paused to draw breath.

'Right. Next. Her home computer showed the same searches and quite a bit of time looking at Google Maps for the best route to take from her home. All good stuff.' he said.

'They've also had a look at her mobile phone. We now have it here to do the same analysis. From the calls log a week before her visit she makes a call to the Premier Inn' he paused and looked up from the file. He nodded to one of the junior detectives at the table.

'Give the place a call will you, find out if she stayed there and if possible what time she booked in. I have a feeling you'll find it was sometime early Saturday evening.' The detective nodded and made a note on a pad of paper in front of him.

'There was one other thing about the mobile phone. It appears it was turned off from the time she left Burnley in Lancashire on the Saturday afternoon, until she got back home later morning on the Monday, by which time Quinn's body had just been found.' There were a few comments from the table.

'And,' Maxwell continued, 'The sat nav in her car plots her trip from Lancashire to Wester Hailes via Lauriston Place, and then back to Lancashire early on the Monday morning.' Another round of grunts of approval sounded from the team. He continued,

'And, the telematics in the car showed she stopped on her way home on the A7, so young Alan had a run down there and came up with a bag of goodies. Scalpel and rubber gloves all nicely wrapped in a Tesco bag.'

Maxwell put the file to one side and took a separate report from it.

'The home computer has a file on it called 'personal reflections.' It seems to be thoughts on her private life.' There was a murmur from the group. Maxwell looked up and grinned.

'Sounds interesting doesn't it?' he said. 'And it is. Apart from the fact she was trying desperately to get a chap from her company to have an affair with her, there is also a record of Quinn's youngest son Gunther, or Graham, staying with her for the best part of a week. This happened about five months ago and it is clear from what she wrote that he was smoking cannabis all the time he was there. She eventually kicked him out after he kept on lying to her. This makes her answers to the questions we put to her at her initial interview a bit suspect. She was obviously in regular contact with him to invite him to stay with her for the best part of a week.' He sat forward in his chair again.

'The Lancashire lads also had a good look at her bank account. Seems like during the time she was in Scotland she never used her bank debit card, though she normally seemed to use it for almost everything she bought when she was at home. The last time it was used before driving north was to fill up with petrol at a station not far from the M65 near her home. That was on the Saturday afternoon. On the Thursday and Friday before the trip, she drew out a total of five hundred pounds in cash. Not her normal cash withdrawals at all. So presumably she paid for everything in cash once she got north of the border.'

He sat back in his chair and looked around the group once more. They were now right up to speed with him and eager to discover what else the boss had to say. Joanne was busy making notes through the revelations, as were most of the others around the table.

'Right. The most important thing they found was the coat she wore when she visited Jimmy. On the right-hand hem of the coat were traces of cigarette ash. It's not possible to say if this was from the ashtray found half under his bed, but considering she didn't smoke, it is more than likely it was from there. Also found on the coat were two small traces of blood.' A few calls of 'Yes' and 'Gotcha' came from the table. Maxwell held up his hand.

'Yes indeed,' he said. 'Gotcha. They are only very small spots on the left-hand cuff of the coat. Enough to do a DNA test, and they are from Quinn.' A low growl of approval and one or two smacks of hands on the table showed the delight of the team.

'Looking very good so far,' he said. 'The spots are on the inside cuff of the left sleeve, level with the little finger.' He held up his left hand so that it was straight and at ninety degrees to his head and pointed to the line from his little finger down to the cuff of his jacket.

'Found just here on the edge of the cuff. Probably got it when she was cutting his femoral artery.' He smiled around the table. 'Well done sir' said Joanne at his side. He glanced sideways and smiled.

'Not my work Jo. Forensics have done a cracking job. I think we have her nailed.' Maxwell eased his chair back a little from the table and looked around at his team.

'You've done a good job ladies and gentlemen. Well done.' he said beaming at them all. He gazed at the room for a moment or two before finally telling them about the discovery on the A7 dustbin.

'The scalpel is being looked at by forensics as we speak. A great result! If the scalpel and gloves come back with any prints or DNA then, I think we have her.' He paused again before continuing.

'Right. One further thing we have to consider though. Have we missed anything? Are there any holes in what evidence we have gathered so far before we make arrangements to get Dr Hawkins back in?' He looked around the table. One or two low-level conversations were going on between various members of the team. Eventually, a question came from the right-hand side of the table.

'Sir.' said a young woman detective raising her hand.

'Go on Annie' he said.

'Apart from the blood under his body were there any other signs of bleeding on his body when he was found? She asked. Maxwell opened a report from the file.

'Seems not. The only blood found on the body was between and beneath his legs.' Annie coughed slightly.

'I was just thinking of a possible reason she might come up with for the blood being on the cuff sir. Just a thought.'

'And a good thought. Forensics say there was no other blood found on the body. Though there was enough of it wasn't there?' he grinned ruefully.

'Anything else?' He looked around the table once more. There was a general shaking of heads. No one could find anything else, so it seemed. Then Jack Dwyer spoke up.

'Sir.' he said, 'What about the knife she used to cut him? That's hasn't turned up has it?' Maxwell shook his head.

'No Jack. I have a feeling that the scalpel we found at her home was not the one she used to kill Quinn, she has been too bloody clever in erasing all of her tracks. The one she used will probably have been the one she jettisoned on her way home. The pathologist feels that the small, neat incision on the artery, was probably a surgical instrument. The sort a surgeon might use.' There was a low moan from one or two of the officers. Maxwell held up his hand for silence.

'However. The scalpel she used has been found on the A7 by one of our sharp-eyed colleagues.' he pointed to the young officer who had spent the day in the lay-by on the A7.

'A nice little job there. Well done.' he said. A mutter of appreciation flowed over the gathering.

He gazed out of the long window to his right. Once again there was a clear blue sky, no trace of the vicious showers they had had the previous day.

'It seems that the good doctor was very forensically aware. No trace of fingerprints anywhere in the flat other than from Quinn and his neighbour Molly Cullen.'

He looked again at Jack Dwyer.

'Jack, you had another word with Cullen, didn't you? Did she come up with anything else that might help?' The old constable flipped through his notebook and at a couple of foolscap sheets of paper in front of him.

'Not really sir. Seems she had been buying his heroin for some time, maybe a year or more, and using his bank card, with his permission,' he added.

'There's enough information from her to help the Drugs guys to stop the supply for the time being. Not going to stop it completely though. Bloody impossible.' he grimaced. He interrupted Maxwell as he was about to speak.

'Sorry sir, one further thing.' he said. Maxwell nodded for him to continue.

'She lifted the money from his wallet, from the last time she did a hole-in-the-wall trip for him.' he glanced down at his notes.

'That was on the Saturday morning, and the pack of cigarettes from his room as well. Gave her the gypsies warning for that. Told her she would be kept an eye on in the future.' he grinned. Maxwell nodded his head and smiled a Jack.

'Nice job Jack. We'll make a detective of you yet. If you've enough time left.' he said.

'Fat chance' Dwyer replied with a grin.

Maxwell gathered his papers together and tapped them into a neat pile in front of his on the table.

'Right. That's it. Thanks for your input and time. Crack on with what you are dealing with. Get the loose ends tied up. Joanne and I are off to see the Procurator this afternoon to lay out what we have.' He glanced sideways at Joanne. 'Then the next step is to get her back up here to respond to her bail.'

CHAPTER 30

J o sat at her desk looking across at her boss. He was swivelled away from her and was gazing out of the window at the buildings across the road. She nursed a mug of coffee, she'd lost count of how many she had had today since the meeting earlier. Her desk was littered with files and bits of files which she was trying to put into some semblance of order. Maxwell was lifting his unlit pipe to his mouth and then dropping it to rest his arm on the side of the desk.

'What's the problem sir?' she asked quietly. Maxwell didn't reply for a moment or two then turned back towards her.

'Do you reckon the Queen Charlotte Room would be any good for a retirement do?' he asked. Joanne spluttered on her coffee.

'What the hell are you thinking that for?' she asked, placing the mug on her desk and scrabbling for a tissue from a pocket in the leather jacket on the back of her chair.

'Just wondering. Nice looking building though isn't it?' he replied. He looked at her though it was apparent to Jo that he wasn't seeing her.

'What's the problem sir?' she asked. 'Something about the Quinn job?' Maxwell shook his head from side to side.

'No. Well not really. Well, yes' he said quietly, his eyes still not focused on her. Finally, he put the mug down on the desk and turned to face her pointing his pipe in her general direction.

'Why did she do it?' he asked. 'Why kill him after all these years? Doesn't make any real sense does it? And why do it in a way which could potentially lead to her being charged with murder? There are lots of other ways she could have done it.' He tapped the end of the pipe on the file absently.

'It's not making sense.' he said.

Joanne pondered what she had heard and waited for him to elaborate further on what he had said. He continued to tap lightly on the file making a brown puddle of spittle appear on the file cover.

'Sir.' she said pointing to the pool coming from the pipe. He glanced down at the mess, small though it was.

'Oh shit!' he exclaimed and felt in his pocket for a handkerchief. Joanne threw over a wad of clean tissues from her desk.

'Use these sir' she said. He dabbed fiercely at the mess and cleaned the file cover, leaving just a feint brown stain.

'The thing is.' he began, then paused, and began again.

'The thing is, if she wanted to kill him then it would have been far easier for her to inject him with something. I mean he was taking, or had in the flat, a pile of Dihydrocodeine which had been prescribed for him. It would not have been all that hard for her to crush a few tablets up and inject him with them. It would show up in his blood as a fairly straightforward overdose of morphine from his prescription wouldn't it?' He looked at her in silence.

'But doing it this way? It seems like she wanted to be discovered one way or another. But why? It just doesn't ring true.' He paused again.

'Something doesn't ring true, and I'd like to come up with some reason before we go to see the Procurator this afternoon.' He sat back again and soon started to tap his pipe on the desk surface.

'Want some more tissues sir?' she asked. Maxwell looked up at her in puzzlement.

'What?' he asked.

'You're going to stain the desk now if you keep that up.' she replied, pointing to where he was again leaving a brown liquid on the desk.

'Bugger' he said and wiped it off with the tissue he still held absentmindedly in his hand.

He pushed back from the desk and stood up, glancing around again through the window at the building opposite.

'Come on' he said. 'I'll buy you a bacon roll from the canteen.' and started to walk to the door.

'I have a much better idea sir,' she said, rising from her seat and picking her jacket from the back of her chair.

'I'll take you for a nice walk to the seaside. How does that grab you?' He smiled at her.

'That sounds like a much better idea.' he said and took his overcoat from the coat hook by the office door. Joanne took her Pashmina from its hook and opened the door for him.

'Age before beauty sir,' she said.

'Cheeky so and so' Maxwell replied,

'Come with me young lady and I'll take you to where the rest of the world begins.'

'Race you.' Joanne smiled and followed him through, locking the door behind her.

They walked quietly along in the morning sunlight up to the junction of Baltic Street and Bernard Street then turned off to the Water of Leith. Neither spoke until they stopped at the side of the Water, admiring for a moment in the distance the floating restaurants and pleasure boats together with the odd commercial vessel moored on the water in the distance. Maxwell stopped and leaned lightly against one of the iron posts with fence lines strung between them on the edge of the waterway.

'Thoughts Jo?' he asked lightly. 'Why did she do it?' Joanne reached into the shoulder bag she carried and fished out a bag of Midget Gems, offering the bag to Maxwell. He shook his head and instead took his pipe from his jacket and started to fill and then light it.

'I was thinking about this last night sir,' she said eventually after feeding two of the sweets into her mouth.

'To me, it smacks of revenge, pure and simple. But why? Why draw attention to yourself if you could have killed him quite easily without drawing attention to yourself?' She paused for a moment.

'It doesn't make a lot of sense does it?' Maxwell drew on his pipe blowing out a cloud of smoke away from Joanne.

'You're right.' he said. 'Revenge. But why draw attention to yourself?' They stood silently, each turning over in their minds yet again a reason why Dr Hawkins should have cut Quinn's femoral artery and then left him looking serene and peaceful in his bed. Maxwell turned and knocked his pipe against the top of the iron bollard.

'She waited until he died. Probably held him down a bit if he realised his leg was bleeding and started to struggle a bit, then when he was dead she folded his hands across his chest and pulled the covers up to his neck very neatly. That shows she was confident in what she was doing and also was not afraid of a neighbour coming to see him. She must have had the place under watch for some time during the evening.' He drew his tobacco pouch from his pocket and started the process of refilling and relighting his pipe.

Joanne folded her arms across her chest and shifted her weight onto her right leg half turning to face Maxwell.

'Sir' she said. 'It's not all that important, but it was something I noticed when we brought her in for questioning.' Maxwell turned his head to look at her.

'Go on.' he said.

'Well, when she was being searched in the station before we took her to the interview room, I noticed a couple of things which I thought were strange at the time but not important, so didn't mention it. In the bag she brought with her, the shoulder bag, she had three pairs of briefs and a new unopened packet of sanitary pads. Not heavy-duty ones, lightweight ones, the sort a young girl would use when she first started her periods. It struck me as peculiar at the time because she must be close to retirement, finished having periods years ago and finished with the menopause as well.' Maxwell held the pipe in front of his mouth and stared at her.

'What do you reckon that was all about Jo? I know my wife is finished with the menopause now, but she never uses those sorts of things,' he said.

'I think it's probably a habit she's had for some time. Something she started doing during her early adult life and never got out of the habit, almost like a fetish.' She reflected again on what she had said.

'Like she didn't ever want urine, or any other fluid, to stain her panties, her skirt or trousers, or even her skin. Maybe it goes back to the time when she was being abused by Quinn if she was abused by him.'

'That is weird Jo. Never heard anything like that before, never. D'you think it's possible?' Maxwell said.

'Could be sir. When a kid is sexually abused, or when they start to have normal sexual relations, there are a lot of changes which occur in the mind and body. I suppose it is possible she picked up the habit then until she was unable to stop doing it. Maybe it started after Quinn masturbated on her, or raped her.' She thought for a moment. 'Still strange though isn't it?'

'Aye, it is.' Maxwell said. 'Anyway. Still hasn't answered the question of why she killed him though, does it?' Once again they fell into a silence, broken only by the odd seagull trying to find its way back to the sea. They started to slowly walk along the roadway called the Shore until they came to Tolbooth Wynd, and turned back to the station on Queens Charlotte Street.

CHAPTER 31

After having to drive two or three times around the back streets by the Sheriff's Court Joanne managed to park her car in a cobbled back street close to the Procurator Fiscal's office. Locking the car she looked around for a traffic warden as she followed Maxwell to the Procurator's office.

A mid-forties secretary with an ample figure rose smiling from her desk as they walked into the reception office, she stepped around her desk and held out her hand to Maxwell.

'Chief Inspector,' she gushed. 'How lovely to see you again. It's been such a long time. Wait here a moment will you while I tell the Procurator you are here.'

'Thank you, Margaret. Good to see you again' Maxwell replied. Joanne made a gentle puking noise as the secretary disappeared into an office ahead of her.

'Catch sir' she said quietly. Maxwell turned to look at her with a puzzled look on his face.

'What?' he asked

'Her knickers sir. Catch,' she said, grinning widely. Maxwell started to go red in the face as he turned away.

'No idea what the hell you are talking about Detective Sergeant.' Joanne chuckled.

The door opened and the lovely Margaret held out her hand to usher them through into the office of the Procurator Fiscal. He was a tall man, some three inches taller than Joanne and about eight years older. Broad shoulders and a mane of sandy hair going grey covered his head and touched the top of his ears.

'Lewis' he said, walking around the desk with his right hand extended. 'Great to see you again.' he said. Maxwell smiled and shook hands and turned to Joanne to introduce her.

'Have you met my Sergeant Jamie?' he said.

'I have. But it's always good to meet again.' Joanne smiled warmly and allowed the Procurator to grip her hand slightly longer in a greeting than she normally would have been comfortable with. This man, she had often thought, was not simply handsome, he was beautiful. He was wearing black court trousers and a gleaming white shirt open at the neck with the cuffs folder over at the wrist. The black coat to the suit and his tie were hanging over the back of his chair. She smiled broadly and felt the warmth of his touch.

'Wonderful to see you again sir,' she said treating him to the brightest smile she could muster.

'And you Sergeant. And you.' He indicated two comfortable upright upholstered wooden chairs across from his side of the large wooden desk. 'Take a seat. Can I get you some tea?' he said.

'No thank you, Jamie,' said Maxwell. 'Got a few things to catch up with in the office. A thought suddenly flashed through Joanne's mind. She suddenly turned to Maxwell and blurted out,

'It's publicity sir,' she said. Then before he could say anything she turned to the Procurator blushing.

'Sorry sir,' she apologised. 'It's just that we were talking earlier about her motive for murdering Quinn, and it's just struck me. Out of the blue. It's publicity!' Her face was flushed, her eyes bright and sparkling.

'I think that's the answer, sir.' Maxwell looked across at the Procurator then back to Joanne, and then back to the Procurator.

'Jamie. I'm sorry. If you could allow Joanne to carry on whilst she has the thought in her mind it might help us all to understand a bit more about this case. Because I'm a bit lost myself.' he said.

'By all means Lewis' said the Procurator. He turned to Joanne and smiled, who by now was blushing with embarrassment.

'Please Joanne, put us out of our misery.'

'I'm sorry sir. It just came to me' she said. 'Out of the blue. We were trying to think of a reason why she would have murdered Quinn the way she did. She had a couple of other alternatives, neither of which would have pointed the finger at her it would probably have been a Natural Causes verdict at the Coroners Court.' She paused to take a breath.

'But that's the reason she did it the way she did it. She didn't want a Natural Causes verdict, she wanted it to be Murder, by a person or persons unknown.'

Maxwell was silent for a moment or two.

'I think I know where you're going with this Jo. Tell us both will you?' he said, settling back in his chair.

'Right. Quinn was found lying in a pool of blood. Didn't have to be that way, she had access to Morphine based drugs belonging to Quinn which she could quite easily have injected him with, and it probably wouldn't have shown, him being a heroin user and all. But, instead, she cuts his femoral artery and lays one of his kitchen knives in the blood when it has congealed a bit so that it lies on top of the blood without sinking too far into the blood. She wanted this fact to come out in the coroner's court, so that it would look like murder, and the Police would be deeply involved. She wanted the case to get maximum publicity so that Quinn's background would have been brought out in court. Or at least given a reporter the justification for chasing up his story.' The Procurator nodded but said nothing. Maxwell looked from one to the other.

'Carry on Jo. You seem to have got something.' he said.

'The one thing she didn't want though was for herself to be investigated for murder, did she? No. She tried to make sure she left no fingerprints, she arrived late in the evening so there were few people about to see her, and she wore surgical rubber gloves so there were no prints. She's been very forensically aware, hasn't she?' Maxwell nodded his head and glanced at the Procurator who nodded his head in agreement.

'I understand what you are saying, Joanne. Almost all the evidence you have is circumstantial.' he said, tapping the file in front of him on his desk.

'Except for the one firm piece of evidence of the blood spots belonging to Quinn on the bottom cuff of her coat sleeve. How is she going to get around that?' she said triumphantly.

'Yes. You're right. It's the only bit of real solid evidence you have, but I think it will be enough to take it to court and get her convicted.' he said.

Joanne sat back and grinned at him and then her boss.

'Meet with your approval boss?' she asked cheekily.

'Aye. It'll do for the time being,' he replied giving her a broad smile of approval.

The Procurator looked from one to the other and smiled.

'I think that you might have covered everything I need to know ' he said. 'I've had a look through the file, obviously, and the explanation you've come up with looks to me to be right. She never expected to be found out, but you've done it. When are you getting her back up here for charging?' he said. Maxwell flipped through the file on his knee.

'Should be the end of next week Jamie, but I think we might be in a position to bring it forward a bit, with your permission.'

'Go ahead. I don't see a problem. Get her up here when you feel you are ready for her.'

Maxwell and Joanne rose from their seats and shook hands and said goodbye to the Procurator. 'I hope we meet again someday Sergeant,' he said to Joanne.

'Yes sir. Me too' she replied and gathered her jacket from the back of her chair.

They left the building without a word being said between them, making their way around the back of the building to the cobblestone street where she had parked her car. The sun was shining and the sky was blue. All in all a good day, thought Joanne. Her pale blue Volvo was still on the yellow lines about a hundred yards ahead of them.

'Hurry up sir,' she suddenly said and lengthened her pace.

'What's the problem?'

'Traffic warden ahead. Coming our way.' Maxwell speeded up. She gave the car a once over as she got closer, no scratches, no graffiti and so far no ticket. However, that could change soon. She flicked her key fob and the indicators gave a satisfying beep. Throwing her handbag into the back seat she slumped down into the driver's side, pushed the fob into the slot and hit the start button. Maxwell quickly closed his passenger door as he saw the warden hastening to catch up and dish her a ticket. Joanne pulled away from the kerb when the official was about twenty yards away. The middle-aged woman held out her hand for Jo to stop. She wound down her window and stuck out her head.

'Sorry, can't stop. Police business. Urgent,' hit the accelerator, and swiftly performed a wheel screeching three-point turn to blast back past her to get back onto Cowgate.

'Close one,' said Maxwell.

'True enough.' Jo replied. She settled back to concentrate on the short trip back to the office in Leith, but traffic was making life difficult, as usual.

'What date are you thinking of bringing her back for her bail sir?' she asked as she settled down into a steady stop-start in the queues. Maxwell thought for a second or two before answering.

'I think I've changed my mind, Jo. Not such a good idea to bring her in early.'

'What's your thinking sir?' she asked.

'Well. No doubt she will have a solicitor with her, yes?'

'Aye. Without a doubt.'

'So if you were her solicitor and the Police changed the date of your bail hearing to an earlier one, what would your thoughts be?'

'Well, I suppose I would be thinking that the Police had got it all sewn up.'

'That's true.' he paused. 'Now. We have to do a full disclosure of what evidence we have don't we? So. Why not let them sweat a bit? They are going to find out about the blood evidence. I am just a bit interested to see what sort of a concoction she comes up with to counter your little gem.'

He turned to look at her but said nothing.

'What?' Joanne said, 'What are you thinking?'

'Little Gem. Midget Gem. Got any?' he grinned.

'Bloody hell' she exclaimed. 'I thought you'd had a brain wave.' Fishing into her jacket pocket she pulled out a small congealed white paper bag containing a few of the sweets Maxwell appeared to have become addicted to.

'Thank you, young lady, don't mind if I do.' he said and dipped his hand into the bag.

Fifteen minutes later they were seated at their desks in Maxwell's office, each nursing yet another mug of coffee.

'Fancy a biscuit sir?' Joanne asked

'Don't mind if I do.' replied Maxwell.

She opened a drawer in her desk and in one smooth movement took a foil-covered wafer biscuit from her secret hoard and tossed it overhand to her boss who caught it as it flew towards his head.

'So that's where you keep them.' he grinned.

'For today. Have to keep them moving around so the mice don't get them,' she replied. She settled back in her chair and unwrapped the biscuit staring at the far wall of the office. Maxwell watched her quietly for a moment or two then said,

'What's the problem? Something on your mind, you look pensive.' After a few seconds, she turned to him.

'Just thinking sir. Something about this job just doesn't ring true.'

'Go on' he said, 'Share it, the answer might come if you speak it out loud.'

'Well. Molly Cullen visits Quinn every day after she's done his messages. She hands over the stuff she's bought for him and they spend some time catching up on things. He tells her of the visit of Dr Mansoor a couple of days before and also of the second visit by the locum doctor, our Dr Hawkins, on Sunday. Hawkins makes her visit on the afternoon of the Sunday, and Cullen visits him during the early evening, by which time Hawkins has come and gone.' Joanne stopped to think, Maxwell said nothing.

'So he tells her that the visit from the doctor is a locum come to try and get him off the drugs. Did he recognise her from when she was a child or perhaps as an adult, or did he believe a story she had told him about trying to get him off the drugs? If he recognised her then it makes sense that he tells her the story of the drugs as he wouldn't want to tell Cullen the story of his past, or perhaps he didn't know who she was and Hawkins spun him a yarn about coming off the drugs. Either way, Hawkins comes back later that evening and presumably lets herself into the flat, because if she knocked on the door then Cullen would probably have heard her and come out to see who was calling late in the evening. So, Hawkins must have had a key. Did Quinn give it to her knowing she was coming back, or did she steal it from the flat on her first visit? She paused and took a bite of the biscuit, brushing a few crumbs from her jumper onto the floor. Maxwell thought for a moment.

'A good point Jo. Good point.' he mused. 'It is likely he did recognise her. After all, she had been in touch with Gunther over the years and he no doubt would have told his dad about her. So when she turned up at the flat maybe she told him she would be back later for some reason, and he told her to take the key. Either that or she pinched the key from inside the flat and let herself in later that evening.' Joanne nodded quietly.

'That sounds plausible doesn't it?' she said and paused again.

'So maybe she promised him some more drugs on her return visit, and that's why he told her to take the key.' She finished off the wafer biscuit and took a drink from her mug.

'So the key is probably with the rubber gloves and scalpel in the long grass on the A7' she concluded.

'There's another problem worrying me. Why does she make it so clear that it's murder by leaving the kitchen knife in the pool of blood? Maybe she did want to cause it to be a good juicy story for the press, but she couldn't guarantee a reporter would follow up on it, could she? And she certainly wouldn't want to risk being accused of his murder if something went wrong. And something did go wrong, didn't it? The blood spots on her coat. Everything else she did was designed to stop any forensic clues being left behind.' She sat back in her chair and stared blankly at her boss.

'I don't think the blood was planned, or the cigarette ash. It was an accident. Like you said, everything she did was designed to leave no forensics anywhere. She cocked up.' Maxwell said.

'Nobody's perfect are they?' Joanne grinned.

'Well not everybody. Anyway. Are we bringing her in early then?'

'No. I've been turning that over in my little brain since we thought of it in the Procurators office. I think we should let her stew for the next ten days until her bail date is due.' Joanne nodded her head in agreement.

'True enough sir.' She paused for a moment then said,

'I'd love to be a fly on the wall of her solicitor when he gets the disclosures though. Bet he wets himself.'

'Bet she will too,' said Maxwell. 'She won't be expecting that.'

CHAPTER 32

The interview room at Leith police station had not seen any alterations to its structure since the building was converted from the old town hall in 1828, other than numerous coats of council paint, and more recently with the addition of CCTV and video and sound recording equipment. It was cold and the walls were bare and solid stone, like the rest of the building. Some time ago a couple of crime prevention posters had been stuck to the wall. The humour did not go unnoticed by either police or criminals who frequented the place. A single radiator lurked against one wall and struggled even on the warmest of days to provide a semblance of heat. A table on which lay a digital recording machine rested against one of the short walls, whilst four old metal chairs were placed two along either long side of the table.

Dr Hawkins was seated in the chair closest to the recording machine with her solicitor occupying the other. She had taken care of her appearance and looked good. A visit to the hairdressers and then the careful selection of clothing gave her a level of confidence she probably didn't deserve.

Joanne later described her outfit to Maxwell as 'layered' which meant little or nothing to him, but she insisted it was expensive. Certainly, it looked good according to his eyes. He recognised expensive clothing when he saw it, being a long-time married man.

Her solicitor, a middle-aged man wearing a dark blue three-piece suit, a cream shirt and dark tie sat beside her, a file of papers opened in front of him.

DS Barker and DCI Maxwell came into the room, Joanne closed the door behind her with a bang. Hawkins flinched in her seat.

'Sorry about that' Joanne said with a false smile and took her place opposite the solicitor. Maxwell sat opposite Dr Hawkins. He too carried a file of papers which he placed closed in front of him on the table.

Maxwell introduced himself and DS Barker to Dr Hawkins and her solicitor before then telling them both that the interview would be recorded. He then flicked a switch on the tabletop machine and after a double beep, a green light shone on the machine and it began to record.

He cautioned her and started his questioning. Almost as soon as he had started the solicitor interrupted.

'Chief Inspector, if I may interrupt you for a moment.' Maxwell nodded his head.

'Go ahead' he said shortly. The solicitor half turned to look at his client before carrying on.

'Dr Hawkins will make only a No Comment response to any questions you might put to her. I offer you this information should you wish to curtail your questioning.' He paused.

'Dr Hawkins would like to make a statement. I understand that this might be somewhat unusual, but feel it would be in the interests of brevity and your investigation to allow her to do so. I am aware of what she is about to say, and she does it against my advice, but she is insistent.' He sat back and moved the file in front of him towards the edge of the table.

Joanne glanced sideways at DCI Maxwell. He was staring at Dr Hawkins directly across the table from him. She drew a breath and was about to start to speak. Maxwell held up his hand and she stopped.

'Let me remind you Dr Hawkins that you are still under caution and that whatever you say could be used in evidence against you. Do you understand?' he said. She nodded her head.

'Please say the word Dr Hawkins.' he said.

'I understand Chief Inspector, I am fully aware. May I begin?' she said in a quiet controlled voice.

'Go ahead then' replied Maxwell. He glanced sideways to ensure that the recording machine was still switched on. The green light was solid.

Staring at him through the brown-rimmed glasses she wore, she began.

'I think I might have been responsible for the death of James Quinn,' she began. Joanne breathed in a deep breath. Dr Hawkins continued.

'My father and James Quinn met whilst they were in Germany in the mid-nineteen fifties. They were both doing National Service, and that's where they were stationed. They met two young German girls and both decided to marry them in Germany. My father and mother had a daughter, my sister, who was born in the Princess Elizabeth Hospital in Wuppertal. Later in the mid-fifties, they returned to the UK, at the end of their service.' She stopped and started to reach down to her shoulder bag which lay on the floor by the side of her chair.

'May I have a drink of water Inspector? I've got a bottle in my bag.' she said. Maxwell nodded and watched as she took the clear plastic bottle from her bag, unscrewed the top and took a small drink from it. Screwing the top back on she gently wiped her lips with her fingers, then carried on.

'On their return, my mother and father came back to Burnley where my father had inherited the family home on the death of his father. My grandmother was still alive but died shortly after his return. Quinn went to Edinburgh where he and his wife, Renate, lived in the city centre on a small terrace off Canongate, not far from Holyrood Palace. It was a bit of a slum really, but I understand they have been refurbished and are now quite smart. Anyway, they had three children over the years. A girl and two boys. The girl was born in Germany, like my sister' She paused and looked at the posters on the wall, appearing to gather her thoughts before carrying on.

'I understand that the two men used to visit each other from time to time, during the summer normally. First, my father would go to Edinburgh and then Quinn would come down to Lancashire, with their wives and daughters. Then a few years later I was born and Renate had two boys, separated by about four years.' She paused and glanced for what seemed a long time at the desktop. She traced her forefinger in a rim of condensation left by the bottle on the wood, then looked up and continued.

'Then my mother died. Of breast cancer. That left my father with two girls on his hands. My sister was put in a girl's boarding school. I don't know where he got the money from, couldn't have been all that expensive, but I know she was moved around a bit. My sister was a bit wild apparently, so perhaps it was a reform school or something like that. I'm not all that familiar with the system in those days. I was only a young child then.' She paused and took in another deep breath.

'So during that time, my father would take me up to see the Quinn family in Edinburgh. It was a terrible journey up there. I remember my dad had an A30 car at that time. Very small and cramped and wouldn't go fast. It would take all day to get there, but once there I would share a bed with the daughter, Margaretha, that was the girl's name, and dad would sleep on the settee in the living room.' She paused again and it seemed to Joanne that the woman was remembering things from that time she did not wish to recall. She started to speak again.

'I'm sorry. This is more difficult than I thought it would be. Do you think I could get a breath of fresh air outside for a few moments? I know I am still under arrest, so if you want to come with me that isn't a problem. But it would help me a lot if you could.' Maxwell looked at Joanne.

'I see no reason Dr Hawkins. Joanne will go with you.' He raised his eyebrows at Jo.

'No problem sir,' she said and turned back to Dr Hawkins as she pushed back her chair from the desk.

'Come with me and we'll have a wander down the street for a while.' she said. Hawkins pushed back her chair and followed Joanne out of the room and through the building until they stood outside on Queen Charlotte Street.

'Thanks, Sergeant' Hawkins said. 'I think I was getting a bit claustrophobic in there. I'll be alright in a few minutes.'

The two women walked in silence down one side of the street and at Dr Hawkins' suggestion crossed and walked back along the other side until finally, they went back into the interview room.

'Alright Doctor?' Maxwell asked.

'Yes, thank you. I'm fine now. Ready to get going again.' she said.

She sat back in her chair and took a small sip of water from her bottle, screwing the cap back on and rubbing the trace of water from the desktop.

'Where was I?' she asked herself.

'Right. When I was about five, I'm not certain of the exact year or how old I was, but I do remember that we had been going to Edinburgh for a couple of years, so I couldn't have been much older than five. Anyway. One evening Quinn came into the bedroom where I shared a bed with Margaretha.

He sat on the side of the bed closest to me and placed his hand on my leg. I must not have thought that there was anything wrong with what he did at that time. It was only a few years later that I was able to understand what he was doing. Almost as soon as he started to rub my leg I remember Margaretha sat up in bed and started to throw her arms around her dad's neck and make a real fuss of him. He turned his attention from me to her and I remember he snuggled down in bed by her side, almost pushing me out of the other side. I was a small child you understand.' Dr Hawkins took a deep breath and carried on.

'As the years and the visits went on and I became more aware of what he was doing I realised that Margaretha was doing what she did to stop him abusing me. She had been abused many times by him, and from what I learned later he had been doing the same to the two boys.' She stopped again. The silence in the room was broken only by the almost silent breathing of the four people in the room. Nobody spoke. She continued.

'He had been abusing Margaretha from about the age of five, then the two boys as they got to roughly the same age. I got most of this out of Margaretha many years later. She refused to talk about it when we were kids.' Hawkins stopped talking again. Her eyes filled with tears. She wiped her eyes with a tissue she took from her handbag.

'We can take another break if you wish Dr Hawkins,' Maxwell said quietly.

'No' she replied, shaking her head.

'This has been a long time coming, so let's get it over with.' Stuffing the used tissue back in her bag she continued.

'When I was much older I gained several degrees in psychology which has enabled me to do the work I do. I work with mentally ill people, as you are probably aware. During one visit I made to Margaretha when we were much older I got her to talk a bit about what had gone on. She told me all about her father.' She took a deep breath and continued again.

'He had a job as a bus driver around Wester Hailes for many years. During this time he would groom young girls, and sometimes boys, and sexually assault them. Remember, this was a time when kids were allowed out by themselves when paedophiles were not known about in the same way as we know today. He used his position on the buses to groom them over some time and abuse them on the buses or in the bus terminal shelters on the estates. This went on for some years, according to Margaretha. At the same time, he abused her, and when she grew older, he would turn on his boys. All three of them now are severely mentally disturbed. One of them very much so.'

'Is this Gunther you are talking about?' Maxwell asked quietly. She looked up at him across the desk.

'You've met him then?' she said, nodding her head.

'Aye. We have,' replied Maxwell. 'Drugged up to the eyeballs and mad as a box of frogs,' he said and hurriedly added. 'Sorry. That was not at all called for Dr Hawkins. I do beg your pardon.' he said blushing wildly. She grinned ruefully.

'Perhaps not at all politically correct Inspector, but sums up Gunther very well. As mad as a box of frogs.' she said.

She started to talk again but Maxwell raised his hand to stop her.

'Sorry Dr Hawkins, but there is something I need to clear up with you before you carry on.' She paused to allow him to continue.

'Can you remember when the Quinns moved from the flat on Canongate?' he asked. She stared at him blankly.

'Not exactly,' she replied slowly, wondering what was behind the question. Maxwell didn't speak but waited for her to come forward with an answer. She did after a few seconds and a brief shaking of her head.

'It must have been soon after my mother died. I know it was just my dad and me.' Maxwell thought for a moment then said,

'So this must have been when they had moved out of Canongate to Wester Hailes, to the house they had there.' She nodded her head slowly.

'Yes, I think you must be right there. It was the house, not the flat.' Maxwell made a pretence of turning over one or two of the sheets of paper in the file before him.

'Let me get this straight. Quinn was in your bedroom abusing you and his daughter, whilst at the same time your father was carrying on an affair with Renate in the next bedroom.' Hawkins went white for a second then shouted at him,

'How dare you! He was not having an affair with her. How did you get that idea? It's not true. He was not like that, never.'

She settled back into her chair now flushed red in the face and breathing rapidly. Maxwell looked at her calmly.

'I got the information from Mrs Quinn, Doctor.' he said quietly. 'She told me what was going on.' Hawkins slumped back in her chair and fiddled nervously with her fingers in her lap.

'She's lying. She is where the insanity in the family comes from. She's mad.' She finally said. After a moment or two, she sat up in the chair.

'I want to take a break please.' she said. Maxwell looked at his watch and the timer on the recording machine.

'I see no reason why that cannot happen. You've been talking for some time. Let's say a break of fifteen minutes,' he glanced at his watch and turned off the recorder. He looked at his wristwatch,

'Say half-past shall we? We'll get you some teas whilst we're away.' He looked from the doctor to her solicitor who both nodded their heads.

Joanne and Maxwell gathered their files, stood back from the desk and left the room. Joanne closed the door behind her quietly and they walked along the corridor to the canteen.

CHAPTER 33

Fifteen minutes later the two detectives, laden with their files and polystyrene cups of tea, walked back into the interview room. Hawkins and her solicitor moved their chairs back from facing each other to facing their opponents.

'Hope the tea is ok,' Joanne said placing the two cups she carried in front of them. Dr Hawkins took a sip and grimaced before replacing the cup on the desk and gently pushing it away from her with the tip of one finger.

Maxwell began by turning the recorder back on. 'A reminder Dr Hawkins that you are still under caution.' He looked into her eyes. She nodded.

'So far you have told us a very horrific story of abuse over the years. Can you now tell us about your actions over the weekend when James Quinn was murdered?' he said. Hawking threw her head back and looked at the ceiling for a moment before beginning to speak. Her voice was calm, a matter of fact almost, without any semblance of the anger she had displayed when Maxwell had spoken of her father's affair with Quinn's wife.

'I went to see him on the Saturday afternoon. I knew his address from Gunther. I stayed for a couple of hours and we talked about his life and my father's life, and their time in the army and how they had met their wives. I told him I was involved with drug abuse in the course of my work and he jokingly said that he would make a good client for me as he regularly used heroin.' She paused and glanced at Joanne before carrying on.

'I knew that he was a user from Gunther. It was him who told me that his neighbour was regularly buying the stuff for him and delivering it almost daily.' She sniffed and looked at the cup of tea deliberating whether or not to risk another sip. She decided against it.

'I decided to come back the following evening after the neighbour had made her delivery. Which is what I did. Came back late on in the evening and let myself in with his front door key. I had lifted it from the door on my way out the previous day.' She took the cup and sipped from it then replaced it on the desk in front of her.

'We talked again for some time. He had taken his dose of heroin and was quite talkative. He started to tell me about the children he had abused over the years, including me and my sister, and his daughter and sons.' She paused and sat back in the chair for a few moments. Maxwell said nothing, just allowing her the time to remember and gather her thoughts.

'He told me about a lot of other children over the years, from Glasgow when he lived there as a child and a young adult, from the flat on Canongate and the house on Wester Hailes, and finally, the flat he now lived in. He must have gone back fifty years or more. It was quite sickening.' She took a deep breath and continued.

'It seems incredible to me that the police never caught onto him. He was a bus driver for many years, had access to kids on the bus who he would molest at the bus terminus whilst waiting to start his runs, and then he started giving them chocolate and sweets.' Her head jerked up as she continued.

'Poor kids from poor households. Hardly ever saw sweets and chocolates. It was too easy for him.' She stopped for a moment and looked into Maxwell's eyes.

'I managed to track some of his abuse though. Looked online at the Scotsman and the Edinburgh Reporter. I found lots of instances of indecent assaults which I thought could have been done by him, even though the information was scanty and never lasted in the news for very long.' Maxwell interrupted her.

'Dr Hawkins. We know of him. We knew of him at the time but never had enough evidence. Neither the children nor their parents would ever help us other than a brief complaint. Sometimes we had enough information to arrest him, but never enough to get him before the courts.' He tapped the tabletop in emphasis. Hawkins nodded her head briefly and made a low tutting noise. Maxwell continued.

'So tell us how you killed him then.' he said.

'Easy' she said. 'It was quite easy. He'd had a lot of heroin and I filled him up with some scotch and just cut the femoral artery in his right leg. As the blood started to flow, it wasn't all that fast, he was weak and almost unconscious, he just slipped away.' She smiled and sat back, seemingly happy with what she had done and how she had done it. Maxwell opened the file and took out the report from the pathologist.

'Evidence of sexual activity.' he read. 'The man had masturbated and reached a climax or someone did it for him. There were some slight traces of semen on his legs. Would you care to tell us how he did that, or did you do it for him?' She looked away and tossed her head smiling.

'I did it. Wanted him to die with a smile on his face.' she grinned.

'It also helped to get his blood pressure up for when I cut him, the blood would flow quicker.' Maxwell glanced at Joanne who looked shocked. She shook her head slowly from side to side in disbelief.

'This is the murder of a human being Dr Hawkins. Not really a laughing matter, or perhaps you think it is?' he said. She looked coldly into his eyes.

'No Inspector, not a laughing matter. However, I do feel it is ironic that you are now finally giving that animal the attention you and your colleagues should have given him all those years ago. Save a lot of children from a lousy childhood and an equally lousy life.' she said. Maxwell stared at her for a moment before continuing.

'What did you use to cut him with?' he asked.

'One of his kitchen knives. Didn't you find it?'

'We found the knife. But it wasn't the one you used to cut him with. It was done with a medical scalpel type of implement, not a kitchen knife.' She smiled and shook her head slightly from side to side.

'Oh dear. Does this mean you haven't found it then?'

'Yes, we have. We found it where you left it on the A7. But the tests done on the body and the knife you left on the legs mean it wasn't the one you left for us to find.'

'Looks like you're a bit in the dark then Inspector, doesn't it?' she grinned again. Maxwell paused to allow her a moment of triumph and success before he carried on.

'No. Not at all.' he said quietly. 'You see Dr Hawkins we found his blood on the edge of your coat, together with cigarette ash from the ashtray on the floor by his bed. Care to explain that?' She shook her head from side to side and then eventually looked towards the solicitor.

'The envelope please Mr Jenkins.' she said quietly. Her solicitor reached into an inside pocket of his suit jacket and pulled out a brown A5 envelope. It was sealed and had some form of office identification stamp across the flap where it was sealed. He placed it on the desk before him.

'Before I give you this I want to say that I have not seen the contents of this envelope. Dr Hawkins gave it to me when we stopped for a break at Gretna Services on the way up here this morning. I took the precaution of getting the manager to stamp the sealed edge with the stamp of the company on it, and I then signed it. I have not opened it, I do not know what is inside it and my client has not told me anything about it.' he said.

Maxwell slid the envelope towards him and Joanne. He looked up at the solicitor.

'So, whatever is inside here you are clear of any misconduct as far as the Law Society is concerned? Is that what you think?' he said.

'I don't think so. I don't think so.' he continued. 'I feel the Law Society might just hang you out to dry for allowing this to happen.' Jenkins flushed red and bit his top lip, but said nothing.

Maxwell glanced at the envelope. It showed the inked stamp of Gretna Service Area and had a signature that said, "Jenkins". He took it and handed it to Joanne.

'What do you think Jo? Worth opening?' She pulled a face and then looked him in the eye.

'Go on Sir. Worth a look isn't it?' Maxwell slit open the envelope and took from it a small photocopied booklet, the pages stapled together by three staples along the left-hand side. He counted them. There were twelve of them, all covered with handwritten notes. As he started to read the pages he noted that the head of each page was written in a different hand from the rest of the notes on the page.

Reading each page took twenty seconds. For four minutes there was silence in the room as he turned from one page to the next. Joanne moved closer to him and read the notebook at the same time. Neither made any comment. The only sound in the room was an occasional low sigh from Maxwell. Eventually, he had finished. He glanced at Joanne to see if she was still reading. Within a few seconds, she looked up and nodded her head in silence.

'For the benefit of the recording' Maxwell said, 'Dr Hawkins has handed me an envelope containing a photocopied booklet of twelve handwritten pages. The booklet has been written in two different handwritings.' He turned to look at the solicitor.

'Do you wish to say anything, Mr Jenkins?' The solicitor, who had turned first white and then was starting to flush bright red replied.

'Yes, I do. First of all, I have never seen this document before nor was I told by my client about its existence. Secondly, I would like to consult with my client if I may.' He turned to Dr Hawkins and she nodded in agreement. Maxwell turned to speak to the recorder.

'Interview is being temporarily stopped for a consultation between the defendant and her solicitor.' He flicked the machine off and pushed back his chair from the desk. Joanne followed him as he left the room.

'Just tell the custody officer when you are ready to start again Mr Jenkins' Maxwell said as he was walking through the door.

Outside Maxwell took his pipe from his pocket and his Zippo. 'I'm off outside for a smoke Jo.' he said.

'I'll come with you. I might want to learn how to smoke one of those things,' she said sourly.

They walked around the small exercise yard at the back of the cells, Joanne in silence whilst her boss lit his pipe. Once he had it going she said,

'What the hell was that sir?' He blew a cloud of smoke out as they walked slowly around the small area.

'That booklet purports to be a list of occasions when Jimmy Quinn was assaulted by a variety of Police officers. From a glance there appears to have been about a hundred occasions and probably forty or fifty officers. At the top of the pages, the writing was in her hand, I'm sure of that. It had a sort of explanation note at the top. There was the date, the police station, the name and rank of the officer who he says assaulted him and a series of shortened words. "Fo" meant foot, "Ha" meant hand, and "Fi" meant fist. Presumably how he was hit.' Joanne was silent for a second or two then said,

'How true is it sir?'

'I've no idea Jo. It covers fifty or more years, and of the names of the officers, I recognised a few. Lots of them are dead or retired, but there were a few still serving.' He drew on his pipe again.

'Like me, like Jack Dwyer and two Detective Superintendents and a Detective Sergeant.'

'How truthful or accurate is it do you think?' she asked.

'No idea Jo.' he said. 'Could well be a pack of lies or a mixture of truth and lies. Either way, I have no idea why she wants to show it to us. Beats me. Any ideas?' Joanne kept step with her boss as they walked slowly in a circle around the exercise yard.

'Couple of thoughts sir. She might want to use it to get us to drop the charges. Or maybe she intends to use it in court if we charge her. The publicity would be enormous. Either way, it does smell of blackmail.' Maxwell nodded his head in agreement.

'You have a good point there, Jo, in fact, a couple of good points. However I cannot believe she wants to bring it up in court, and she must be delusional if she thinks we are going to drop the charges. It would destroy her career and her reputation.' The door to the exercise yard swung open and the custody officer was standing there. 'Sir,' he called out. 'They're ready to get cracking again sir' he said. Maxwell raised his hand in acknowledgement.

'Right, we're coming. Thank you.' He said as they turned to walk back slowly to the exit from the exercise yard. 'Jo' Maxwell said as they had almost reached the door.

'Don't suppose you have a candle on you do you?' he asked.

'A candle? No sir. Why?' she asked puzzled.

'Well if you did then you could perhaps make us a wax image and stick pins in the bitch. Might help.' he replied.

'Wouldn't dream of it sir,' she laughed mirthlessly.

Back in the interview room, Maxwell turned the recording machine back on. He looked up at the solicitor and then Hawkins.

'Well, have you sorted something out?' he asked. The solicitor cleared his throat and began.

'As I said earlier I knew nothing at all of this booklet. My client wishes to continue with her statement, against my advice.' he said.

'As you wish Mr Jenkins.' said Maxwell turning to Hawkins.

'So, what now?' he asked her. Dr Hawkins sat upright in her chair and placed her hands on top of the booklet which now lay on the desk in front of her.

'This booklet was given to me by Jimmy Quinn.' she said. Maxwell interrupted her.

'Was that before or after you murdered him Dr Hawkins?' he asked. She hesitated for a moment and then smiled wanly at him.

'It was shown to me before he died and he asked me to make use of it.' she said.

'You didn't answer the question, Dr Hawkins. Was it before or after you killed him?'

'I was shown it before he died and took it from his flat when I left.'

'When was that? The first or the second time you visited him?

She hesitated. 'It was the second time.'

'So that was after you had killed him, at which time he could not have given you his permission could he?'

'He had already given me his permission.' she snapped.

'Well, you couldn't say anything else, could you? Having just slit his femoral artery open.' She flushed and stammered,

'He told me that I could have it before he died.'

'Right. Understood. His last dying words were, 'Take the booklet doctor.' he paused and glanced down at the file, tapping it gently with his forefinger. 'Thoughtful of him to make a copy wasn't it?'

'He didn't, I did. I have the original at home, in a safe place.' She stared at him in silence. Maxwell leaned back in his chair.

'So you are asking me to accept that he gave you the booklet, you made a copy of it and have kept the original at home? Have I got that right?'

'Yes. Despite your best efforts Inspector you have got it correct.' she smirked and folded her arms.

'At what point did you write your few words along the top of each page?' he picked the booklet from in front of her and read from it. 'Information relating to abuse on James Quinn by the Strathclyde and Lothians Police. You wrote that?'

'Yes.' she said.

'Those forces no longer exist. We are now Police Scotland, Jimmy would have known that. However, let's continue shall we?' he added softly and replaced the booklet in front of her. For a few moments, he said nothing but simply looked down at the file before him.

'So what do you wish to say about this booklet?' he finally asked. She drew herself up in her seat before she began.

'James Quinn was a serial child abuser. You know that and I and his family know that. He had been for many many years. You were never able to charge him with anything as you couldn't get the evidence.' She paused and then said,

'So each time you brought him in you simply beat him up in trying to get a confession from him. Am I right Inspector?' She stared at Maxwell and blinked nervously a few times.

Maxwell simply stared back at her. He cocked his head gently to one side and said quietly.

'And your point is?'

She tapped the booklet in front of her hard.

'This evidence shows that you and others over the years abused and assaulted him. I want you to face the outcome of your actions.' She folded her arms and sat back. Maxwell continued to look at her with not a trace of anything showing on his face. Eventually, he took a deep breath and said,

'Dr Hawkins. The evidence, as you call it, is not worth the paper it is copied on. There is no proof James Quinn wrote it, for all we know you could have written the lot. Your actions are simply a rather nasty and pathetic attempt to muddy the waters of this investigation.' He paused and took another deep breath before continuing.

'You will shortly be charged with the murder of James Quinn. You will probably be offered bail. I suggest that you use that time on bail to your benefit and best advantage. Consult with your solicitor to get advice on the use of this document. I cannot see it being ever allowed as evidence in court. Not on this charge nor on any subsequent charges which might be brought against surviving officers in this force. Many of the names mentioned here are dead. Some of the names do not bear any relationship to officers I knew or served with. They are fictitious. They did not exist. All you will be doing is dirtying the names and reputations of some former officers of this force, and their surviving families. This does sound like you are attempting to blackmail Doctor. I don't like blackmail doctors, and neither do the courts.' He paused to allow what he had said to sink in, then continued.

'If you could find an Advocate here in Scotland to defend you, and I'm sure you will, and he decides to bring the booklet before the court for some reason then this will allow the Procurator Fiscal to cross-examine all the information contained in the booklet. And the witnesses. Because there would have to be witnesses to verify the information. Witnesses like Quinn's family. Renate, Margaretha and Gunther. Can you imagine what an advocate would make of a witness like Renate, and the affair she had with your father whilst her husband was in the next bedroom abusing her children and others? It would not be pretty, would it? It would all come out, not only the allegations about policemen beating up Quinn but why they did it. How much sympathy do you think the court, or public opinion, would show you or him?'

He sat back in his chair and picked up the file in both hands, tapping it on its edge on the desk.

'It's not going to work Dr Hawkins, it's not going to work. You and Quinn's family will be reviled through the press not only here in Scotland but throughout the UK. It would make a wonderful story which the tabloids would jump on from a great height, and keep on at it for weeks on end. You and Quinn's family would have a permanent following of reporters and photographers no matter where you went. Your reputation would be in tatters, your career would end in disgrace.' He paused once more and looked kindly into her eyes before speaking quietly to her.

'You should leave this alone Dr Hawkins, leave it alone. It will destroy you.' he said. 'Now, we must along to the charge office and get you charged. I will not oppose bail. You should be back here in a few months. Think about what I have said doctor, think long and hard about what I have said.' He led the way out of the interview room with Joanne and stopped finally at the charge desk.

After she had been charged and released on bail the two detectives went back to Maxwell's office in silence. Joanne made them a mug of coffee each and they sat at their respective desks drinking it. Eventually, Joanne looked across the office at her boss.

'Sir,' she said, 'A question?'

'Just the one Jo?' Maxwell asked.

'How true was that document?' She looked across the lip of her mug, fearful of what he would say. For a moment or two, he looked out through the window. The sky was still blue with only a few white clouds high up in the atmosphere moving in from the North Sea. A blue sky day. He took a sip from his mug.

'How important is the answer Jo?' he asked quietly. She thought about the question for a moment.

'Quite important sir,' she said eventually.

'I think everyone knows about the 'bad old days', but how much of that document do you think was right?'

He smiled ruefully at her.

'The answer Jo is that I don't know how much of it is true. I do know what I did to the evil bastard from time to time.

It's like I've said in the past, the odd slap to try and get him to cough to an assault, but from my side, nothing more than that. I promise you. That is the truth. As to others, some of which are made-up names, I just have no real way of knowing. And neither does anyone else. Those days are gone, thank God. Don't want them back in any shape or form.' He put the mug down and reached for his pipe.

'There is one other thing to consider Jo. That document highlights the number of times he was smacked and kicked and thumped. A hundred of them is what he wrote. A hundred where he was suspected of abuse, but what of the ones we didn't suspect him of, what about the ones which never came to light?' He paused for a moment before continuing.

'Not good times Jo. Not good at all. But remember this. If the beatings noted in that booklet represent a beating for each offence he was suspected of, then there are at least a hundred kids who he abused over a long period. A minimum of a hundred. And think too of his own family. But what about the others, those who never complained, what about the families he destroyed, the parents who had to try and give those children a normal upbringing after Quinn had had his hands on them? The parents and siblings had to try and cope with what their brothers, sisters and children had been through. It's the past Jo. One which we can no longer resurrect, whether that is good or not I don't know. What we did was a small thing in the whole scheme of things. Small things Jo.' He stood up from his desk.

'Fancy a smoke Sergeant?' he grinned at her waving the pipe before his face.

'Aye go then. Beats hard drinking doesn't it?' she replied and beamed him a smile which understood everything he had said, and perhaps everything he had omitted to say.

Printed in Great Britain
by Amazon

53782722R00209